THE COURT BLAMED ME
a novel

MURPH DONNAN

Copyright © 2012, by Murph Donnan
The Court Blamed Me
Murph Donnan
mdonnan.lightmessages.com
Printed in the United States of America
ISBN: 978-1-61153-020-9

ALL RIGHTS RESERVED

No part of this publication may be reproduced, stored in a retrieval system, or transmitted in any form or by any means, electronic, mechanical, photocopying, recording, scanning or otherwise, except for brief quotations in printed reviews or as permitted under Section 107 or 108 of the 1976 International Copyright Act, without the prior permission of the publisher.

*To Dr. James R. Rice,
who gave me the freedom to write this book
instead of looking for a job.*

Chapter 1

"I'm going to point to the one who's guilty. It's that one right over there!" And I, Ben, had always known when the turnaround of a court case met the signs of the road, I was on my way back home. I had signaled out my brother, Tod, the murderer of our dad, who had been drawn into the steel-belted path of a bus in the middle of the day downtown. He had to be blind to cross the street exactly when the heavy bus rolled by, but my brother had figured this out. And so had I, the elder of the two. But there was a gap there I had to fill in.

"We're not here, uh, for the question of, uh, homicide," said the judge, leaning over, stretching another wrinkle in his robe. He wasn't beckoning to me with his embarrassing patronizing tone. In fact, he talked softly, so the volume of his courtroom decibels couldn't be heard much past the courtroom recorder and maybe the attorneys on either side if they leaned in a bit and cupped their ears.

The room was at best typical from the choice of this one to the catalogue of the rest. It was like they had to secretly mow down a whole dry forest to have it built and decorated with so much wood, not to mention having to unplug and dump five or ten tractor-trailer loads of sticky varnish inside, so it coated the walls and furniture as it drained. Not to be left out, the thin curtains were keeping the outside light at bay, so everybody looked their best. So we wouldn't be left totally dark, soft and indirect yellowish hue from the lights on the wall also reduced the shadows, and that was enough. The crowd contemplated their leftover advantage from the complete courtroom glow, which produced, and took the credit for, ninety percent fewer wrinkles, scars, or puffiness around the eyes, and complications of all grey hair—not like the bathroom glare you noticed from the stupid mirror in the morning.

I wondered how anybody read their notes. The ones looking at their sheet music gave their page turners flashlights, so the fugue could continue. But there was a man on trial here—me. We didn't need an orchestra. Television always had one. There are background tunes for every show. But ours put their instruments down. And I had to quit directing. The judge looked curiously at me and wrote something down. He gave a look to the jury, too, and turned his thin lips into one cheek and down from a smile. And the judge ordered the flashlights off. At least I thought so. I put my arms down and quit daydreaming.

Great! The judge had his own wiry adjustable collegiate lamp. Good for him.

"But he's the one who did it!" I said. "And now he's blaming it on me, and I don't like that!" Tod was not only the one I pointed to, but he was also the prosecutor of my court case.

"I, uh, know you have trouble," the judge said, "being it true your own, uh, brother is not on your side, and the court—I don't really ascertain whether, uh, this means just me or the concept of me or me and the concept or plain something else drawn up in the four walls of this room inclusively...let me tell you, uh, in confidence (I'm not angry yet) you, uh, have to concede the proceeding court case has exonerated the prosecutor, your kin, from, uh, any hint of murder. You can't continue to ride in this avenue. The case here, uh, is to determine whether you're a schizophrenic or not. Any other outbursts you, uh, have on the contrary, and I'll have to hold you in contempt. OK?"

Schizophrenia was on trial! And it was mine, if there was any.

"I'll have to have a smoke on that," I said. And I pulled out my pipe from my front shirt pocket, some tobacco in a pouch falling from my pants' pocket, and lit it all up with an opaque-colored lighter. I was in the witness stand and got ready to ask if I should step aside not to offend the nonsmokers.

"OK, Ben, I'll try again," the judge said. "You take one puff, uh, from that kiln-fired hardened glorified cigar, and I'll, uh, put you in contempt of court!"

"A grown man should know the etiquette of a court in session," said my brother. There was real blood between us, counting the knife in his back or the gun or whatever he coaxed my dad with, so he crossed the street at the wrong time.

"Sit down!" The judge said. I lit up and puffed some billows that overcame a few flies, dropping them from the ceiling.

"Ooo, that was a good one," meaning the taste from the smoke I had.

"Now the judge is mad at you," Tod said, and laughed.

"The joke's not over," said the judge. "You, uh, Ben, are in contempt! Take him away!" And the security men led me off to jail, where I continued to puff. I learned what contempt of court was, and decided not to do it again. I told the guard I was done smoking and thinking, which usually goes along with it, and was ready to go back. So he unlocked my bars and guided me back to the witness seat. The judge's docket was so large he had to let me out of his jail in a slow blink.

"OK, back to business," said the judge. "Did you get enough of a good smoke?" His whole body was speaking through his teeth. You know how awesome judges feel when they put their robes on and climb up the ten-foot bench.

"Yes."

"Great, now we can continue. We'll, uh, have recess until ten o'clock tomorrow morning." And he banged down the gavel. "If, uh, for some unexpected reason you prove you're not mentally ill, you'll, uh, be free from any litigation. But, uh, if you're convicted, there's no way you can walk out a free man." I nodded, and then waited for permission to leave the stand. The judge was the last one to evacuate, and this wasn't worth a smoke, but I'd rather be filled with pipe than fear. I gave up the habit a little later on. After a while I was alone, and time was filled up with nothing but itself, so I finally left on my own recognizance.

I was a productive member of society, at least until half my world collapsed. My dad was dead, and my brother was trying to blame me for it. I was a soft target, and thought this was my brother's way of hiding another crime behind his back, which could be worse—really? And how? If he earned the high ground of blaming somebody else, and was successful, a happy but unhealthy plague of society would emerge. We may need a thousand more doctors. And with only a few smokes and mirrors, nobody would ever focus their reach toward the thorns and brambles of what was their past. Stuffing me into jail forever would keep all doubt from attacking him, the great prosecutor. So you may turn the world enough to know this case was a survival issue for Tod. He was pleased to know he wasn't convicted for his dad's demise. He'd think of this murder in his daily life, and not have to do anything to quiet the shadows of the other crime, except worry that I hadn't lost my case yet. Maybe I'd win mine and send Tod to hell in broad daylight.

Tod had killed two people, I deduced, and he needed society to release him of the blame and anxiety and the look over his shoulder and the plain fear he never predicted. He knew me and was acquainted enough to know I was kind of weird. And he was partly successful, the only one in his mind asking all the questions. But he didn't ask how many bodies it took for someone to sniff out the stench and investigate. For the present and only in its peculiar definition, I was the only one standing in his way. All he had to do was prove I was schizophrenic, and I'd go down for murder, even though I was innocent. You see, he could build on the court's verdict that he didn't coax Dad to his death. Somebody did, and I was the only one left to have done it.

When our good-old dad was led into the path of the bus, I had forgotten through the trauma of the event, that I was where my brother was, or crossing the street behind the bus where he wasn't. Thus, the blame of schizophrenia. Which way was it? I focused on one scenario and then the other. I was sure, and I wasn't sure. I made up my mind one way and then changed it to the other. The longer you knew me, the more confused I got, and the closer I really got to schizophrenia. It could drive anybody nuts thinking of the emotion of the circumstance. My brother thought I had conveniently invented in my mind the innocence I couldn't have led my dad anywhere. Minds do that with schizophrenia masking the fact and the pain that you were a true murderer. Somebody, knowing he was temporarily blind, had to give signals to help him cross the road. Either they were Tod's signals or mine; someone guided him the wrong way. He was hit and died. Somehow Tod had put the responsibility on me. Knowing I couldn't remember, Tod saw his chance and determined to switch blame from his past crime to me. He pulled some strings, and we were in court. My schizophrenia would be blazing a trail in my brain by then, knowing I would never remember if I did it or not. And his case would win. Until then, I had my own angle. And it would win.

Chapter 2

I had a wife, a home, however cramped, and a job handing out donuts and coffee to policemen on stakeouts. My court case contained every blame there was, including the amount of money I made to the point of barely sustaining my wife and myself. I tried to stay ahead of it, but we had been drawn through the nose trying to stay in the upper middle class at my old job at Hamerston and Owen. It did provide more security. The hours weren't that great, but the money, as my wife put it, was much greener on the other side; and this is where we tried to be. I don't think she ever completely understood my career change. In fact, she probably had a breakdown of her own, because of it.

Even so, Loro, the wife, and I had decided we wanted to grow old together, where the real love was, starting when we were elderly. We knew old age would be a long time, so the fear of dying was thrown out of our present relationship, for practice, for when we got there. In fact that was the corner stone of our "love." We only got married because of peer pressure, so if we aimed at growing old, we'd beat those crumbs and let the dog have its feast. The only problem was we'd play practical jokes on each other that would look really mean without context,

The Court Blamed Me

because the goal was years from now. We would risk anything, knowing our unrequited love would eventually take off like a rocket. If you put our marriage in the blender, you'd see a fight to the finish to keep panic and the jitters out of the bloody mix. Anything but fear of what old age brought. You'd be surprised how much death was out there in the middle of love and in between the cracks of what was good and safe.

But how old was old? No girl ever divulged that. Since I was married to Loro and had a job with the cops instead of being rich, it was like a free-falling state of mind, ending with a hammer punishing the peace and quiet I used to love so much. Ouch! The daydreaming had taken over my semi-engineering job. So I had a problem, but nothing could right it.

Danger with the cops had taken over my new city in space, replacing my old world with fear. And that wouldn't stop. I had not progressed, at least not with money. I could see my marriage fall apart in pieces, even the real part that had just begun. Fear went right into bed with me every morning on the end of my shift and curled me up like a hatched pink-stained shrimp. The scare of everything in general lasted until I stocked my car full of goods, and cranked it up to get right out there again. This was very unusual even for me, and I tried one idea over the other to use my fire to melt some of that frozen nervousness. I had to chase my tail for and light it up. I blamed my choppy feelings. Why for instance couldn't I be the rested turn of a frayed nerve or its relative while I was sleeping? I tried that, but nervousness and fright had to be alive, and I was sensitive to their personal needs, for they had taken away my last job and replaced it with an employed gutter ball. This was them and not me. I was convinced my mind went through nothing but a temporary break, but the truth relied on what the court proved: right or wrong. That was life! Or was it?

My old job had to go. I was daydreaming too much to stay in sync with my buddies there, and I was fielding too many doubts to keep up with being rich. They told me to make friends with the supervisors down on the job site, or that was it. Why did this bunch have to be Tod's old friends? They gave him cases when he was starting out! So I defended my day-dreams to my boss, citing them as a tool for my imagination. I didn't need more reality with these guys. The second or third time we had that discussion, everything got "hot," and I was fired.

I was full of guilt, since I was the only one responsible for my feelings. I was the cause, no matter how much I blamed everything else on my "nervous breakdown." My mind hadn't taken the corner gracefully from one job to the next. I found out with many probes into the meat that I hadn't worried enough as a child. Knocking on the door to heaven used to be the only living common moment if you lived high enough off the hog.

Having grown up—there was a real door and power was who was behind it. Your thoughts grabbed attention from the doorman, and he had pearls to put around your neck if you made the climb up the stairs—see now, there were stairs. Life was a lesson, and I should learn from it. The more I thought about it, more details emerged, no matter how slow the focus was. That's what happened in concentration. It only moved more forward than backward, and sometimes braked. I was stuck thinking about it all. Why murder? Really, why? I might want to catch up with the figurative rolling stone with his new adventure of the mind, but I desperately needed more of the moss. I wanted to be able to deal with the present. Things were falling apart, and it all began with Tod murdering our dad. I didn't care if he was exonerated.

My wife had a stomach full of the dark-green stuff, and she knew it; and she knew of its importance. Wasn't she a woman? People like her have intuition on their side, but as little as we know about the opposite sex, they might admit each supposition spelled out in the company of men didn't have concrete reason behind the illogical. They just wanted to be believed without an

The Court Blamed Me

argument! I wanted to, but I couldn't rely on Loro to piece both of our lives back together. I'd be too easy for her, knowing death, to punch me in the face. You see, it was my side of the family that brought the trouble. Our life was intercepted by the death of my dad and the subsequent change of my job. This described my "nervous breakdown" in a nut shell.

But I would be the best donut and coffee man in the free skies of the world. So things hit home. Loro became more of a mother figure to me, and depending on her was touchy. Typically, she was genuinely ahead of me in the most general of ways. But I discussed it within myself and believed, one emergency to the other, that there were fears stopping me along the way down––fears of finding an incompleteness not capped from conversation. There were legitimate worries, feelings filling the gap left by the absence of words. That was half the problem, maybe—let's believe it. She must have had those concerns before and worked them out, but I didn't.

It was a man and a woman thing, OK? I loved her, and should prove it with a slant on old age, of course, but waited for the drama to build up to a high pitch before I earmarked the bill heading for the fray. You see, it was already true half my dwellings inside walked off the job and pulled everything with them for the goldfish bowl. Too bad.

All I had wanted to do concerning the last half of my problems was to hide. Isn't it true the more light you pour into something that wants attention, the more light will come from it? It was attention my wife needed, especially now. Usually, I'd give her a scratch, and then one would come my way. You know I needed her light, but this wasn't our relationship. As we got started, there was no mercy invited. So like Jefferson's Ten Commandments, this mercy had to be struck in our hearts or anything could be planned and executed without a single thought or consideration for the other person—a smart example for grudges, obstreperousness, or apathy all over again. People go for the smaller battles if they see their rug gently slipping, sliding away from them. I was hit with a force of hypocrisy, a definition of what marriage wasn't, why I was so lost in these answers. Oh, well.

Maybe this was what got me into a mood. I just wanted to talk about it. But I only got so far. We didn't console each other as a rule, like "mercy" would have it. Living at the old age we promised ourselves was such a cheery on top, being below meant playing around. And seeing it in the future was like viewing love itself––enough to save up for it. This is why it didn't enter the conversations. Mercy didn't either. We were practical people. If the goldfish bowl was sent outside, maybe it would, but I'd have to lead Loro into putting it there. I was sure she enjoyed watching me squirm, so give her a medal: hope was still alive.

"Am I right?" I asked her. "I can still work tonight and easily be back to court by ten in the morning?" There was hope, and being so cheap, I'd find another one if this one faded.

"That's your job," Loro said. "Does it scare you to death?" She knew how to sneer and smile at the same time.

"A job is heaven on wheels when you enjoy it. But it's a job if you don't," I said. "We're closer now that we're poor—no distractions of adorning each other independently." When-ever I hinted about the money problem, I got accolades for beating around the bush.

"Watch out for that poet. You'll take his job away," Loro said. But I couldn't send my operable words through the mill. Something stopped me. I couldn't embellish. In fact it started a conversation I had no finish for.

"Yeah, yeah," I said, and made a funny face. I wanted to win enough of her heart for a kiss, but Loro wasn't even looking in my direction. It took some thinking, but I made it through the barbed wire. "Will a donut kill you?" OK, now I'd have to fall back in love with her to make everything right.

The Court Blamed Me

"Bribe me. I want to keep you here," said Loro—to hear more poetic wisdom. "We're talking about paying the bills, happy or sad about it."

"I'll go get one. But let me say poor people are usually shocked into poverty. If it weren't so, we'd have guards and warnings posted along the money trail. Don't pretend you're the only one surprised." I wasn't too sure what she heard and would say next, but she did say it loud enough to reach the adjoining room where I was. And it wasn't about bills or money. It was about donuts!

"I'll believe you took it out of the mouth of the fattest cholesterol heart-attacked cop on the night beat. Then I won't feel guilty. He'd still die before I do," she said, loudly. "Would you care if it killed the both of us?"

"That's Con," I shouted. "He's on a diet. If anybody got killed, it'd be me. I'm the rookie." The chips were flying out of my mouth, at least the ones she was chiseling out.

"You know all their names, don't you?"

"You're trying to be human for me, aren't you? Divinity had no place in getting me to understand. That's way too high. The prince and princess of Who Knows Where were still heirs to the throne if they had money or no money, and had to eat out of the garden to stay alive. We're not that bad, so it's less trouble to find the royal side of things, especially when you think about dying all the time and have never worried once. Wouldn't it be great to find an error in judgment that will cause us to change? Money comes from virtue, Socrates sort of said, but virtue takes human relationships and we don't know anybody." Now whatever the goal was, that had to be a good start. Her sawmill found my wooden mouth without cutting up my tongue this time.

"Yep. And here's what you wanted, I hope," I said. I gave her the donut.

"You treat me so good," she said. "Maybe I do love you." And she hit me with those piercing eyes.

"Con might not be there," I said. "Donuts aren't enough to draw a man to work."

"Then you'd lose a customer. Tell them the truth then. Tell them your wife ate one when you weren't looking. Turn your head so you can say that." I had moved to her room.

"They don't care," I said.

"Do it for me."

"Fine." Then I turned my head. "I can hear you munching."

"That don't count!"

"Die! Loro, die!" I said. She ate it up.

"I'm dead," she said, and came up from the gritty-soiled grave with a smile that stretched around her head.

"Then we have mercy with each other?" I asked. "And in how many passed years?"

This was going to be the final end to arranging Loro's molecules to group up to the acceptance part of her brain, saying it was alright for both of us and time to go to work—at least trying for each to be accepted by the other. But she didn't answer me.

I had calculated on catching a couple hours of sleep, when I got back. She would have to be on silent enough tip toes for the compacted snooze to fortify itself with the iron needed to keep me in bed. It became necessary, and I caught myself just hoping we both had some leeway on taking a little of each of our ways for granted.

This wasn't the mercy we both needed, but it could be used for an introduction. There was no need to convince her on helping me sleep in or out of bed. I don't think we ever got past this attitude, relying more on the newness of being our-selves when old age actually happened.

We were both thinking about it, I guessed. It was a sweet thing to dwell on. It was true my schedule, that took away my sleepy time had just begun, but maybe this was the last straw for Loro. I never had time with her. But anybody knows the start of something new is a beginning that acts up until all of the surprises are nailed down—nothing dangerous I would hope. Hope was all over the place. She had bricked up all the higher virtues. But there had to be something brewing that would help to ease our minds.

Chapter 3

I said, "Till death do us part," as a goodbye to my wife, and I kissed her lightly on the lips.

"Till death do us part," she said. "Make dying your servant, OK? Goodbye." I didn't let on that I was leaving an hour early as I made my way into the dark. I wanted to get away with something that made me think I was the secret agent. Hence, I took my gun.

There had been a veil stretched between me and conversations with my wife, and I noticed it, whether she did or not. She was always cute the way she looked when we first met; and getting a little age on her vintage, she carried this trait through what she said between her lips and the gusto after it. I had always taken this in stride, but now it was blistering me the more I moved her way. I put light in her when I spoke. There was no way of stopping it, and this opened the curtain for more. So when every little thing wasn't practiced or done twice, I was lost: first to shield myself—I was so unsure of giving, not knowing how to track it down—and second to fully understand. Who talked like that?

But she had to have caught on, which made me constantly shocked and paranoid. Cutting through the veil was first on my mind as a reason to go beyond the call of duty on the job. My firearm was to do the work, I thought. It was time to make a difference, and I wanted to be a hero. That's how beautiful she was—heavy on the "was." Before I left there were two socks draped over the drawer lid. She rolled them up and deposited them inside. I was probably choosing socks and accidentally left them, she would think. She really didn't even have to know for sure. They were a sign of my instability, and she had guessed but kept it under wraps.

But I had depended on them being right where I left them. They were the entire world on edge connected to a trigger that changed everything. If you can't change yourself, then change the rest of the world and bring it along with you. Weren't the cops after criminals?

The suspects were five neighbors in a row. A steady drip hiding there in each one of the five leaky houses side by side made up the neighborhood easily on one side of the street—the others across from them were in tip-top shape. Nothing was sacred when it came to criminals in your front yard. My goodness, they had to face them every day. The orders from the police captain were clear once they sank down into the experience the guys on stakeout compared to what was really going on. Of course, a bite of refreshment helped at about the stroke of midnight. They sank their teeth into a chewy decision and swallowed to represent what really was no less than the process of belching out more than what went on. Nothing but donuts and coffee. They hoped the next stakeout was ordered for the daytime, when at least they could witness the five suspects grab their lunch boxes, or a few bucks for the cafe, and jump the transportation on their way to work.

But the genius of the captain's operation was that these five had been recently released together from the local mental hospital—all at the same time. And one of them was the murderer! That's as far as "Mister Wanted Poster" had explained it, as if it was drawn up and printed a century ago. More truth was in the lead, but nobody knew which one of the five it was. It sure made it easier for them to live on the same street though in houses next to each other; complicating the real estate were five of the twelve jurors who lived in a row across the road. Each of them had a stakeout of their own. It was called, Go to Your Mailboxes at Your Own Risk. The same went for mowing the lawn or any other activity. Their lights consecutively went off in the dead grave of the night—after the suspects' went off. One side was overly interested in the other.

"Let's take all five of them in," said Mon, the lead cop. There were only two badges in the car. "You listening?"

"Then we'd have to have a bus to take them in. This piece of junk won't fit but three in the back seat. The other two would have to sit up front with us. You probably wouldn't want that. I mean one in your lap, and the other one on the gear shift. C'mon man. I don't want one on the seat with me, even if my name is Con. And I'm listening."

"OK, you made your point. Let's just take three of them in—all in the back seat," said Mon. "I think you're listening."

"Well, the thing about that is the rest will hear of the bust, and we'd have to split the country. We can drive down to Panama, but who would want to? I mean the tires alone have to be new, at the start—"

"OK, I get it," said Mon. "And we wouldn't even know what country down there they split to."

"They'd be chasing us, dummy...so more tires bought in a foreign country; how could we trust—"

"You and your tires," said Mon. "Answer me this: why don't they all just leave and set up residence in Chile, say? What's comfortable about the cops breathing down their necks?"

"We're on stakeout, Mon. They don't know we're here," said Con.

"Now we both can say it. Ready, go!"

"We're both listening!" They chorused together.

"But don't make any extra noise, all right?" asked Mon.

"We're a true product of the twenty first century. We can stick it to you," said Con. Then they high-fived each other, hit their shoulders with a slap, and fist bumped. "Fine." And this he believed was to shut it up. But embarrassed at this point in time, he got angrier and angrier and then just popped. "But I'm getting hungry, aren't you?"

"Hi, guys! You hungry yet?" I asked. I had pulled my car alongside the cop's car and got the third degree.

"We're not going to pick bananas and hitchhike, are we?" asked Con with a look at a car worse than theirs.

"Get that car outta here!" said Mon. 'They'll notice a traffic jam!"

"I was thinking I could sit inside with you," I said.

"Sit anywhere you like, but park that car—behind us or in front! I'll give you a ticket if you double park."

"And he means it," said Con. "He gave me one for taking over the wheel when he went to stretch his legs. Well, I didn't know he didn't have it in park, so letting out the clutch, I almost ran him down. Consequently-"

"That's your new word, consequently," said Mon.

"Well, he took it personally, like I had attacked him," said Con. "That's what you get for being promoted. They gave us this new car—"

"You have a license and should have read the manual," said Mon. "You should know most of the time murder isn't personal. That's what keeps you alive!" Mon had his own way of explaining things.

"Cars are no more than wheels and peddles," said Con. "Wheels and peddles. You set me up. I believe to this day you take a little pocket change from the ticket slush fund. Don't you?"

"I need my donuts and coffee!" yelled Mon. "And I've been a veteran of three wars of stakeouts compared to your meter-maid experience."

"These are free donuts and coffee," I said.

"So park the car and bring us a box!" said Mon, who did calm down some.

"But watch out if Mon stretches his legs," said Con. "The car could roll backward on this hill, he'd prove to us he's learning, and we'd take the guilt for running him over. How-ever, it rarely happens, but Mon has a chance to break his own record. Ooo—I mean bones. You got insurance?"

I needed insurance? Surely these guys weren't that rough.

Chapter 4

In this neighborhood, Green Street and its houses were built on a slant. And like any cosmopolitan city where the skyscrapers weren't but two inches apart, the houses were similar, not unlike condominiums taking over a whole block. But each of the five owned this much. And if you didn't know you were in the good old United States, you'd think you were in Germany or Sweden with the architecture and the accordion music coming through the winter-proof boards—coaxing the beer patrons to come inside. Over there, picnic tables were surrounding the crisscross facades and giant white angled boarded eaves, stacked no less than three stories high. On weekends the whole town turned out. They could do that over here. Everything was the same except for the language and the people hidden inside. If we got truly neighborly, somebody would dare open their home; but with the mistrust we have between each other, this would not happen on Green Street—where you'd actually want it. Maybe it was possible a couple of generations from now when that one criminal we didn't catch stopped counting his money and built an honest business. Maybe then a beer business could see good times with imported music. It would be like a celebration of catching the crook. A new fable might be just keyed into literature for eons.

People keep repeating the idea that crime was invented just to let off steam. Kill enough innocent people and the scoundrel won't be angry anymore. But our nation was built by immigrants. If war broke out anywhere in the world, its violence would bounce through our system to the related ethnicity, and some part of the United States would have to be braced for a hit. So if the houses in this row were so long and built to evade the most casual of pedestrians on their sidewalk, the opposite of a beer-business trend, how did they have an inch of noticing an extra car parked outside? It didn't happen unless the one skunk was pressured to the gills, and his mother country turned to violence. War broke into his heart, so he attacked, and we'd be right there in his sights. But the cops weren't taking any chances.

"Don't slam that door hard," said Mon, as I climbed into the back seat with my stash of goodies.

"We can't see but two or three of the houses. Why don't we pull up?" asked Con. "Gimme some of those donuts."

My mind was racing from one thought to the other. I strived to have my brain back. It was possible. Wouldn't the teeth-clenching change of jobs be enough to disable me from the fruition of insanity? Knowing I wouldn't want to go backwards? To what was peachy in a worm neighborhood? The destruction had to be over. I used to be safer in this context and checked each part of a brainstorm to make sure the result was genuine. I wanted to speed up, but I couldn't deny that my restraint made a more accurate pulley for heavy hearts and minds. Before, after one piece of the puzzle was laid down in my noggin, I carelessly degenerated to comments from a paragraph of ideas saying, "That thought was good enough," or "That'll pass the test." Running up to the next logical step to assimilate the entire sequence, I backed up my grey matter with actions. Having been debated for some time now, my mind's sensors had improved and felt free from any kind of crazy compulsions that had nothing to do with what I wanted. I had to tell myself this to keep from sinking. My other job was so perfect (if you ignored the worms).

Everything stupid was lost in the dark to make way for the new quicker-thinking platitude. I was building a better mind from what I had previously. I had enough evidence to admit in court that something exactly like mental illness struck me down. It was an impostor, and all traces of it would soon vanish.

Everybody would be happier. But logging the thought that I was a schizophrenic into that little notebook or court-held diary or whatever the judge had in front of him wasn't what he wanted. He wanted my truth and the reasons the murderer, if I was the one, was a schizophrenic first. This was the only evidence necessary to prove I was guilty of killing any good-old Dad. The court case my brother went through, the one that acquitted him, was a blur, and I didn't even remember what I said on the stand; except to say I thought he was innocent. He was my brother. But now to everybody's surprise, I was fighting for my life. And if I had to blame him to survive, I'd see it through. But since he won his case, that was a hard muscle to cramp.

"What if you were the murderer?" asked Con. "We've heard of the court case. Now we're eating your donuts and drinking your coffee."

"I'll have a minute of warning from poisoned pastries or laced coffee, hot or cold, enough to put a bullet through his head," said Mon.

"You worry more than I do," I said. "I haven't even thought about that." And then I became a worried man. The freshness of meeting new people shattered like broken glass. I knew it would hound me all the way through every thought and penetrate every survival mode built so delicately in my mind. I was messing around cops and dangerous criminals. I didn't want to convict myself of insanity and subsequent actions like high jacking the car to Cuba when they hadn't even built that bridge yet—or having quintuplets each in a different state by the miracle of transportation. Or the abuse of it—just look at the picture I'd drawn. I quickly worried that the lack of keeping my donuts and coffee safe from poison had not been calculated or backed with any deed or guarantee. Maybe they should read me my rights before eating or drinking. What would the Lord think, hearing the law in place of his blessing? A fool hadn't any worry he was a schizophrenic, but then he proved he was not a fool. I quit worrying, presently, anyway. I promised.

Actions beat paranoia, if you thought that way, so there it was laid out in front of me. Fool or no fool, I had a challenge.

"Guys, I gotta go," I said.

"Already?" asked Mon, "We were about to pick up a couple of high school chicks. They love men with extra donuts and coffee. It's good you have so much. You aren't at your last drop off, are you? Listen, we depend on you!"

"He's just kidding," said Con. "We've all got wives wasting away at home, and now that the shift's at night we can't blame anything on them anymore. In fact we don't even know what the heck they're doing these days. There I go again. It's not the days that count for all of us.

"It's the night that's hit the fan, and we're in the middle of it. Just think, how many jobs do you know that pamper you to death on a shift change? If I were to bring my own donuts and coffee, I'd end up shoveling the whole store out of my bowels. I'd gain weight like a balloon on its way to New York City. There'd be contests on who let out their pants the most to embarrass us not to volunteer for another stakeout.

"That's right, (I had already left) to perform admirably under the watchful eyes of someone like the captain meant he saw the good in you. And if you're good through and through from the hard work you chose, that respect you had as a shameless youngster on the streets went in an ant hill in a crack of a sidewalk. Being a man meant to dispose of your childish ways. It communicated the message with all the other ants that a shoe was on its way. And watch out! Smash! Now how did they survive that? The answer was that the deeper down antenna colonists knew the hill's history, and they would survive at such depths. You could call it the memory of what you didn't want to admit in those young times. And somewhere down there, there was this little lonely ant that remembered you backwards and forwards. Who knew that a certain juicy grape on the kid's vine conclusively said your offspring was criminal material? They just worked hard. And who do they answer to but us? And we have to have respect for the good in us to be seen by the captain to be known by the neighborhood. Now pray to give us the spine and general good health to get plenty of assignments like this (I was halfway down the street). We'll work hard to save those kids growing up in troubles, who only the parents knew, to bring them up like that."

"Well!" expressed Mon. "I heard ya, but then Ben disappeared down the road. He didn't take his car."

"But he had a gun," said Con. "You know I can tell little hidden secrets like that. Who's on top of things more than me?"

"We better put a move on," said Mon. And he stepped on it after cranking up the old piece of junk.

All five of the houses couldn't be seen from one parking job on the residential road, so they were right in thinking I went to the furthermost home of a suspect. There the cops were out of sight and any fight would be done alone.

"Pow!" went the gun I took out of my pocket. It hit the lit-up window of the semi mansion, and spread glass crinkling everywhere. I stood a short while looking at the damage. The light flipped off and then on again. A siren was faintly heard at a distance, and then the front door was cracked, scaring me into walking back to the car. I couldn't go fast enough, but then I realized I didn't bring the car.

Mon and Con rolled up along side of our brand new crime fighter.

"Get in this car!" said Mon.

"And put that gun away," said Con. "We know what you did." They all looked at the broken window where my hard bullet had made its assault. I sat down behind them like a common criminal and closed the door. But my somber turtle head was only superficial. After both of them in front and the culprit in back had finished stretching their necks, they burst out in praise. "Wow! That was great! We didn't know you could shoot. Yeah, cooking donuts gives you perfect sight!" But they held their happy laughter.

A unit of their own police department pulled alongside the front yard of said possible lawsuit. And all the policemen, including Mon and Con, piled out the proof that all overweight people are suspended by tire pressure and shocks, as illustrated by the creaks and groans any car gives until one foot is planted firmly on the ground. In other words, the cops took their time but got out of the car.

I stayed in with my head hanging low, but before Mon and Con depended on that one last pivot to swing the rest of their bodies out, I had my say.

"I don't know what the heck got into me, but look!" I said. "That guy at the door is in shock. He's so scared, he's shaking. Look at him tremble. What I did gets us to admit that he couldn't be the murderer. Have another donut. He's much too scared to be hardened by anything. He's afraid of going back to the mental hospital by any traumatic event. He could be terrified of dying. A murderer wouldn't be like that. He'd be living with the fear before it all happened again. Wouldn't he be worked over enough by his own conscience to remain stable in the next confrontation? Here it is, and he's not ready."

"Maybe," said Con, who was still on speaking terms with me. Mon walked ahead of him as both doors closed, and I sat back believing they had already caught the man they wanted—or didn't want, and I had helped. My coffee and donuts were the freshest in town! But why would the suspect fawn all over these two particular cops and treat them like kings of their own kingdom, a kingdom he had been given the keys to for business and family vacations? That's what I expected. They liked him; and all they had to go on for this was from what I had said.

The four cops stood next to each other and waited until they saw the owner of the house approach looking like he needed crutches. He was trembling on his way over to them. Then one of the houses across the street had a similar lighted window that went dark. Three others lit up.

"Sir, can you tell us what happened?" asked the tallest man in uniform. And they all gripped the pavement with their feet, bracing themselves for what he was about to say.

"Somebody shot out my window!" he said. "I was shaving. I could have been killed! I'm scared to death." He may as well be scared of life. I nodded.

"See?" I told myself. He was more afraid of being himself than being nuts. But I kept staring, like that pet bird that never blinked.

"Weren't you committed to a mental hospital, because you were so paranoid your windows would all be shot out the day you moved back into the house with your tent set up in the backyard? And all the neighborhood complained you never turned the lights on, which attracted bums and deviates to the area?" This interrogation was from the shorter cop. They called him "foot long."

"No, I never did any of that," he said. I cocked my head to the left. "Excuse me." He did something like calisthenics, trying to work the nervousness out. "That sounds like my man next door." He pointed toward the fourth possible criminal's house, going down the line the five suspects were living.

"Sure it wasn't a football?" asked the tall cop.

"No, it was a bullet."

I cocked my head to the right.

"It would be easier to trace a football than a bullet," said the same cop. "Maybe it was a baseball or even a rock. How about your neighbors? Do they practice golf shots at this late hour? I've noticed a couple of golf carts in some of the houses. If the little thing has a sign painted on it, we would find the owner."

I put my head on a spring and bobbled it.

"You know, why don't we just forget it?" The owner said looking wide-eyed, and it ate him up that the cop was using his own way to get to the bottom of things; then his eyes did everything but fall out onto the grass. Had he taken a peek of me through the broken window? I had stood there for a good long time, and right now he was looking directly at me without wavering! But I imagined he had to put his eyes put back in for that. He couldn't be looking at me. Anyway, I ducked my head by shoving it down a little.

"What about that guy in your car, Mon and Con?" Oh, no, you know the truth comes out in the end of days. All secrets must come to light. "Has he anything to do with this?" asked the stilt. "He seems to be hiding his head."

That's exactly what I was doing.

"No, he's the coffee and donuts man. He's been with us the entire time. I mean he wasn't with us until we noticed the infraction. He got into the car on the way. We know him. He thought this was his own car. We needed some donuts and coffee. You want some? He'll eat some," said Mon.

"Looks like you ate them some time ago," said the pole.

"Yes," said Mon.

"You mean to tell me you heard the shot?" asked the two by four.

"Yes," said Con. "Gimme a donut, Ben." And I complied. "See how good his ears are? Ours are even better. The windows of our car are rolled down. Do you say rolled up these days?

They're electric."

"Screw your windows! The one in question has a bullet that smashed his to pieces--while he was shaving!" said the tall one, and he was angry. They all looked at the victim. "Isn't that right?" The anger didn't go away.

"Yes."

I put two of my fingers each under my eyes and pulled, making them look bloodshot. I hoped he looked at me again.

"We could dig the bullet out of your house," said the tall leader. "We don't have many matches in the computer, but we could get lucky."

"You know," said the owner. "It's less trouble to fix the window myself." Was he getting scared of the cops? I thought so. Liking them backfired.

"What's your name?" asked the tall pine.

"Done Shotit," said the owner.

"What the stupid heck!" said the skinny column.

"That's my name!"

"Get out!"

"I'll prove it."

"No, you won't."

"You get out!"

"We will." And he and foot long plumped themselves back into their car, tore the leaves off, revved it up, and left the forest. So there.

"I didn't give up before you did!" Done Shotit told them as they saw what the others did to the road by squealing their tires. The giant straw and foot long were gone, but as Done opened his door on his way back inside his wounded palace, he fell dead. Our cops were already walking back to their car, so they missed the new and improved bolt of the building industry used to attach windows and people behind them, which was his old job. If you picked up the pieces first, you'd find Done wanted to die earlier than most and could be trying a little too hard. The argument hadn't died down, and if it were an early demise, he was sure to have no screws in his casket. Otherwise, his body would have spikes of jerks in the open and viewing part of the funeral. Bolts would do just nicely, thank you. For that he could be trying too hard.

"Let's listen to what Ben said," Con said, as the dust was settling.

"I don't want to hear anything from him until ten pounds of coffee and donuts have its way in and out of me. But I could tell you Done wasn't the murderer." People die in an alternating sequence, dying one second and living the next. More repetitions of dying, and you're dead; more of living and you're alive. He had not exactly died peacefully on his lawn--or lived. Which one was it?

"That's what I was going to tell you," said Con.

"What?" asked Mon. He hadn't been listening.

"Ben loosened him up to come out of there," said Con, "and as nervous as he was over one little bullet proves he wasn't the murderer. But he could've been the accomplice. You see him laying dead over there?" Mon looked. They were lollygagging back over to the car, but when Mon saw the dead guy, they sped right up as if the neighborhood was ready to break out and circle around. Then Done twitched, and they saw that, too. One of his live seconds in time took control.

"We got to get the heck out of here!" said Mon.

"Good thing your bullet didn't kill the suspect," Con said to me as they quickly sat down in the cop car, turned it on, and threw it in gear.

"I must have had another nervous breakdown," I said. "I don't know what came over me. It won't happen again." They drove back to their spot. I was going to take the blame, because I wasn't afraid of death or dying. My wife would be proud. I didn't get any real danger from the job I lost. Maybe after all this trouble, a cop's life was my calling. I hastened to say I was really doing some good. But I didn't trust my cohorts completely.

"You were great!" said Con.

"What a pistol you pack!" said Mon. "And you're a good shot! You might have blasted his shaving cream off his face. He didn't say."

"He can't say anymore, if he's dead," said Con. "Let's go back and see if half his face is creamless."

"Do you remember him coming out with cream on his face?" asked Mon. Mon was stuck on not moving an inch.

"I guess not," said Con. "I'm listening."

"I gotta go, guys," I said, incredulous that they were praising me. And that was the same thing I told them before the action happened, so they didn't know what to think. Was I that bored of everyday life? To shoot out something? I said my good-byes, jumped into my own car, and rode back home. As I passed Done, he wasn't twitching or anything. I told myself I was too moody, so before I saw my wife, I decided to become more jubilant. I wasn't mixed up. If I had missed, and Done shot his own gun at the same time, he could've broken the window himself. After all, his name was Done Shotit. I was perplexed enough to be concerned and meant to check it out when I returned. And those cops—what a couple of guys! They didn't pin the broken window on me, because since I was like a donkey with a horse making a mule. I had no cover. And the barn had collapsed from age. The injustice of it all lit up the remaining windows across the street, until they all quickly went out again. So what if Done was dead. It was easier with one less suspect.

Chapter 5

How did the dead man in the graveyard turn into a ghost? The answer is quite simple, and you'll hit yourself when you find out. He was voted in by a majority of his peers. This might be the lighter side of the issue, but I was a dead man petrified that the shock of my psychological breaks, taken life-long in my marriage, would deaden my wife's feelings day by day until the eventual divorce. I was at a loss to love her out of it, because my stature had diminished so much to the point I was ten times less the man. And I couldn't grow out of it fast enough. In fact, I was still falling. The people at my old job had wanted nothing but my best, which is what I was doing here on the donut and coffee trail. I thought about this introspectively on my drive back home, and knew I had laundered this subject many times, until I couldn't turn it off, breaking washer after washer. Was there a clue of the good life hidden way back in the creases of my brain, or was my thinking process obsessed with the hurt, making no progress toward a solution?

I was a worried man again, but this morning given my insecurities, a celebration was on the menu, like being offered a thin reference book in place of the two large pages the best restaurant in town would give you. And for me, being so dogged out by the new events becoming normal living, a true optimistic turn upward promised twice the happiness. Couldn't I mop the deck of a boat in high seas with a rogue wave or two just about capsizing everything? I had forgotten I was an optimist! Deep subjects were a challenge, only because I knew my whole mind had the ability to right itself.

I pulled up in the driveway with my old fifty-three Cord sedan. No telling when it would fall apart. To get another one would take winning the lottery.

The insurance payment needed to go down in price, like the car did, but it didn't. We sold the newer car to pay the rent.

So I stood myself up out of the front seat onto the ground and told my eyes I would be looking at my material world. It could be construed as a perfect reality check for some of my optimism, which was right on cue. Take me on when I was in a good mood, and that way it wouldn't hurt. And when the chime on the clock was right, I'd dance with it—not much explanation here.

There was the spot where our wind chimes should be, looking around before I walked in. Yes, they had eyes. Nothing was better than hopping along getting to know myself. I had some depth. And there was a place for a swing or a ham-mock. She'd give me a battle for one or the other. And how about that front door that needed painting? I wanted it deep dark red. I'm sure that was my job. It would hide the scrawny roses covering each side of the way and create a comfy path to what was the neon sign saying, "Enter," an idea my wife never let happen, despite how perfect it sounded to Mon and Con. Their houses were drawn up and planned and made real by the architect, who took classes in bushes, trees, and ornaments—until it became natural.

Possibilities turned quickly into apologies, and then into punishments. Loro had the guts to fine me a couple bucks, and I didn't know how much enjoyment she had in molding me, but it didn't seem like much. Maybe I just didn't see it, but I expected if she were a potter, I'd find my wet clay self on the floor and stepped on. Then she'd sell tickets for a real trampling.

She wasn't evil. She was just using up her mood swings before the thought of them tore my heart out in a more real circumstance. What if at this very moment we turned old? Would there be kindness, or would there appear hate and disrespect not yet experimented with? Those roses needed some water, didn't they? Yeah, why not look at that? Other people's roses were OK We had to make cuts to keep ours in the budget, and this wasn't Congress. I gathered a little energy and walked toward them with my sharp fingernails, ready for an insignificant test, you know.

"Come in." I jumped and sprung back as my wife's lovely voice interrupted me. I collected myself and got ready to wander in. On the inside there wasn't much space, but we had planned on saving enough and even had a surplus at one time to join the vacationers in Mexico, where the ceiling was the sky, and we'd be overcome by the spaciousness—a trick that didn't cost us extra. We'd seen the brochures. Yep, there would be the blue sky, ready for us. To this day I never knew what happened to that money. Maybe it thought it was out in the open, too.

And we didn't have many windows—one or two here and there that used to have transparent curtains. I thought we weren't in the sights of any crummy gunman who wanted to find ourselves full of bullets and blood. I was an expert working with the cops now, and we hadn't predicted any work, like covering all of them up. I found myself digging into a female prosecutor's defense in Loro's court for lacy-thin curtains to be repealed. The neighbors signed the list for covered-up windows, and Loro won the battle by dragging one neighbor after the other to see her, before she took it to a real court. It was only a small-claims court, but she had forced it on me! My hands were tied, because she didn't have to love me until our old age. I forked up the money.

When they were all replaced by shades and lit up in the darkness of night, the whole neighborhood of square houses end on end, counting ours, looked like a windy crooked stationary train. It's hard to hit an object in motion, but with everything stopped, nobody wanted to smash our windows. The litmus test to prove this would take years, enough to keep my opinion. Bless my wife. I wanted the argument gone, but I learned love does things on its own.

The train idea was kept under wraps. To me, it moved. Maybe Done had a well-covered window. I remembered he didn't, or was this the schizophrenia removing his trauma? Loro would go as far as complain that I killed her, I thought, but there was a little problem called evidence. If she knew I was mentally ill and waded into the open sea of what I was labeled, she'd tear it off and get ready to do battle—in case it rubbed off on her. Oh, how slowly love grew. Would we ever make it to our old age?

"Come in," said Loro, the second time. "I heard your car pull up." Now she knew something was strange, as I gingerly wiped the dirt off of my hands. I used my key and barged through the portal of what was now no new life. Our apartment wasn't a haven of ecstasy anymore. But conversely I was in a happy mood. I thought of a joke gained from worrying about my state of mind.

"Loro. Why did the principal give the masochist a punch in the head?" She didn't even look interested. "Because the teacher had caught him daydreaming." She wasn't interested for sure, and not laughing proved it. I had nothing for a come back, so I looked twice at my good mood. The joke was neither here nor there, so I went with plan B.

"Good morning," I said.

"Good morning to you," she said.

"You'll never believe what happened to me last night," I said, with a thousand smiles hidden one behind the other.

"One guy ate too much and exploded?"

I shook my head.

"You brought home left-over donuts?" Loro asked.

I shook my head again.

"You know this week I gained two pounds. If this keeps up, I'll need new dresses, and you'll have to show me around town first by waxing the car."

"That car needs more wax than Jack and the Beanstalk's giant hundred pound scented candle," I said. "Have you asked a mountain climber how it smells up there? Of course I don't believe anybody has. But that's not the surprise."

"What is it?"

"You're not going to guess?"

"I already guessed."

"Oh, yeah."

"Well?"

"I killed a criminal last night! Is he here?"

"You what?"

"Is he here?" I demanded.

"Nobody's here!" she said.

"You know I always said I may work up the ranks to be-come a good cop-something more brutal than my last job—but I'm more brutal. I could be a real policeman soon... Say, what's wrong here? Where are my two socks I let drape across the edge of the drawer?" This was bound to be ineffectual, but I tried anyway.

"I put them in the drawer," Loro said.

"What?" I asked. "I left them specifically over the edge of the drawer!"

"They're in the drawer where they belong!" she said.

"They belong where I put them!" I said.

"They're only socks," she said.

"I could've been killed last night!" I said.

"Because I placed the socks inside the drawer?"

"Yes!" I said. "I could've been killed! That lug didn't go down with the first bullet. I used the H-bomb on his house. He leaned one way, he leaned the other way, gave me the thumbs up, and turned to his big front door—then fell dead. You'll have to apologize."

"You weren't in any danger," she said. "You're not scared of dying, remember?"

"Yes, I was."

"Did he have a gun?"

"No."

"I'm sorry," she said. Now she knew something was wrong. I had lost my bearings. They were in my skates, but I thought running around in my socks was good enough.

"I'm not going to be so easy on you the next time," I said. "I'm going to go to the car, start it up, and run back into the apartment to see if you've messed me up." I left it at that, while the seething turned to a bad mood, and then I knew I'd have to forgive her. But what good would it be for her not to have a husband? Maybe this was her endgame, and her push in this situation was only a prelude to worse weather in the future. Maybe she had enough iron inside to have a hand in predicting my death, and finally found in a better man the family she always wanted. If this were nothing but a soap opera, I'd head for the bar and make friends with Catholics. Did the Pope need a bodyguard? The Vatican happened to be one of my languages.

After killing a few more criminals with rocket grenades or boiling oil, the policeman's job laid before me made more visible the mercy of staying alive. The lock was off for this new space, offering many more rooms of happiness. But it would give both of us the politeness for me to leave her. I knew it. She deserved better. She couldn't live with a cop. However, stray moments of being alive with her could add up to her getting what she wanted. But this was only conjecture. Most likely, she'd rent a forklift, in case I was against every-thing she did.

"Well, I owe it to you. The man I killed was one of the

suspects we've been watching all night long, and there are only four left," I said. "I'm a happy man now that I'm still alive––no thanks to you." I was very indulgent in this happiness, thinking what I said was true, but I didn't mean any harm.

"Sorry!" she said. "Got a donut?" She was happy to gain a few pounds to roly-poly land, and also live through the pain. "But lookie here. If you killed the criminal, the other suspects are innocent, aren't they?"

"I can tell you know so little about police work. As soon as that bullet hit the window, he was a nervous wreck. Any murderer standing tall with an attack on his life feels like a million bucks because some errant pillage was against him. He's for the fight. We figure that since this never happened with our subject, he was innocent. Plus you're making me nervous right now, so I'm in the clear."

"I'm treating you like a murderer?"

"Yes."

"You shot an innocent man!" Loro said.

"He was innocent, but then he turned on me. I saw it in his eyes. The other cops thought it was a baseball or a foot-ball or some kid cutting across the yard with a rock; but it was a real bullet. I shot it in self-defense. The other four didn't have the choice, and one of them is a sick unrepentant murderer—!"

"But did you see the new fence constructed around the fifth's guys house? I was in the neighborhood (actually there was a phone call). It had barbed wire on top and leaned in, as if it kept him inside. One lady across the street told me he didn't put it there himself. Are we testing the temper one of the suspects? If he was the one, there would be knives and guns and sticky things to put a hole through his enemy or saw it in half, so he'd be torture to live with. Our appraisals had the entire neighborhood subject to his whims. Are you ready for that?"

"He has no plan," I said. "I heard the cops talking. They're going to eat enough donuts and coffee to barf on his front yard.

The Court Blamed Me

A murderer is too sensitive about too many things, so he'll obsess about it and come running. He'll be ranting and raving, and when he pulls the gun on us, we'll shoot him down in cold blood. Maybe I'll be the one who does it—and be that much closer to a real job."

"I pity the cigar and cigarette man they hire next when it comes to a shooting match. Maybe they'll sell beer and pea-nuts. You've left quite a legacy," Loro said. "And I thought we both weren't scared of death."

"Am I?"

"Then I'll keep your socks in a drawer."

"You treat me like a child!"

I thought the mercy she gave the criminals should be applied to me, if she cared at all. Nothing but silence and time ensued in our bedroom, where we both were, but that's as far as sex went. I had made the proceeding night sound as dangerous as trying on the proverbial hat with a nail in it (the hat had to be hammered down to fit), but did that work? No. I'd have to come home wounded to please her. And instead of the common sense we used to drum up and whistle out for our-selves in the smoldering confines of our loving arms, there blew in free and living disturbances, like the closest electric cloud; try to have sex with that oneness of nature. The cumulous rain machines, too, generously spilled everything every-where. The rest of our day was rained out and flooded. We couldn't make the precipitation warm enough, so it seemed my lady was dismantling our sex life. We were shivering witnesses to other people moving out because of our noise, but where was our energy spent? All we had on the shelf was nickels and dimes. We were on the way of quitting, but they didn't know that. And the prognosticators didn't want to put our names on television. Somehow I got her to settle down to a simmer—she always was afraid of the weatherman; and we both were sleepy, but she didn't change her mind. I was the criminal.

Chapter 6

We were on the edge of being so immersed in the ignorant vastness of space, as marriage should be, that we had believed nothing of each other, focusing solely the scare of death. We saw it take over or at least encroach. As soon as my break with reality happened, we reaffirmed the common sense that insured no break of that kind would ever happen again. We still hated death, but it was a hate that was light enough to the touch. It wasn't a savior. It was a simple proponent of our love. And there was so little of it that it was possible we hated everything. We had our feelers out, but there was a tunnel that tempted us, knowing we were falling into something—as if an enemy had built it. Hired men dug a bottom that didn't go all the way to China. If they did, we would eventually go "whoosh" like a Roman candle into their air out the other side, when we fell far enough. If we didn't get out of falling, it'd smash us like a runaway elevator. A body in motion needs electricity, so if you wanted to stop, all you needed to do was to pull the plug.

It was getting close to nine o'clock, which was the cut-off point for using up the time to make it to the courthouse, as I wanted to get dressed and go. Loro's night wasn't fitful since she had already been to bed and up again for the next day. She had carefully climbed out from beside me and sat in the kitchen, a few feet from the front door. It was locked with help from a cheap chain, the odds being small if we were broken into that the home invader had enough of a bulky-hardened body full of likeable pecks and certain obliques to smash our door down.

So Loro was lovingly staring at the clock the same time my alarm went off. She was so settled in her big heart that she didn't even budge an inch, preparing for me to wake up by myself. My timepiece was on the other side of the bed, so I had to get up if I wanted to turn that dang thing off. I wanted that incessant ringing to stop. But then there was a knock on the door. It was probably flowers I forgot I ordered for my woman. Small jokes kept me going.

Startled, Loro opened the door a crack. There was no bouquet or anything like it.

"Open this door!" said no familiar person in particular. She closed it back again, or tried to. The rush of this stranger busted the door down, the chain flying off its screwed-in base. And a man in a white uniform carrying a white piece of stiff-cotton clothes charged into the apartment running after Loro! Another white uniform chased his lack-luster future down looking for me. He surrounded me, who wasn't even trying to wake up, and held me down while the other forced a straight jacket on my wife!

"Who are you?" Loro asked, incredulously. She was trying to communicate with a wild man.

"Your mama!" he said. That woke me up for good. Calling somebody that was the most indiscreet offense said to anybody.

"Can you please turn that alarm off?" I asked. So the attendant, who was ready to hold me down to give room for the higher-up man to stretch his muscles (they were extra big) on my wife, made his way a half turn toward the alarm. He came right back and said the obvious.

"No, no, no, you're trying to trick me, aren't you?" He grabbed my shoulders again and held me down.

"Listen, I need to go to court, or they'll lock me up! If anything, I'm getting dressed, and then I'm gone. Please, I don't want to go to jail. Aren't you sick of me already?"

"Ben!" Loro screamed. How were they doing? This moment was filled with strings of death that wanted to strangle us, but that was a chokehold meant for much later on. Maybe I'd infiltrate the straightjacket company, and when they weren't looking, put ripcords in each one. If you're smart enough to get out of one, you're smart enough not to have to be in one. I must be a goon like these two if I couldn't concentrate on my wife's bristled hairs. I guess I wanted to ask, but something else came to mind. And it was the last recourse to keep up. Fear wasn't the problem. I didn't think so, anyway. But maybe I needed to know that.

"What are you doing with my wife?" I took it there might be something important going on.

"Take it easy, Ben," said the higher-up white-starched man. "You know, and you have to accept, buddy. Your wife is taking your place on the witness stand today. You have to go back to bed." He tied the ropes of that jacket tight and led her to the black-wheeled van, but not before I could smell his armpits, even from a distance. But body odor was not on trial.

"Ben!" she cried, and must have been in the same position. I didn't have any extra deodorants lying around. We'd have to go to the store.

"Listen, do you folks go on stakeouts?" I asked, while being held down to the bed by the other goon. He was struggling some, but what they said about going back to bed was enticing or interesting or down-to-earth plausible. I wished. I really did. It wouldn't shame me any. I'd be trusting in the world and not the spirit. She could handle the spin. I trusted her.

"Why yes, of course. We staked you out for an hour or two,"

said Jon. I heard the attendant say his name between mini-altercations of the psychiatric kind. But none of this kept me from my well-earned amorous nature. Sometimes the system had kinks in it. They're retroactive if we won a case in court. I could expect a sizeable settlement if I was named the victor. But I needed to think that over.

"Well, you're not getting any donuts or coffee from me!" I said. "Let me go. There must be a law against this!"

"Blame it on the prosecutor. I just follow orders," Jon said. "We're going to prove schizophrenia is contagious." And then the other let me go. Loro was already in the old van, and the door was slammed shut. The attendant jumped in, and they were off. I meandered around the kitchen for a short while, thought about going back to bed, and then did it. I couldn't handle the stress. I realized after hitting the sheets that the alarm was still blaring, so I slid out again and stepped over to it, turned it off, and got back under the covers. Maybe it was a dream, but I'd decide that when I woke up. There was a long time to go. I took my two socks and lipped them over the drawer lid and buried my head in the pillow. Justice was served... with a kink... and no pepper on the table. But there was something trying to spice things up.

Looking between the ears and eyes of the imaginary thing suddenly in front of me, as I was neither awake nor asleep, I stopped. Its wedge was pushing against me and had me hopping to get out of bed. I jumped out, forced the time to let me get dressed, cranked the car, and headed to court, not knowing what that thing was. But why be so flippant against common sense, when the kidnapper had told me essentially to lay down and die like a dog? Why trust criminals when my marriage was at stake? I raced to the ten o'clock deadline, so I didn't know how much time I had wasted or lost sleeping. I didn't stop to look at the clock, and then I was concentrated on driving.

Why was my wife beautiful? I had invested in her from the beginning, and the beauty had grown from little additions and subtractions to a genuine relationship. At least, I used to think so.

Did it happen to this day? No, they all boiled down to agreements or disagreements, like we had an eternal debate waiting for that day of freedom that would fit like a tailored suit. And if I forgot during the heat of the day what had started the convergence, I would fall from her grace as a husband. But we always agreed love took longer than a few years and maybe much longer. Most of a lifetime for sure. And that's exactly where old age was. But to pin it down to a certain time was a problem.

Was she relying on me for her beauty? She may be trying, but I didn't know it. It was a constant start-over since the clumsy trailblazer in us quickly brushed aside the spider web of love. We had to guard our trepid expeditions into each other, which were rare but necessary. We knew our marriage was simple to nothing, but we had the right idea. We wanted to be with each other. No explorer and his or her violent march through us could ever see our primary understanding and drive. Things like happiness shined through victoriously. And if she or I did get close to figuring out the other, we'd act as old as possible. Being beautiful for each other was just another thing thrown out to die, until our old age unearthed it for survival.

Did she lose her beauty when I fell? I only noticed the wrinkles, looking forward to being elderly. And if nothing else, which wasn't the case, she gained a few having a growth spurt of age. My happiness of the grasp of her age bullied my sense of survival, wanting it to head forward to a pace I could accept. I had a partially unswerving rate before, but now there were fears attached that she'd look old before I did. I wasn't going to destroy the main attraction, was I? Even thinking of her was a warning I might stray too far from what she taught me. But there was a lot an old man forgot. And if I saw through the gross and callous when we were old, I could be given mercy for recognizing her beauty now. A lot of good points were there. Growing up with both of us learning to use practical eyes, there would be a slice of truth guiding us away from a "goo-goo-ga-ga" sort of love. We'd have some of it—different from many marriages.

Was beauty important at all in our old age? Every line or wrinkle or sag or jiggle had a story to it. There was a day set aside (and we had guesses about when) for a party celebrating the moment we both came of age. This might be my retirement, so the giddiness could continue to the next day and the next, instead of being interrupted by work. We were serious that we had to look our dead-level best. We could look wasted. We could look emaciated or dried up or shockingly sad or even downright hideous. Our eyes could look dishonest or evil. This was us. Youth catapulted rocks to destroy the castle, where we lived, but nothing was really noticeable to the normal person. We were going to be satisfied as terrible as that sounded. Love was interpreted to be the leaves from our two trees going through the seasons until they took on the fall and buried the ground, which was only a few feet away. But there were many leaves, and each was as tender as the breeze that brought them down.

Chapter 7

If anybody told me or my wife that we were at the peak of beauty, we would either deny it or laugh. Our transposition through life, be it hard or downright impossible, was one we held in trust. The secret was ours, and we knew no other couple like us. When we fought tooth and nail to get what each of us wanted, old age was our deadline. We would have to be nice then. We'd have to care for each other. We'd not even be scared of death. We wouldn't get mad at one another. We'd actually not be scared of living. Many people were, but if we had more of this hook on life we wouldn't need much convincing to clasp it to what would be another failing job by then. I had retired and had new power to beat the crap out of the competition. I didn't need a lot to keep on climbing, anyway. That's all she wanted of me. I hadn't given up. It was either our marriage or her that kept me going. "Envelope, please."

A grand commitment made a longer note on the piano. That's what I should have. That's the answer, folks. The note would linger as long as possible and never alter, playing with sheer reflexes. I wanted to put a hold on the present job, listen to this note held, and then bang my fist down on the keys,

The Court Blamed Me

expressing my bitterness! The suffering was solitary until we were old, and only then it'd be completely dissolved. Wouldn't a crowd eat this up? I was there in my mind. I had the tux, the grand piano, and everything. Maybe I would retire at fifty from my anger, because my new position with the donuts and coffee might kill me before the benefits kicked in. I'd strive to work up to my social security check. The prospects of being a cop would never mine gold, though. That was a dream I'd rather stay asleep through, ready for each step to be an endless morsel of information about why money wasn't the answer. Each of the other cops had already put the banquet to their lips.

I stepped on the gas. I was on my way with a beat-up car, but I'd make it by the ten o'clock court session. I thought. And don't think the worst of me for being late, because I already did.

Loro was led to the admission's desk at the mental hospital. A policeman had joined the group. While she was sup-posed to be signing papers, Jon took the policeman aside. They walked away from earshot.

"I can't sign anything with this straight jacket on," Loro said. The desk monitor gestured at the attendant, and he began loosening the jacket until it came off. Loro wiped her forearms and hands and shook it off, making herself comfortable with some mean looks to the attendant and the lady at the desk. "I'm not signing anything!"

"All right, I'll put the jacket back on."

"I'll sign," she said. The lady shoved a few pages to Loro's end of the desk. Loro looked at it and read. "I'm not signing this," Loro said. "It says I got here voluntarily."

"Here's your jacket," said the attendant.

"I'm signing," said Loro. He took the jacket away. "I'm not signing."

"What is she doing?" asked the brutish-looking attendant. "She's always changing her mind." They shouldn't underestimate my wife. She talked about death like a golf-tournament pro—

without a molecule of nervousness. "Fore!"

"She's a woman," said the other lady. "Maybe she doesn't have one that fits."

"Jon!" the attendant yelled. Jon had thought she'd cooperate at the release of the straight jacket—her freedom was that valuable. They didn't need a cop to force the issue. If Loro played ball with them, she'd be treated like someone who won the Masters. Now the Green Jacket might fit, but that wasn't the color. "Ladies and gentlemen : Loro driving," with a green paint can. Didn't she know the court was appointing her first in the witness stand this morning? His royal mama must have forgotten to tell her. Time would tell and say too much and crack stupid jokes and whisper secrets, if the day grew curious enough.

Jon was dismayed at what the attendant had told him. To him the jacket wasn't that much of an issue. You could save it for Halloween, but how'd you reach for the candy? Simple. Tell your kid to say, "Trick or treat. Give my candy to the attending desk at the local mental hospital, and I'll pick it up on my way over there." Now why wouldn't that work?

Jon had already told the cop he didn't need him, but then he did—with one foot on the floor and the other taking its place kicking side to side, he worked up his nerves, seeing the policeman slam his door shut and crank up his car. He wasn't in a Western where they broke glass all the time out of the saloon, where Jon saw him straight out the window. So after the basic semi-maze of rooms heading out the mental hospital's door, he ran after the man in blue, which took a whole lot of waves and shouting.

"Stop! Comeback! Hold it! You've got to come back!" But the city's finest was concentrating on Main Street. By the time he ran through the first intersection, and Jon's feet a growing block away, he gave up. Why didn't he give out hooks on life, if he had plenty? That one run had possibilities of a thousand post cards of what the city was like. If he gave every patient a camera, they'd naturally have enough for a contest on whose to send to the printer. Contacting the stores would be fun. Jon had more hooks on life—more then what he just lost.

"There will be two cops committing you without your signature soon, if you don't go voluntarily," said the desk lady. "You must go without that straight jacket. It's only for an hour. They told me all about it. We've been expecting you."

It was the cops that changed Loro's mind. If she escaped, it'd be easy to catch her wandering outside in the streets. So after Jon had phoned in two other badges, they and all their importance came in the front door, while she was signing.

"You didn't need us, you did need us, you didn't need us," said one fuzz. "Which is it?" The creaking of his tight new leather belt also wanted the question answered. Jon made his way back, a little out of breath.

"I'm sorry." She got out the straight jacket. "We've a need to check it. Here, put this on," said Jon, to one of the policemen. He held it out like a tailor at the men's store. Isn't it strange only one store in the entire mall had "men" in its name? All the rest of the stores must be for women.

"I'm not putting that on," said the cop.

"How about you?" to the other cop.

"You've got to be kidding!" said the other officer. "Put it on him." He was pointing at the attendant.

"No, no, no, no!" said the attendant. Trying on straight jackets was not in his future.

"It'll only be for an hour," said Jon. "Come here!" Jon had authorization to fire him if he had to, so the attendant acquiesced, and Jon wrapped him up. Then he gave him a kick in the pants toward one of the wards of that floor. "Find a merciful nurse or something. Now get out!

"Where did your partner go?" Jon asked one of the cops.

"Is there life after straight jackets?" asked the attendant on his way. "I'm looking it up in the library!"

"Now as to you, Miss Loro..." said Jon. He wasn't complaining, because he had more dumping to do on my wife. The cops jiggled their handcuffs. "Would you rather go to a ward for people like yourself, have an appointment with the chap-lain who knows you're gone to hell, or to the beauty shop?" He was serious.

"I'll take the beauty shop," Loro said, defeated.

"Good choice!" said Jon. "Follow me." Flap, flap, flap. "Maybe I can take the rest of the day off to fix my shoes, broken from that run." Flap, flap. He rubbed his calf muscles as if he was contracting an insect bite. Flap, flap. "Here we are."

"Yes, can I help you?" asked the stout lady in charge. The place was a mess, but very organized. There were ladies starting work on shampoos and hair cutting, a few bold driers over the heads of some who were finishing up; and mirrors every-where. They were there with Miss Hock, the stout lady boss, to impress you with what you wanted. It pulled in all the area's expertise captured with their hands. Loro had an appointment before the willies hit her on the stand. It wasn't too late.

"Give her the usual," Jon said.

"You sure? The usual?" asked Miss Hock.

"I'm sure. And then we'll take her to her court date," he said. "She needs to look her best."

"She will look just right. I guarantee it. The usual. OK, you're in charge. Loro, I have to follow orders."

"Is there a shampoo included?" asked Loro. What? With all the change lost on describing "the usual" why not doubt that? It didn't invoke confidence in what was going on. But there was real hair at stake here.

"Hop up here. There sure is a shampoo. You'll like that. I'll do it by hand—the best for my favorite girl. Hop up now. Mother will take good care of you."

Loro did the hopping. There was a feint squeaking that put Loro in premature shock, but everyone else knew that sound, and everything returned to normal. Despite it all, Loro felt like somebody; somewhere, somehow, someone was finally paying her some attention. There must be a song for such great relief. Self-indulgence costs a pretty penny, not like her husband who only took it out of his hide. But if she could throw me around with one arm tied behind her back, she could take on this inactive group. She'd ask Hock later on if there was an extension to her business that applied plastic surgery for a small eye lift. It was wrong for her marriage, but I might not even notice. And if that was true, she'd get away with other minor touch-ups. She had found an innocuous deliverance from a dead husband barely making it and killing a bad element on the side. She didn't believe they were all criminals who I fought. She just thought the lower forms of life were all competing for some breathing room—forced by higher forms, meaning myself, to shoot it out. How base! The beauty parlor was her reward and glory. I didn't complain. I didn't even know. Anyway, all they did was talk.

Chapter 8

There was no song playing through my head anymore. A memory of a good heart-liberating musical moment with my friends or family, or a mellow feeling of why I had made it to the bottom of the world on a mountaintop cracked the egg in the morning—told me to give it another chance. Every healthy teeny-weeny happiness I could see gave me the energy to keep going. Any space for optimism was great, but my territory was a crawling thing with feelers wanted dead or alive for a child's bug collection. So I had to learn to get out of the dirt. What gave it a try were my small happinesses sandwiched in-between moments that pulled me toward everything else. I couldn't concentrate on a good thing if it fell on angel's wings. If I wanted to preserve anything worthwhile, I had to jump into my mind, and lose the rest—possibly something important. And these things distracted me from the basic happiness of getting what I wanted. There was opposition some-where that didn't want me feeling naturally happy. I would make the wrong decision over and over again, but that's what I wanted until I would finally find space to ride one moment to the hilt. So you can figure not much went my way. It was like a volley out of a cannon, with another right behind. My brother, the pirate, was firing at my ship. The high seas weren't big enough for the both of us. He chose to attack. If he didn't, I'd never have had any desire to pick up a sword against him.

If peace would awake after its long sleep, it would have to rise out of the block of my life, which I had built strong through the blocks of others. On each face of the cube there was a radio, my job, my wife, and the world in general, with which I was in constant touch--or at least I thought so. I'd soon explore those practical images. Two faces were left blank. Taken all together and without exception, these items, held in my hands an example of my heart and how wonderfully it beat. I was trying, consumed by reality, building blocks of life that walled off or exposed what was going on with me—nothing if I didn't uncover one of the blank faces. See how peace would awake? It had enough life within me to find a couple places to live. But don't we worry anyway? Didn't we? It would control at its best one third of my future and the riches of getting there.

So far on another face, we got nothing but destruction and crime that the news broadcasted over the radio; a constant all-points bulletin of criminals and their insurrections, which concerned my job. And then came the next that said I had strayed away from the general view of the world, which brought complaints from my wife and her fears. I guess if I spun the whole block fast enough in my hands, the blur would be how I translated its worth. I dropped it and it broke.

I guess you could say I was technically lost, but only the sunny side of it. I had to get to know myself to catch my fall. I had made the wrong turn, somewhere. Was it the divorce I imagined that cared for Loro more than I could? Her face on the cube had the strength to burst through the blur and grab me. Now that was a half hour already sifted down the hour-glass. I was reminding myself of the time pressure I was under. Nobody was around to turn the hourglass back over again--unless we could get some help from China, on the other side of the world.

Since everything was ready for modern man and machine, peace, given more time to unravel the puzzle of what may not be divorce, was more certain if they dug a hole to the good-old United States, jumped into it, propelled themselves through it hard enough to pass the middle of the earth where gravity wanted to keep them the most. They'd grab the timepiece for their upside-down shelves. This would work! Maybe there was an incremental hope of a live molecule, if we launched a few holes to the other side of the world, dug to coincide with the one coming toward us. They'd shelve our hourglasses, and we'd shelve theirs. A whole new cosmos would erupt. The Swiss Watch Company would have to go back in time to reboot. There was no need to compete with time travelers. Going back in time meant to use old timepieces. Peace had roots in time.

I quickly needed to learn about the world directly around me, though, by arriving and entering the courtroom for a back seat right when they were bringing in Loro to the witness stand. That's what time it was. Who cares about China? They'd probably tell us if they were digging a hole that deep. And I hadn't heard anything. A delivery man was wheeling her in on a dolly! She had bubble wrap around her from head to toe. But remember peace had more than its one side. Just don't pick up the faces of the world from where I dropped it to give it a sizeable shake. People's lives were at stake, if they had started digging. Like the waves of an ocean, its beauty would bring tranquility, knowing many of its parts would be working together.

"Hold everything, boss," said the package delivery man. Everybody had been waiting. The judge was already there ordering the people to stand up or to sit down. The jury was sitting and looking at each other. The prosecutor and defense stood on their feet. And behind me in the last row was the hospital's beauty-parlor employees. We all wondered what my wife would do. "Boss?" The mailman couldn't get anybody's attention.

The shampoo and hair-cutting people made me turn around and stare. They said, "Her hair came out just right. It was never so easy. And not one complaint. She saw the best in us. I hope she tells her friends. The usual. Never was there a more perfect fit for her type."

I turned back around after a couple "shushes" a row ahead of me.

"I, uh, hear the lions roar," said the judge, in Loro's direction. "They're hungry, so let's, uh, pass out the meat and help chew it up. But, uh, that only means we would be left to smell. What's cooking, Loro? Why are you in bubble wrap? Get it off of her! Tod, is this your big idea?"

"No, sir," Tod said. "Flap, flap, flap," went the steps of Jon who took the place of the mailman in order to tear down the bubble wrap.

"Was it one of you who put that packaging on her?" I asked the stout lady, Hock, who I knew was in charge. It was hard to turn around, since the pews didn't move.

"Yes, now it's like the unveiling of a famous sculpture," she said.

"I know where I'd stick mine if you bent over," I said.

"You'd lip it over a drawer. I've heard of you," she said, and before she said more, I took out my gun and aimed the barrel at the lady's face. She coughed the rest of her words.

"More lip, and you won't have any," I said. Somebody shushed me again, so I pointed my gun on him and said, "Shut up!" Those words took the floor of the slick-hardwood thickness of boards and nails so resonantly, I acted like nothing had been going on. Exasperated, my two victims tried to signal security, but only confused them. I didn't make a scene? Heavens no.

The mailman said, "I'm outta here. We only deliver. We don't do bubble wrap." And he left.

Jon tore it off of her. "Satisfied, Tod?"

"Boyyy, if you're a part of this, Tod, I'll, uh, hang you by your nostrils," said the judge. Somehow this had a humorous touch. The judge had pushed up a smile. His nose was getting more prominent, his hair was rustled by the constant shaking of his head, and his tongue was mashing on down his throat like he was about to choke. Somehow, the judge had a little more than a family figure going on next to Tod.

"That does represent her entire existence," said the parlor ladies. They giggled and laughed. I turned and looked.

So when the plastic packaging was off her, we all sucked air and oohed and ahhed. She in her unregaled glory was my wife with a handful of hair that looked like she had stuck her fingers in an electrical socket. It was in strands, each pointing in a circle imaginatively around her head. The hairs were straight but sticking out perfectly each in its own direction-solid, like you'd cut yourself if you ran your fingers over them. She was a true porcupine curled up in defense. And her hands, like all women do, patted the sides of her head and smiled. She looked crazy.

But she was sharp. Before the prosecutor or judge struck a verbal blow to her intelligence, she said, "My husband's breakdown happened because of his daddy's murder. He was fine until then."

My soul was defective. My wife showing all the people her ridiculous hairdo made the case. I slinked down. It wasn't going to be over. And where was that old age, when you first spotted it?

"That proves it!" said my brother, the prosecutor. "She's schizophrenic! Now we know it's contagious. She can't deny her looks. He contracted it from her to hide his guilt. Now he has to live with it."

I can't be schizophrenic. I just can't be, I thought, slinking down in my seat even further.

"I object!" said the defense. Was the judge playing ball with us?

The Court Blamed Me

"Lady, if you don't get rid of that hairdo, uh, on the top of your head, you'll be in contempt of court!" slammed the judge.

"I can't do anything with it," Loro said. "If I break one hair at a time, it'll still take an hour to go bald."

"You're, uh, in contempt of court!" said the judge, and he banged down the gavel. "Bang, bang. This trial is continued, uh, at, uh, ten in the morning."

"It's ten in the morning right now, judge," said Jon, who thought hanging around with the judge would add a step to his ladder. "We must have convened a few minutes early."

"Do you want me to confine you to the mental hospital until, uh, you've proved to everybody there you're a clock?"

"Not really, your honor," he said. And he knew the judge's next words were something to the tune of "scram," so he left, taking along his giddiness of actually conversing with somebody so real. Slap, slap, slap, and he was gone.

I had one more thought before I left, and I wished I could tell Loro.

This happened all the time. Say a just man has something torn away from him and he spends half his life trying to get it back. But since he doesn't force air into the bubble gum, metaphorically speaking, you had to admit he must not have been just. Anybody can blow a bubble with the right gum. There's no sense in being satisfied with that one solitary goal when there were so many others.

Since I left my job—well, they made me leave--my soul was just. I didn't narrow it down to the sharp point of a sword, thinking the war had only one enemy for me, and the other thousands were sent to fight my comrades. This would be selfish. My last job was the enemy. There was no way to conquer it again. So I improved my fate and even reached for accommodation at the donut position.

My soul was at rest, but my breakdowns kept me in the slave ship. Relating to them was easy enough: we were the lowest humanity on the sea, rowing for some idiot playing the drum. A few miles, and we were out of our minds! So communicating my trances based on imagination, I thought, fit into anybody's mind. I didn't know mine weren't true, and that they didn't know what they were talking about. My burden was I didn't believe them, until the motorboat replaced us, and the fishes in the sea were also ours.

Nobody convinced anybody. I was back where I started. But later on we would meet at the dock and talk about old times. I wouldn't recommend rowing on a slave ship. If you had that much imagination to share, go back in time and change history. A new life would keep me out of court.

My life's building blocks had cracks in them. But that didn't mean I was wrong. Who builds them? God? It was his fault then. I had figured out earlier that a human couldn't have compassion on God if He was so perfect. Maybe He wasn't so impeccable. Jesus broke rules like the rest of us—his fault officially. Maybe if God saw peace on one side of the block, He'd be there to give it a push.

My darling went to jail, I was telling myself. It had been eons since I called her anything chummy. Tod hadn't left. We crossed eyes for a moment too long, and then I turned for the door, asking the doorman the direction to the prison. I hurried on over there. It was like she was single again and giving me the chase once more. In the past, "The Usual" must have felled in one swoop a few others on the line stretching from Tod to the judge. The beauty shop certainly wasn't foraging around in the woods for a medicinal reversal.

Chapter 9

My wife had figured out I had new breakdowns after my job change. Since I was busy all the time, my grief over my dad had busted out through my mind. She respected this, but also knew it'd take a lot more time to work itself out. I didn't put the grieving first in my life. There was the rent to pay. And I really didn't know the harm a little imagination would do. There was snooping in my job, and there were rocks to re-move all over my life. Surely after a while they'd work together. I'd find energy in the incredulous. This is what my trances were about. I'd see a spot of one chance in a million, and I'd take it to the limit. What's the harm in that? It only meant I could explore the worst of undergrowth from the tiniest of clues. All I should worry about was going forward in a world consumed with the past. Yeah, let me try.

There was that one time in the intermediate past I was almost without a mind, when I came home and told Loro I had killed someone. It took a while to see my mistake, but she didn't believe that. Her good mind was saying she caught me with some kind of a disease. And how long was she deter-mined to let this ride itself out—to an inch of my life? I guessed the past had strength enough to bite. I wanted three or four feet or a hundred inches, enough to walk around the apartment. I recollected the issue of Done, the one I killed to an inch of his life, or the other inches to get to that last one. Going over and over the event completely changed it—to life, then death, then life—whatever. I've had times when the "clouds cleared" and something terribly different told me to wait for the reality of the event. It was so easy to forget what I thought was true, and I didn't want to see Done again no matter what side of life he was at. I just charged it all up as a bad memory and dispersed both sides of the argument. But it was like keeping a secret from myself: the first slide of the projectionist in my brain was the best one. He was a suspect, and my mind should respect that. If there were tricks, my job was to figure them out. If I had to trick the truth in and force it down the pipes where it'd grow, then so be it.

There! I saw the penitentiary at a distance. It looked like the Torg out of a Space Trek movie come down from space to sit on a flat plain of one hundred zillion cups filled with grains of sand. Some of us took time to count. It was the only thing living or dying for miles around—a ten story piece of a metal cube with engineered pipes coming and going through a steel base. It had picked this desert to stay away from the rain, which would undoubtedly rust something. I parked the car and presented myself to the receptionist. She was on the phone.

"No, we don't give pardons to anybody if they know the judge," she said. "Yes, it's true he comes over to visit contempt-of-court prisoners. Yes, they languish in jail up to a year sometimes. No, we don't make any exceptions, because he visits Green Street. I'm hanging up now. You got nowhere." Bang went the phone!

"May I help you?" she asked. But I was plastered to the picture window. I saw the judge! And he was emptying some boxes out of his car.

The Court Blamed Me

"He donates food each Thursday out of his own pocket," said the receptionist. "You're surprised by this?"

"I certainly am. He doesn't seem to have that much mercy on the bench." Then I heard a "Flap, flap, flap," coming from the side. A door was opened, and I knew who it was—Jon, dressed in striped prison clothes was going out to help him.

They met in a friendly manner, and the judge said, "Tell that, uh, Ben I see glued to the window, uh, looking at us, not to jump to conclusions. He knows, uh, what's good for him." I had no talents of reading lips, and the window glass was an inch thick.

Jon took a box and went inside where we were. He put the cardboard container down and came right over to me. "There are fifteen schizophrenics on Green Row, and you'll be the next one—number sixteen!" he said. "The judge said so."

I didn't want to talk to the judge anymore. It was obvious he told Jon to say that, or the consent was amicable to both of them. It was a pop-up in my mind that schizophrenics go to jail: they didn't have two court cases? One for "Far Out There in Maybe Land," and the other to get down to business? I ran for the lady behind the desk. There was only one, and I con-versed with her while Jon stacked boxes. Since that horrible morning Loro was forced to go with him and his cohort, Jon had said it was orders from Tod, my brother and prosecutor. They all must be in it together!

Jon had corrupted the mental hospital and the prison with the judge's consent, and Tod had corrupted the court with the judge's approval. If he had a beef with me, Loro might be in there forever. Oh, well.

"Flap, flap, flap." That Jon needed new shoes more than he needed food.

Bulldozers like Jon and Tod would have voracious appetites, considering all the dirt they had to move so the judge could have his way.

I asked the lady where and if I could visit Loro who was

penned up.

"We're all on a first-name basis over here," she said, "for a slice of a little friendliness, like at home. You said her name is Loro?" She got her computer ready.

"Yes."

"There are three Loros, unless she's a triple schizophrenic and the other two are just make believe. She looked bigger than a little spaced out when they admitted her." I just ducked that snide comment and kept going.

"You know who she is?"

"I guess I do. Victory! The others have been here longer than a year," as she rustled some pages. "She's started her visit in the last few days?"

"She was admitted today," I said. This was a stretch. I had quickly driven over here, and they got here first?

"Today," she said. "Right…OK…" She got back on the computer. "She's on the left as you enter the double doors—"

"Yes." I had moved my feet already, but then there were more directions. I had to come back to hear them.

"Go down the long hallway, turn at the elevators—"

"OK" I braced myself and didn't move forward.

"Walk up a flight of stairs, where you'll take a policeman with you to the crosswalk—"

"Sure, I understand. Make a nice guy's day."

"Pass the lunchroom—"

"I visited there once."

"Open ward thirty three, wait until the bars close, go right, until you see the elevator. Go to the color red on the walls, and then it changes to green. There she'll be—"

"I was born here. My mother and dad shared the basement."

"You'll see her in room six ten. Aren't colors just the thing for jail cells? I think they put a little brightness in one's day."

I had time to say all my brothers were the security men in this building, when it came down from the sky. But I was gone!

The Court Blamed Me

"You forgot to sign in!" were the last words I heard of her.

It was like a true maze, but I did it. I ran up to her cell and saw her slumped over and crying. "It's me, Ben," I said, and she bolted up to the front reaching for a long hug with the bars in the middle of us. We both cried for a short time.

"You won't die in here," I said, and she knew what that meant. I had dipped into our reserves. I meant of course that our marriage was secure and old age was coming despite the circumstances. I don't really think she saw it that way.

"But how? I'm here for the ages according to some people. I've seen other contempt-of-court cases, and they've been locked up over a year. We do some communicating, you know," Loro said. "I'll just die!" She hugged me more with the bars pressing our torsos.

"I could prove to you by reasoning that there's life after death," I said.

"Our marriage isn't what's important right now," she said, "or else I'd tell you to fix that splintered door lock on the apartment. Did I tell you? No!"

"But a strong marriage has some love in it. Don't you want to be comforted?" I asked. "Squeeze the life out of what you got?"

"I could feel better?" she asked. "What happens when you leave?"

"As soon as I know you'll be doing well, I'll go after a lawyer who'll make his own keys. That's what they do in these circumstances."

"If I fell from the top of the Sears Towers, and had all my confidence in you to catch me, I would still die in two seconds flat. Give me a year in here, and the same thing would happen. Open up this door! Get me out of here!" She had the bars in her fists and was trying to pull the building down.

Then I thought I saw trumpets with red and green flags attached to them embroidered with gold tassels. These were like the flags flying over the penitentiary, itself, somehow on the roof. If you didn't see them, your eyes were down. And who was looking up that high, meandering in for a visit? People are downcast just thinking of prison. Anyway, the trumpets blew a fanfare like they were introducing someone, and the waist-held red, green, and gold drums were keeping the beat.

They came from around the corner forming a line. Once they were in front of our cell in question, the philosophy of a kingdom came to mind. Maybe a king was coming. And then they quit—silence—the trumpets were sidelined, but the drums kept drumming. Then we saw him. The trumpets didn't blare out anymore. The men holding them yelled out with their big super-tonsiled voice makers, "All hail! All hail!"

The judge came out of the drifting smoke. He had a king's robe on. It was red with two rows of white fur, and it trailed along the floor with a train of golden cloth. He let someone take the robe off his shoulders. It was taken care of. And then someone put a crown on his head with jewels and gold bands, and red where the cloth stuck through.

"You've, uh, heard of the genie in the bottle?" He was talking to us! "Well, uh, I'm the king from his court."

"Long live the king," I said, excluding what I could've said of the jury. "Loro, here's a king who could help us."

"I've heard you, uh, need help," he said. Then the trumpets blew out more fanfare notes. "I've come to let Loro out."

"I could catch the notes," I said. "Is one of them shaped like a key?"

"Yes, you know, uh, we could blow, uh, the jail door open," the king said.

"Blow it down! Blow it down!" yelled my wife.

"But wouldn't you rather I open it up?" the king asked. Then the trumpets stopped. The drums did too. He was on his way to the door lock. "Contempt of court cases are, uh, at the most a week. We'll let this one out."

I was having another breakdown. None of this was true. I

blinked my eyes and looked for trumpets and drums like I cared, and I did. There weren't any. I looked for the robe and crown and found none. Was there a fat stout king nearby? No, nothing. And what about my wife? Did she say, "Blow it down! Blow it down!" The bridge to my imagination was just that, but what was the harm? Something was wrong if I traveled two hundred miles an hour to reach this place so crazy. Am I manic? I didn't slow down at anything. I should under-stand the breaking point. But I had to laugh a little. She was sent up for a bad hairdo. That's exactly what happened.

"Did you see that king with the small entourage who said that for your freedom he'd blow down the door?" I asked Loro. The Torg was all around us, metal everywhere and invincible to attack. Hacksaws broke, and there were a few scattered around. Then I saw a split-up drumstick and footprints on the dusty floor, like the king's troupe had actually been there. I'd just figured out the wrong timetable. Or else I couldn't do anything right. What if they were here before I was and had opened her door. I was crazy if it wasn't unlocked.

"How could any wind blow hard enough to open my door? You got to be kidding," she said. "What are you doing?"

"I'm thinking the door is already unlocked." It wasn't.

"Then I'm dead, and nothing I say matters. Don't you know the process? Trumpets make music, not door keys," she said. Why or how did she say "trumpets?" I didn't say they were there. Was she lying, having something askew with the mon-arch? She'd have to teach him about old age, and he'd get offended. He wasn't the one to save his love. He needed every ounce of his good sense, backed up by the emotional care of a loving wife, not to die of fright from the sentences he dolled out every day to people who'd kill him in an instant. Waiting for old age he'd lose his concentration, and some murderer would slip through. But how could Loro be that love sick—being so old in a while that she'd reach out to somebody else? Old age to most people was unbearable, having to remake yourself with all the extra hours with your spouse. It wasn't easy, and this must have scared her. Being out of the territory where everything was going on, to the few square yards of what was hers, what was the normal change a person had to go through?

So we lingered there together loading up our "gasp machines" to intermittently charge the air with them. I didn't know what to do. I had the whole day off, was a little sleepy from lack of bedroom time, but tried to comfort her with strength.

"You can't be scared to be here," I said. "It's only a little death, the bars and all, compared to real death. You can take it and break it into little pieces. You won't be truly happy until then. You're..." I fell asleep in her arms. I had needed the comfort myself, and now I was getting it.

"I'm sick of our marriage!" she cried. "It wasn't fit for death and its challenges. I'm sick of it! Understand? It stinks!"

My teeth went backwards, but I wasn't awake.

"If you can pull off a little happiness, that's you!" she said. "You're a measly little man, and half that, once you lost your job. You stink!"

"Like a hibernating bear? Roar!!!" That was the mama bear, not me. Who wouldn't wake up? "You look like a crazy person with that hairdo," I said, trying to hide the fact I was competing for her love and failed miserably.

"And the prosecutor thinks I'm a schizophrenic," she said. Was that mama bear still around or could I stop talking? I had to talk.

"Well, that doesn't mean I contracted it from you, like he also said."

"I didn't know you were there," she said.

"I was, and my opinion is you didn't fix your hair on purpose," I said.

"You're right," she said. "I was tricked."

"The prosecutor could have had his hand in it. He and Jon,

who straightjacketed you, are in it together. And just recently I found out the judge is in cahoots with both of them. I might be able to blackmail one of them and bring the whole case down-after I get you out of here, of course.

"Well, lookie here," I said. "Here comes the judge."

To our astonishment, he ran, not walked, right up to us with a key in his hand and unlocked the cell with Loro in it. Then he ran back just as quickly without saying a word. He was trying for a mute favor for me, but I didn't buy it. If he was in deep with Tod, the prosecutor, and Jon, a criminal in the slammer, he may have killed someone or helped. I was thinking I didn't kill Done Shotit. My wife was right: he wasn't a guilty criminal. I finally cared about what she said. So why was he just laying there on his lawn as we left the scene? I liked to depend on little things, so was that a bunch of non-sense that a guy could die for a second and then relive that moment on the next second? Life has its own order, and it may be justice that Done had to bear a few of the dead seconds. It wasn't my bullet. He might not be dead! But he could scare us, the more we worried about it—or at least I did. He surely wasn't dead. And I depended on it to keep myself from an upset stomach. But Loro was out! This was not the time to be worried about anything.

Chapter 10

So she came out of her cell in an expectant mood with her eyes making peace going on a touch of apology--and a smile that pulled her high cheeks down. They all worked together like it was possible to accept some of the happiness I had for her. She was the kind of woman who deserved a date—a time of showing off. But I had no money. There had to be a trick why she lasted this long. Love was what we both were sick of, even more than we thought of the giant mousetrap at the front door. Successful mice won their freedom if they passed the maze. Maybe I was like the knight in shinning armor, but there was always something she did for me. What she said in court was probably the best thing that ever happened to me.

Well, I already had it. The moment was over, so we tried to make our way back through the maze of green walls and red walls and doors and elevators. We did everything but get out of the dang place. We were quickly lost! If the wicked witch was in residence, we hoped she didn't have ownership of a cast iron people cooker. You know how dangerous gas ovens are. Maybe we were saving our own lives. After all, we both liked cheese instead of gingerbread.

THE COURT BLAMED ME

We saw many people behind bars, some violent, some resting, but mostly all yelling their heads off. The jackpot was Green Row, where the schizophrenic ones were confined. There were about ten of them, and the complicated way out was tailor-made just for their taste. It was easy as the Gospel to round them up—they would get lost even easier than we did. I asked what their crime was, and the ones listening said, "Contempt of court." A couple other heads suspended in a sleep-like daze turned my way.

I didn't want to ask, but I thought carelessly and did. "How long have you been here—a couple days?"

"Try a couple years," said what I guessed was their leader. He came right up to the bars in front.

"I got out in less than three hours," said Loro.

"Don't say that..." It was too late, so I embellished. "First was a peal of high drama from the trumpets, then there were flags, and then the king showed up—"

"What are you saying?" asked Loro.

"Go on," said the leader. "I'm Gomez."

I whispered at Loro. "If they thought the judge let you loose, the next time he came over to Green Row, they'd kill him!"

"Get out!" she said.

"I know my murderers," I said.

"You sure do," Loro said. "Next time you go out to the stakeout I'm grabbing a bag of chips, and I'm going with you!"

"No, you don't," I said.

"Stop me!" she said. Then she patted her hair like all women do and smiled.

"What are you two whispering about?" asked Gomez, a man who should be placed on a pedestal for everyone to see and remark that we had such a great immigrant society, and so diverse. We could finally cage the air as a country and replace carburetors. I wanted to get to know him personally along with his Cherokee past and Irish lineage and the German story, the

English connection, the French help and the Spanish plot. He was a real guy, so how was he a stupid mouse who got caught by the maze? So I asked questions. I didn't pretend schizophrenia, even though Loro wouldn't stop me.

Gomez told me he was the head chef of a fine restaurant, but he didn't like the others depending on him. Things hit the fan when the air conditioning went kablooy. It was like a steam bath for all the cooks, and he threatened them with violence if any went out into the customer side of the building, where the air was just fine. And then came the questions. On and on his workmates pelted his horse and mule, until they hit the desert.

It was scorching hot, and anything inside an hour to fix it was left over to the diligence of the boss. Our head chef didn't resort to any hitting, clawing, or kicking and knocking the closest object to smash over their puny heads for their persecutions. He began to believe every order was one in the same. Anything the customers said for the waitress to ticket up was the same as the next order was. He cooked and filled the bill with the same food—no matter what they asked for. A few hours of this, and he was fired! An argument ensued with the owner, and the chef could've won it, but the taped-up proverbial camel's back broke and through modern engineering was pieced back together—he, the head chef, now with his wits in control and his brains beside him dumped a half-full trash can loaded with mistakes over the boss' head. I guess you can say this fired him for sure. But the boss didn't stop there. He had Gomez institutionalized!

Based on information dug out of the cooking crew, the overseers of the mental hospital decided Gomez had committed a crime, so they put him on trial. He lost, but they couldn't find the legal infraction. So they tallied all the votes and put him away until he came to his senses about why he had made all the dishes the same. His sentence was to think—the same as the rest of them. Just knowing their punishment drove our new prison residents deeper within and farther to the outer reaches of the mind. It was so unfair all of them had to be locked up. After a while of being incarcerated for absolutely nothing, they each believed their imagination to be reality. It was a vicious fall straight to the fires of hell, and I knew exactly how that felt. These were all working people, and if forced to do no labor for a substantial length of time, rigor mortis came early and infiltrated their eyes, noses, and mouths. The rest of the body had grill marks magically appearing. "Flip us over! Flip us over!" Did I really hear that?

The judge had a brain storm. If the bars were strong enough, he'd have the chefs with their backs to the wall. This would force them to think normally under pressure, a quicker length of a sentence than the meddling mind-breakers had with experimentation in the mental hospital. So far this didn't work. According to one, two years had passed. But the judge wasn't a quitter, especially when he wasn't the one locked up. Jail seemed to strip away some of the basics of life, not make you think of them. Worrying would do most of the tinkering up there, and a moment of this was never enough. Since he thought he was producing a batch of geniuses, the judge would erase what shame he incurred when he locked them up. He thought their intelligence quotient had already hit the point you couldn't understand them.

"How did you get out?" asked Gomez, looking for a word he probably heard before. He wasn't satisfied with the story of the king. However, he didn't say so.

"The king had a key like a genie out of a bottle," I said. Loro didn't argue against that.

"One day I will," he said.

"I'm just like you," I said. She didn't argue against that either. "I have stories I just made up."

"No..."

"I do," I said. "I was in contempt of court, but after I finished smoking, I was released."

"Then give me something to smoke," asked Gomez.

"I don't let anyone puff on my pipe but me," I said.

"But what if it worked?" he asked.

"That's not how it's done," I said. Gomez had practiced this conversation as soon as they closed his door. And his reward for getting his way, if it happened, was a cozy convenience store—a pound of donuts, candy bars, cakes, and cola.

"How then?"

"You've got to have something on the judge," I said. "You know Jon with the flip-flopping shoes?"

"No."

"Well, it may not work like you want it to, but you can try something I know to be a sure thing. Look at that schizophrenic remark: it may not work, but I know it's a sure thing." I laughed.

"What's a schizophrenic?" Gomez asked. Oh, well. He should've learned that in school.

"You don't know? We'll get to that later," I said. "Does the judge actually come around to visit?" I was slowly beginning to be something for him to hang onto—not like a friend or a minister, but like the tit to the suckling child.

"Yes, every day or so." But his words were clear and full of daylight.

"What is he interested in?" I asked. The other guys had picked up their heads, too. They had begun to listen intently; like when the wheels of the train had smashed the coin out of shape, and they were on the verge of grabbing it, and running away.

"Well, he's asked a bunch of questions about our families, but none have come over for a visit."

"That's something," I said.

"Yes." He was going along with me. Maybe I had a clue to this mystery forming.

"What else?" I asked.

"He's asked us, do we like the prosecutor enough to go to

trial again," said Gomez. "We don't want to go back."

"You don't like him?"

"He has that patch on one eye with that funny curved black hat on his head. With that hook on one of his arms, he looks like a pirate. I was afraid he'd shoot me. The court lets in those ancient guns, since they figure they don't work. But I've seen him sitting down pulling the trigger for practice. Flintlocks still fire bullets even at this late date."

"That was at Halloween," I said, but I had barely remembered.

"I can't keep up with all the holidays," Gomez said. "I can at work. We had a calendar. I must have had other things on my mind."

"I'll grant you that hook on his arm looks pretty real. He's not a magician. We haven't been in contact. He's got a lot of shop equipment in his garage with saws, but these days they can reattach an arm. And I hate that big black mustache, myself. I know it's real. Maybe we should search his ship down by the dock. I'm just kidding. Let's tie him down to the mast, set the thing on fire, and run it out into the harbor. Surprise you?"

"No, I want to sue him," Gomez said.

"How?"

"I don't know. We don't have lawyers," said Gomez.

"I know some policemen who are dying to hear about you, but the help might not come for a week or two," I said.

"So between now and then, we'll get back to cooking," said Gomez.

"Cooking?"

"You don't think we don't cook here. I'm the breakfast man. How were your eggs?" He was looking me straight in the eye!

"It was good," I said. Loro changed a frown to a smile, like whom do we have here? This must be the real Ben, her dear, dear husband making alliances.

"Next will come lunch," he said. "Larry, do you got it yet?"

"A half a minute for the scallops! That's all that's left," said

Larry.

"Pronto. Get it done, George. You know!"

"Vegetables up. Presentation with the scallops on standby," said George.

"You can go home with a taste of the good life," said Gomez. "The steak exploded. Wanna lick? It's all over my face." He stuck his face up against the bars as much as he could. I looked, but only remembered that commercial on television about acne.

"No, we've got to run. Be back for dinner, I guess. Do you know the way out of here?" And he told us, only knowing because he had run away thousands of times, until he knew the route. These people weren't anywhere close to dumb, and their smarts were just wasting away in a corner of no man's land, a human pool of skin and not much else.

"You know, we've all got a flawed soul, Loro," I told her on our way out.

"Yeah?" she asked.

"Until death does us part, our soul is in need of our inherent body. We've got to live, so we feed ourselves food, entertainment, exercise, attraction, lies, and inconsistencies and complaints—all corrupting the soul. There's no way out of it, until we die where the soul is separated from the body. We'll never gain perfection, until death––more to look forward to. Like with a warm blanket, we'll go right on down the road after it's all over. And it's the body's fault we don't die earlier. See, it's backwards what we used to know. We blame the body for expiring too early. Hang with me, Loro, and we'll be old and in heaven for years to come.

"So we're married for life, but we're just as bad as those schizophrenics on Green Row; and helping them out has to be our goal in life. The judge knew what I'd do to him. That's why he let you out." Loro's head was a hundred miles away. I looked over to her, and it was missing. But why was I whispering? Were the guards listening? This was a maze for mice, not humans. So they should be spraying for such, not making it impossible for humans to visit.

"I may be like them, Loro," I said. "I've got my lucid moments, but I've lost so much life lately, you must have gone through a beating. If it's true I'm a schizophrenic, the court will find it out, and they say the next one would already have my confession—when I'm up for murder. I would have in-criminated myself just enough for a hanging. I don't know I don't have the disease. I've always supposed I was just a little weird. Isn't that healthy? They kick the little guy off television, so what we see is mostly millionaires. Why follow their example? There's a gap between relating to them and our own life. This is why I'm so insecure (I was going in all directions) and why I can't remember anything. A bad memory can't win in court, which I'm aware of after watching such a rich television set. Once the reality shows take over, we'll be safer. It probably won't work, now that I've made such an unpopular decision. Anything close to it will be a guilty verdict. But it's one end to our free life, except for the scallops. Did you want any?" There was no turning back. I had forgotten we were now in the maze to leave this place.

"You may as well say what you're afraid of believing," said Loro. "You killed your dad and forgot you did." I quickly glanced at her, and with her eyes baring her insides, she looked remorseful.

"You're a potato in the dark, Loro, dead until supplied with butter," I said. "All you want is a spread and someone's stomach to suck it in. Well, I'm not accepting a cherry pit in a raisin of your logic. I don't have to please you. I'm waiting until we grow old. But you'll agree I'm doing more than that. I got you out of jail, didn't I? Isn't that enough for now?"

"Was it for me, or was it because you don't want your wife behind bars?"

"I probably won't please you to a T. My disposition is that I react to your fears. And if you're afraid every day of your life,

I'll love you more than enough. I'm not out of reach—out of service—even if it destroys our goal. Seen farsighted, our finish line is to love each other—one way or the other. I have mercy."

"You know what love is?" she asked.

"Yes. It's hard to keep it in, but seeing you try to get out of it gives me strong giggles," I explained.

"Yes, that's true," she said. "I've heard you when you thought I didn't. But how do you know I was trying to get out of it, because I didn't love you?"

"That's not our marriage vows? We promised each other, with words we both spoke, that before we got old, we'd act anyway we wanted with—I'll go ahead and say it-love, hate, anything. And when we reached old age, not defined as yet, true love would blossom. We'd rather have a time of growing old together and enjoying it more than forcing the expectations of either one of us through big arguments. Normal marriages shove the old age ideal on each other to force the relationship to go to one of them. We don't force it. We live it! I've seen too many marriages fail because they couldn't force enough love out for one another. Being starved without love for so long, we won't be able to wait for it to start. And being old, there'd be more time to live than how much time we'd have left."

"I don't have to love you, because I don't," she said.

"No. Do what you want to do. Be yourself. You don't love me?"

"That's what you said I could do," she said.

"I deserve it," I said. "There are exceptions, but I won't get into that. Who knows what I risked springing you? And there's much more love where that came from. It probably relates to that. And I feel there's such an abundance of love you don't reach for. But we're not ashamed to make love from time to time, right?"

"Yes, I'll OK that," she said.

"But there's such a difference between a man and a woman,

it's like embracing the world when we go at it, you see?"

"Yeah."

"Being the world, there are people in their arena, people who know intimate secrets of this marriage. It's like our friends are physically in-between us."

"Yes, I agree." But we had no friends, thank goodness. This ended on a serious note.

"And as time goes by, and they age, everybody gets set in their respective ways—maybe at different times, right?"

"Right."

"Therefore, the distance is broadened between our couple issues and wants, not exclusively directed at the marriage, but devoured singularly with each individual wanting more of the pleasures to themselves. Being of late age in general isn't so easy on them anymore. Right? We've lost some privacy."

"Right."

"So our friends fall out of love, while we start loving one another."

"Yes."

"But we can't be that different from anybody else, can we?" I asked.

"OK"

"So our love could fizzle like the rest of humanity that came in between us. And we'll try not to stop loving each other? What happens?"

She slapped me right on the face! But how could I apologize from such a lengthy dissertation?

"If we don't work on our marriage," which was my point, "our house will burn down." She slapped me again! Did she unconsciously see "mercy" rear its head and slapped it down before she consciously saw what it was?

"Should we love ourselves the regular way?" I was groping. Then she slapped my brains out. The little green pieces exploded out of my open scull and were automatically peeled like miniature bananas. She was eating my head!

"I was working for the good in us, not in a destructive frame of mind," I said. Didn't she know that already, or was she so filled with hate she couldn't see straight? I didn't want to think about it, but I had to, because taking only a slice of her love to heart was the limit for my people. If our volcano of devotion blew right away, would there be enough to last through old age? I didn't know how close I came to losing her affection.

Translating it from the French, I was sincere, but I had lost the argument. She thought more of old age than I did. I had talked myself out of learning that. She just didn't want me to lose my grip. Like Done, this was going to take a while.

We waved at the receptionist and filed out of the penitentiary without seeing any trap or cheese. Making it to the car was no work. I revved it up, and we were on our way. I thought some of what we talked about. In my opinion the old way of thinking was born by my big mouth. But this was before marriage. There was still some extension of the truth that my mind with channels and defenses made a child of Loro. I must have forgotten I was only talking to Loro, my loved one, and not trying to impress the world at large. She wasn't in that world. Work meant digging the trenches some-times, so I learned to hand her the shovel. This is where we both were at that moment, and no telling how many others.

Chapter 11

I thought I should receive a blue ribbon for releasing Loro from her jail cell like I did. Otherwise, there would be an all-out war against a loose Jon and an even looser Tod with the powerhouse sentry, the judge. I had no armory compared to the corrupt ones owned by the robe. I was sure to guess their motives. But what light at the outskirts of the Milky Way had a chance against this garden of thorns that stood inflexible as the money stuck to each penetrating smelly-green trail of it? There had to be one, and I'd find it. I wanted payback. How many hours was she there? It was way too many.

We were casually driving. She was in the passenger seat, and I was behind the wheel.

"What exactly do you think the judge is up to? He has to be the benefactor of those schizophrenic prisoners, but how do you think he makes any money?" I asked. "They're only chefs."

"I bet millions pass through his hands. You haven't asked me what I think he does," Loro said.

"I just asked you. I'm asking, and I love you."

"What he does is prove that the husbands of fairly good-looking mates are schizophrenics. And with the fear of them populating the jail and languishing there forever, he sets up the women in an international-dating service based in the Caribbean. If the husbands don't give up their wives, they can count more days in jail, for who knows how long. A date monitor combs the world for multi-millionaire prospects, and the judge takes a cut from each successful match. They get married in a chapel subsidized with franchise money from the Las Vegas love-in-a-minute business there on the strip. There's also a casino to warm up at and twenty liquor stores parked on the main drag—pragmatically buckled in for the fastest pre-flight nuptials. I suppose the judge is going to retire there after he uses up his wife—not a hard thing for him to do. I know personally. (I coughed.) The plight of us women is to trust our husbands. Trusting you gets harder every day (I coughed again.) You may be schizophrenic before the judge forces it on you."

"Thanks a lot," I said. "Sorry, I've a cough."

"Did you go back to bed after I was kidnapped? Jon said you did," asked Loro.

"I got back up," I said.

"So there! And I still trust you," she said. (No cough?) I looked over at her and saw a survivor.

"Touching! Do you want a donut?"

"Wait, Ben. I'm not done yet."

"The judge told you all this?" I asked.

"Between him and Jon they made it clear. I'd push you away, as you faked schizophrenia, and then clear to marry up, I'd be free to dream about what a million dollars in my pocket feels like."

"And you turned them down?"

"I'll take that donut now," she said. "But you don't have to fake schizophrenia, do you?"

"What a great day that will be when we grow old," I said. "I'm going to have to fight this, you know. I'll drop you off at our place—"

The Court Blamed Me

"No, you won't! I'm going with you. Drop me off at the supermarket for a bag of chips. You need me more than ever."

"Yeah?" I wondered. I was glad she said so.

"I won't let you argue," she said.

So I buzzed by the store and also killed four or five minutes swinging by our place. I went inside alone, and for good reason. She saw nothing of my good-luck charms. I draped two socks over the drawer, put the teapot at an angle over the eye, closed and opened the closet door until I heard a squeak, and turned the television on in between channels until there was snow. Then I escaped to the car afraid that by some magic somewhere they'd return to normal if I wasn't looking. I got to the store as she was coming out.

"What took you so long?" I asked. "The more daylight, the more we corrupt what the scene is going through to keep the cops from losing valuable evidence or good information later on. Having the donuts—"

"Or the chips," she said.

"Yes, and not forgetting the coffee—it could make all the difference," I added.

So we drove over there to Green Street. It wasn't much wear on the tires. Rich people didn't live too far, practically speaking, from the poor. I'd wage a bet they had thoughts of us resurrecting an army to attack them with plans put halfway into action, as if we were that horrible. Crime was enough of a burden to bear, even if you only counted the waste of time the news anchor went through on television at six o'clock. Nobody knew what useless information they had about us, but I couldn't complain. Loro's parents were rich, and we never saw them.

"We'll park right here in front of the fourth man's mansion. The fifth man wasn't inclined since he fell over dead, but look, some of his windows are lit. Maybe his family graciously took up the final cleaning," I said.

"Or he's not dead," said Lore, and I heard a chip crunch.

"Pay attention to the fourth house. That's the focus," I said.

"Don't you have a camera?" Loro asked.

"No camera," I said. My eyes were a blur here and there from lack of sleep. "How about some coffee in my hands. I'm about to drop off."

"I'll take it from here. If I see some action, I'll force him to the ground, take away his gun, and call the cops on the radio. Piece of cake," she said.

"I need coffee," I said.

"I know, you're looking for a murderer, and I don't know any, but I can imagine. Isn't that what you do?"

"I need some coffee!"

"You know, I have an idea murderers have fragile constitutions. They don't have any spirit of togetherness that we share as common individuals. The spirit of us all gives you strength. So they have less, and I'll have the edge if I tackle a suspect," she said. She was just like me, and I didn't want anybody to be like that.

"Coffee!" And I yelled so loud the house window across from the fifth dwelling went out. Then a couple of good-looking women crossed the street from the fifth mansion and seemed to be in a hurry to the fifth juror's residence. Then the dead guy, now alive, returned to his house from the one the young girls had sprinted to.

"Oh, boy," I said, with a sigh. I caught on. He was alive, and he was back on the list of suspects. Is life going to be like that balloon toy you pinch and twist and never, no matter how much you contort it, make it pop? He had something to hide, faking death and whatnot in his show.

"Have a chip?" Loro asked.

"I want some coffee," I said, politely gritting my teeth.

"I'll go after the one who just went inside his house," she said. "You wait for the next house down, for the owner."

"No, we'll both wait for the fourth house to come alive," I

said. "Two at once is beyond our means."

"What if he never shows?" asked Loro. "Oh, well, I understand now your impetuosity being in a hurry with all the patience in the world keeping you back. I've got it myself. And there are no cops coming over for a while?"

"Not until dusk," I said. I should tell her. But maybe I wouldn't have to. Maybe he'd come out noticing us, and turn himself in. Or maybe he'd died on the spot again and stay dead this time. Maybe he was allergic to me. Maybe all criminals who got physically close to me died. If he knew this, he'd warn all of his buddies, and they'd flee the state. Job done.

"You have proof you didn't kill him," she said. I was startled to say the least. If she kept working so diligently she may be with me on stakeouts forever. Yuck! I learned later that he had stuck his head out of the door and waved his hands like moose ears. And his name was still posted above the door.

I laughed. "No, he's not dead."

"You didn't shoot him," she said.

"I don't know what to tell you," I said back.

"Figure out the truth, man," she said.

"Oh, well, I give up."

"It was another breakdown," she said.

"I'll try not to repeat it, but if it were meaningful, someone had died, and he was trying to tell us."

"You probably have no power to do anything about it, except with your imagination."

"I have no power in this establishment," I admitted. "Now look! My trances protect me—they're in such a different world, nobody sees through me."

"What?" she asked.

"Never mind." Nobody looked back and front and on in, except Loro. But I wasn't going to explain everything that had passion interrupting good sense.

Then two party-looking women appeared out of a cab,

paid the fare, and ran into the front door of the fourth man's house. My eyes were blurry from lack of coffee—it had to work its way in to dissolve the sleepy part of myself. And so I had no purposeful or non-brittle way of deducing what their looks represented.

"Look at their hair!" my wife exclaimed. I cringed. I was blocked by my own fault from what she was talking about, and I had a hard time discussing this with myself. My strength wasn't enough to protect Loro, when it was my responsibility to keep her safe. They had shocked and colored splayed-out hair like Loro's, and it hurt me to the core the longer the do lasted in contemporary fashion. Who was next? Our future children? We sat up on the edge of our seats and waited for more.

Like all the other long-range goals of long-suffering people off the curb, we had time on our hands. So let's say I liked to see myself philosophize. I worked on Loro again.

"You know what love is?" I asked. I needed this to give room for my intelligence to breathe. Maybe I could regain the brain cells needed to at least convince my wife. The fourth man's visitors weren't facing severe "legal" punishment, so we had a break.

"You going through that again?" she asked.

"Hear me out. I set it in motion to please you, and I know what went wrong," I said.

"I can take a truck and wheel it into my smarts, depending on my own opinion," she said. She meant to brag about how open her mind was. And if the truck came in and parked, it wasn't me at the wheel, because I wouldn't do that.

"You can drive four tires into my brain any old time," I said.

"Well, what do you have?"

In the meantime we both kept our eyes pealed on the neighborhood.

"You know what love is?" I asked. It was the second time I asked, so I must be serious.

"Yes," she said, reassuringly.

"And it's usually between a man and a woman, right?"

"Yes, that's true."

"Well, there's more love where that came from. It happens to be substantial as the years go by, OK?"

"Well, that's different from where you were earlier, but I agree."

"We continue with each of our own selves, which grow apart to the point of hate, and then we hit old age, right?"

"Right. I feel a little of it now."

"You're not old looking," I said. Actually, Loro was pretty. She had plain features, but they had personality.

"But I've sprouted this ugly hairdo," she said. "It was meant for an ugly court case."

"OK, we've grown old, and the rocket blasts off. We're in love so much we can't stand it. If we did hate each other to raucous levels before old age came down, we'd throw that away and feel the power of gravity being unleashed as the giant heavy rocket leaves the earth. Our whole lives were waiting for this. Wouldn't you be watching from under the covers where nobody detected you for this special moment?"

"Yes, and your philosophy has gotten better. I agree whole heartily."

"And that's how our marriage should work," I said. "We'll be in euphoria as soon as the old age bell tolls."

"I don't care too much for you now. That's the way it is," she said, "but all the more to care when we're old." She had got it!

"And you can continue to feel nothing for me, exploring your own opinions for who knows how long," I said. "I'll argue them to bits most likely. And anything you do, I'll try to top it."

"I won't work it out. Let hate ride. Maybe you'll grow some grey hairs or go bald," she said.

"But I can ask you why you hate me."

"Shove it up your armpit," she said.

"Not any philosopher can take that without begging you to interpret," I said. "But that's my Loro. You have an inhumane side, front, and back."

"What's a philosopher?" she asked, wanting to shoot one, I supposed.

"Someone who loves truth, loves learning, and loves things eternal that never will change," I explained.

"You're just pretending. You can't keep it up. I never knew any philosopher. You're just trying to impress me to put a cast on that broken job you lost. You lost a lot of money," she said.

"You're partially right: I've forgotten I won't be able to please you. Bending the old-age string down can't pluck sweet music for your ears. And there's no way to tune it. There's not a whole lot of people who pack their bags for the beauty of old age. We do share that together."

"You bastard! That was my feeling exactly," she said. "You believe in feelings, don't you?"

"Yeah, of course," I said. "But I must lie. You don't know where I'm coming from."

"Is it not a lie if I do? Tell me. If I had a feeling, and you had a feeling, they wouldn't touch for fear of a happy marriage, right?"

"I guess," I said. "I'll tell you right now our marriage is in the dumps."

"So we better forget all our feelings until we've grown old, where it's easy to forget anything. Our happiness will not be built on feelings. If that makes sense, I'm a philosopher."

"You are," I said. "I'm just agreeing with anything."

How did she take over?

"Darn you, I'm not!" she said. "There's no way. You just go on your high-minded stuff, and let the very real and genuine qualities live in me. If I hate you, you've paid attention. It couldn't be too serious, like an ax to the neck or a chainsaw to the torso. I could dream away on killing you, but that's only half my problem. You'd probably play dead and trick me like Done

The Court Blamed Me

Shotit. How are your live molecules?"

I laughed. It all came down to my old job and how good it used to be. She was my wife, and I didn't have the dominant role. What a kick that cereal-box prize had in it—meaning Loro. We might make it, and I wanted that rivet to count if I had a hope of plugging those holes in my brain and reaching the height I was before as a man. The only real difference between the job I worked in the past and the one I had presently was the timetable. The job I had now was an amount of issues and controlled choices in teaching and pure experience, like one had piled up a sizeable runway, including two planes.

One plane landed on the multiple instructions I needed to do the work on time, risking my life. The other plane was in the day, and it dug into the past that led me to the job. But I had to put my nose to the grindstone more than the other people there, and I constantly had to stick my neck out. This was why one job wasn't bigger than the other. Years later if I was still working for them, they'd chop my head off, and I'd roll out the door like a bowling-alley tomato. I was depending on it. I had the ball rolling on a decision way up in the future to plead for fireproofing. There was no money tied to that hardball game, and that's why they'd turn me down. I wasn't working for the money outright. And you couldn't pay to remove me from the stadium for either job. My life was a double header. Handled by the usual magic, the money would come. Having any job, my happiness stood a good chance of being just as bright and fulfilling as my heart could take it. And Loro wouldn't have to believe this until we both got old and rocked our lives away.

What scared me was that some people aged faster than others. Whoever that one was, he or she should take the lead. Compared to our marriage, others give it up to one person in the beginning. But shouldn't one of us follow the other, earning the privilege? And get old but not die? Then we needed to believe our potential. And we'd get rid of the "falling," since one of the jobs had been way up into the clouds. It had consequences that I wouldn't spike her coffee with. By the way where was that coffee?

Chapter 12

We had all kinds of things to discuss while we were waiting and waiting and learning more patience. For all intents and purposes our marriage was actually tightening up, despite some irrational plan against it. How, we didn't know. We were so different.

"Have a donut?" I asked.

"Thank you. I do suppose I will," she said.

Then it hit me. A tree fell on the road, and three monkeys fell to the ground, made jungle noises, danced around our car, picked up the flying giant ostrich eagle-eater's eggs, and juggled them amongst their hairy selves. Afraid they'd dash the eggs onto the car, I took out my gun, ready to shoot, but they didn't drop or crack or eat any one of them. As perfect as show-stoppers in the circus, they separated to an unbelievable distance; not damaging anything, increasing the number of eggs until there were about twenty flying back and forth.

The mama bird swooped in like an owl, sizing up its prey, and clawed one of the round white, freckled objects in its grasp and built a new nest on top of my car! We were anxiously waiting, or to put it more succinctly, I was patiently playing with the trigger, fighting on the side of the big bird. After a few moments counting the slight thuds on the roof, I knew it had rescued ten of them. The rest were still being juggled by the monkeys.

I would also retire when I got old.

Then another car was sighted. I took out my binoculars and saw it come closer. It was bright yellow with a sign that read Bird Rescue Service Control. It parked straight across from the fourth suspect's house. I didn't want anybody interrupting the mother fowl with her potential chicks. She'd never stop protecting and gathering her own, and I didn't want her to. So I took my gun and rode the cavalry to the yellow car. Loro saw me leave but hung back. She hesitated, huh? I felt my manhood come alive as I moved into position—not as a first-rate sleuth coming from a family of coral snakes, but as a husband shouldering the yoke for his marriage and his wife.

The back door to the auto was already opening as a huge middle-aged guy stepped out. Then he saw my gun. The man who was sitting next to him in the back seat was the judge! He waved him back in, but it was too late.

"Don't touch that mama bird!" I said.

"No, I won't touch it," he said, as he plumped back into the car. I waved my gun all around keeping them from scurrying away, and then I noticed: they had to have driven through the tree to park there. And the bird-control sign was replaced by a cab advertisement. And there were no monkeys or birds. I'd had another mental breakdown. I didn't care for shooting anybody anyhow, but the judge had seen and heard every-thing. The big guy got out of the car again as soon as I put my gun away and apologized. Who was that philosopher who said we're all in the same boat? I needed to quote him some to relieve myself of being a zipped-up heart-in-the-right-place thrown-over-board fool. And my wife was laughing.

"Why are you in front of my house, and what bird are you talking about?" It seemed he said this with his last shiny dime he slipped in the tongue slot, getting his unmatched-money's worth. Then it was over. That's all he said? He stood there eyeing me up and down, solidly, like it was my turn. We were playing a game? I looked at him, rolled my head like a top, and extended my hand. He didn't accommodate me. He was angry for many good reasons. The blood was rushing to his head. I wasn't going to say anything. I had to remain objective if I was going to pin the tail on him. But I really didn't know if I had good use of my faculties. I made the table tilt from the beginning of our meeting. And then there was the judge?

"Wanna donut?" I asked the big man.

"No."

"I'm on stakeout in this neighborhood," I said.

"Are you a cop?"

"No." He looked at the judge. The judge looked back. Then he looked at me again. Hard to say, because I put every bit of my gut into concentrating my powers on this big guy, but there was a growing thunderstorm, and we heard some rumbling.

"My name is Smith, and I'm a psychiatrist," he said. Everything was an emergency now with red lights flashing on a stairwell going down. What, I could only imagine. Somehow I recollected the two girls who had entered his front door with the qualifying hairdo and realized he was pandering his genitals, breaking up marriages like the judge was doing. They must be friends, and he must be on ground control here at Green Street. I could blame him some and get away with it. I was very optimistic.

"You're a psychiatrist for broken homes and the left-over wives you send to the Caribbean where you match them up with potential hard bodied multi-millionaires. Am I right?" I was right. He had to lie not to receive any blame. But I was all by myself like a journalist alone in a city that never proposed any news, minus what was happening now. I had headlines, but I had no camera to back me up. There were too many questions and doubts about a gunfight. So I continued, having the dicey integral information for blame already set in concrete—instant stones, because that's what he had. Anymore was kept under wraps, even if he was a criminal.

"You need to see my wife," I said. "Loro, come out! You have to meet this guy." I was a tangle of nerves. "Look at him." She stood by me after leaving the car behind, along with her senses. She looked crazy. That hairdo—how would we get rid of it? But I was glad we didn't.

"I got her from your match-up scheme, and look. She's the ugliest girl I have ever seen. I mean drop-dead ugly!" He looked. The blood had reached his face by then, and he was flapping his arms like he swallowed it and couldn't breathe. He was going to vomit. I mean a lady can take a little constructive criticism, but...

"Let's get out of here," the judge told the cab driver, and they left the psychiatrist standing alone. Everything stopped. The birds stopped singing, somebody finished mowing, and the gentle hum of traffic on a nearby expressway disappeared enough for our man to throw up. As if thrown from a sling-shot, the third man on the Green Street investigation threw open his door and ran over to the psychiatrist, studying his puke.

"Oh, it's in your yard. Sorry," he said. And he ventured to go back to his daiquiri, but the psych caught him by his shirt and implored him to stay.

"Her hair is ugly, her arms are too long, her hair sticks out way too much—" I tried to say, but I was a little woozy all of a sudden.

"Tell him," the psych said. "Tell him about James."

"Her lips are too thin—"

"Hey!" my wife interrupted. Now would she bring me some coffee? I should wash down what poison was in me.

"Her forehead is too high, her feet are too flat."

"James?"

"Yes, James. Tell him what James does," the psych said.

"Her elbows are gigantic. Don't hit me, darling. I've got to show him money can't buy you everything. He took a cut out of my savings," I said. I was only kidding.

"James put a fence around the murderer's house, and then he painted it with pink polka dots," the new man said. I was at a loss. One of the houses stuck out? I was standing at the moment, but how long would that last?

"I'll give your money back. Let me explain. You're looking for a murderer?" the psych asked.

"Yes." We both were throwing up. Did he share a date drug with Loro when she was in prison? And kept some for me?

"Well, I know there was a murder, and I'm not a police-man; but I know for sure the murderer lives nearby. So I hauled in my whole block to the mental hospital, in control with charges I forged myself. They brought them in, but we couldn't hold them for too long. On superficial testimonies, all preliminary of course, we narrowed it all down on the surface to the man on the corner. But one of them was sure. James knows it's the man on the end—the corner. We also called the cops, and they're having stakeouts. I get reports from them, but they don't know me. Thanks, Bill. I'll give you a call."

I threw up. Bill came over to make sure it was in the street, and only then went away. He walked back to his fine spread and the libation he would try carefully to incorporate.

"His wife was the one who was dropped into a shallow grave, we think."

"You mean the one on the corner?" I asked. I was still seeing double.

"Yes. She was set up by my dating service, and I gather both sides of my brain say her husband wasn't impressed. But I can't run a business where the girls are scared to contribute."

"You can't run anything that depends on the head of the family being forced off to long sentences of schizophrenia! Innocent people can't be freed from their jail cells, because of you," I said.

"But he couldn't wait for his wife to join us," said the psych. Do you see he had two different ways of looking at it? The psych hinted the man on the corner was schizophrenic, and probably didn't even know.

"The one on the corner?" I asked.

"Yes," said the psych. "Here. Take twenty thousand. That's the price of a wife matching up with one super-rich guy. Cash," he said, as he went for his pocket. "You're only looking for a murderer, aren't you?"

I took the cash. Loro shoved me. She hoped the drug would last much longer, at least up until she could take over again. But I didn't blame her at all, and that was the end of the issue.

"We have to, Loro," I said. "Anyway, I'm getting matched up with another. You're history." I quickly saw my mistake before she did anything else. "I'm sorry," but the meaning of the apology shaved both ways and sounded insincere. I was OK, but she saw her chance.

"You don't have to be sorry," she said.

"Not to be a meddle in your life," said the psych, "but you have a problem you should look into. Remember calling me a threat to an imaginary bird?"

"Yes."

"That's all. I don't know the whole scenario, but you should invest in a good psychiatrist. You had a delusion. It's a sign of schizophrenia. Just a thought," he said. I wasn't going to believe him, thinking he knew so much about the murderer, bud didn't really. Then it began raining, lightly at first. We both just stood there, awkwardly. He didn't move, and I didn't know what to do. A couple doubts came into my mind and ideas on what action to take, but I wasn't a policeman. The rain came down harder, and he said, "I'd like to go in now."

"You'd like to go?" I asked. I didn't like the rain, either.

"Yes." He was getting away with so much, but I had Mon and Con's ear in just a little while. The thunderstorm caught up with us, and the wind was whipping. Before we got too drenched, lightning hit Smith's shoes! Knowing that must have hurt, he looked like a jumping kangaroo high stepping it to his door without saying anything derogatory about God and mother nature; he must have been thinking that if he made it inside, the fire would burn out between his toes—both the big ones. A few drops of rain made them sizzle like he had found a new way to cook shoe leather. You had to have a psychiatrist's mind to figure out what this would do for our taste. But surely there wouldn't be a fast-food restaurant coming soon to offer this delicacy.

Ever since this meeting with the head psych and kidding with him about joining up and throwing out my wife, she had decided anything done to me was fair, and I had to endure it—anything! Turn about is fair play. Would I have enough faith to stay with her? Would she do something that challenging? I looked over at her; the rain had smeared her mascara to show anybody looking that she was old and sagging. Yes, I thought about asking her, but I was sure she had one trick left over. It had nothing to do with the noises that came back. They did though: the birds were singing, distant cars in the expressway hummed again, and more mowing churned the grass. Our vomit was the climax of a recommendable day.

Chapter 13

Time went by, and Loro and I were back home. There were the normal few hours to work just ahead, and I bagged enough donuts and was finishing up on the brewed coffee. I always percolated the best. I had to pour it in the thermos, and then I was off. Loro let me keep the socks over the drawer. The other things askew I didn't tell her about, and she might not ever have noticed, if I didn't talk about it. And I didn't. I had fallen into a delusion where I had thought of monkeys and bird eggs. Maybe I didn't have the right combination. I decided to use a different pair of socks, and not so much disturbance of the other materials. But this could last forever. The last combination was for the birds, I guessed. The monkeys probably knew this and took advantage of me. The snow on television or the tea kettle off to the side was well known by them, and they knew how to fight it. I read a magazine that said so.

I could've killed someone! Again! Was it the beginning of a horrible trend? I could've shot the psychiatrist! With nothing working how could I survive? What was my mind? Had it tricked me all my life, making me have false hope that I could depend on it right up to the crucial moments I needed it? And then it'd turn

The Court Blamed Me

on me? Did it want me to die? Was my mind trying to kill me? Where was I? What did my senses require of me? What breath of brain juice would reason with me for it to ease up? But this took some thinking, and thinking was from the mind—and the mind was the trouble.

No combination would work. I decided not to do it again. I broke into a sweat from the insides out and held myself where I was shaking. My faith from all sides was consistently eroding. It was not time to depend on Loro. We didn't do that. Anyway, it was time to go to work, and I'd have to do away with my childish insecurities, the ones that wanted to go with me. I thought of Loro when we'd truly be in love. Man, we'd have some stories to tell; and like I thought, I'd have to learn to have patience.

What would you do if a common vine were creeping its way into the barrel of your gun to block the bullet from coming out? But I pretended everything was all right. This took intestinal, pancreatic, appendectomyic, liveral, and spinal fortitude—and I didn't know how much to run with it, or what. So I just blindly did it anyway. I went back on my change and moved everything around. Maybe this would defuse the fear that they were building a two story replica of a Colt 45 aiming through the bars of a secret cell I would end up in. The barrel was three feet in diameter, and I would have to reside there with the gun cocked. There was hardly anyway to move about with that weapon ready to blow you to bits.

Under the prying eyes of my wife, I hurried with no shame- that was just a line, wasn't it—and set the socks out, the tea kettle off the eye, a suit in the closet off center, the television on snow, and two clean plates set in the dishwasher. I was gone, in more than one way. I had no faith of it working. Maybe that was the beginning of a sound mind.

In fact, I was just a wind-up toy walking in circles for only a short while. I needed my idiosyncrasies. I wasn't forced to go to work and accomplish what other men wanted. Thus, I'd come home knowing I did some good, what success was full of. It was topped with victory; and with chocolate on top of that, I'd be a happy man again. I cranked up the car next to the house apartment. It was unbelievable it was still working. I forgot to go back in for a final check to see if my wife had put everything back. I had two good steps behind me, and I was on my way to Mon and Con. I was the king of late-night snacks!

I drove up and parked the car right behind them. Getting out was understood. They accepted me in the backseat of their car by opening the door for me, my coffee, and the donuts.

"Hi, guys," I said. "I've got some more good news you may not want, but I'm sure you need it." I introduced them to my problem as I got comfortable.

"Hi, Ben," said Mon. "Shoot."

"You've had a busy day, I take it?" asked Con.

"Well, before I tell you, give a listen to this. Here's some donuts. Just think it's breakfast, and the alarm went off. Try to decide if I'm the donuts and coffee, or the alarm," I said. We shared a laugh, but more them than me.

"It don't matter. We're alone," said Mon. "We like you. Shoot away."

"Yeah, knock it out of the park," said Con.

"OK, then listen," I said. I didn't know if I had a chance to pull it off or run myself out of town. I respected these jerks, and they defended me that one time against the fifth guy, Done, who had evidence to run me in. But that was once, not twice, or any other number in a higher sequence. I did know that was a major breakthrough, an opening for more concessions, not fewer.

"A car needs oil, doesn't it?" I asked.

"Yes," from both of them.

"Well, if it runs out of oil, it doesn't work, right?"

"Right."

"And if you take a good car that doesn't have oil, and you put oil in it, it'll run then, wouldn't it?" I hadn't planned every question out to be in a pure sequence for a remarkable result, but since it looked that way, I'd gain respect.

"Yeah, OK," said Mon and Con.

"And if that car is old and beat up, and you make sure it has a change of oil, and then it doesn't work, it's not the oil's fault, is it?" I asked.

"No."

"Do you prosper in life knowing me?" I asked.

"Yeah, sure, Ben. You're the best. Hand me a donut." I put the bag holding a bunch on their side of the seats.

"I'll take some coffee," said Con. I poured it into his cup and left the cream and sugar with him.

"You may even say I'm better than a dead-old piece of junk, right? Something that doesn't work?" I asked. I didn't know I was pulling their heartstrings too much for a rookie, but I was, and it was quite uncomfortable for them.

"Yeah, sure. This is easy, Ben. If there's a punch line, we'll chase it around the corner, through the fence, up the stairs, and on down the roof. I'm sure I'd laugh," said Mon.

"Like catching a criminal on foot, say, Mon," said Con. "It's too long for a funny joke."

"OK, look. Oil is something I need, like your permission," I said. "You come to the conclusion, and I'm not interpreting this with bias. You said I'm better than a dead-old car. But sometimes if you put oil in it, it'd come to life. You agree?" I was getting nervous. My heart was flawed. There was no other explanation.

"Yes."

"How about putting some oil in me? I may be old and dead, but with some of your hard working greasy fingers, we could fix this car, and let me run with you. I'd like to be your point man—the one in front who takes all the danger. What do you say? I've got plenty of gas, and if you don't humor me, I'll be worse than that dead-old car. I'll never be dead and gone to you, though. I trust your words and will always believe in yo

I was good the first time. We made the right decision that Done wasn't the murderer, remember? What do you say? We can keep it under wraps. It's only for the stakeout here on Green Street. How about it? Yeah? Yeah?

"Tell me you will. I'll hug you. I'll do anything. You know, I want to be a legitimate cop. (This is where my foot came down.) You don't know that?

"Well, I do. I know a lot of stuff. OK? We're pals or brothers. Which one is it?" I was losing it. What would shut me up? I had passed the point of convincing. Was I looking for a dead horse to beat? Loro had changed something around—maybe the socks needed washing. I didn't check for that.

"I didn't bring my ugly wife with me. And I've got lots of nasty stories to tell about her," I said, and I was finished. The next all-consuming fire was coming from their coal-eating energetic lips. "I hope I didn't lay it on too thick. Maybe you don't want to hear about my wife."

They didn't say anything, and the moment lingered with each of them giving the same look to each other. And this was when all the wrinkles (girls called it character) counted on their faces. I'd never take a sad look on somebody's countenance to actually mean someone was down on his luck. No matter how crinkled and worn, there was a use in its reflection coming around the corner. She'll be coming around the mountain when she sees my ugly face.

So I spoke up, or else we'd live and grow warts. A whole week of deciding had enough ammunition to kill me, as many chances as I took. So the decision was now or never. But I still had to pull down the hand of Almighty God. That would work.

"sus is the fire in my smoke," I said, and I had to reach was desperate, but I could explain. "You see, let's smoke my pipe, I get all high and mighty; and my 'e like I'm something great. It's a lot of fun and when I'm relaxing in need of a little confidence.

I work on something that isn't pulling in any great amount of money, so I have these little celebrations, you know, in praise of myself. The potential is there. I smoke quite a lot, so instead of heaven and the angels getting jealous knowing their glory can't be challenged, the Big Honcho has to consume the picture of me—the highest and mightiest, in flames. But he doesn't let it get out of hand. I'm not going to hell, except in some evil man's imagination. So casually, He wanted an excuse to work with this being. He is there. I know, because I can depend on it. And what I can tell you is I need to light up extra and keep on smoking. I just want my presence known, and that's how I do it. I could have more than enough, and I'd certainly be smoking if I got the job." I motioned for them to have more coffee and donuts, but they waved me off. It looked like I put them between a rock and a hot place, and they didn't want to be burned. So I kept going, even if all their importance was shown next to my pettiness. Maybe if the ladder had a place for oil?

"Now one thing leads to another, because we're all related, said Einstein, probably articulated differently, but what do you think?" I was pitiful. "Are you sending me to some slippery slope, where there was supposed to be a clear road over the mountains? Or down some well, where I'd have to wait for enough Native Americans to rise from the rocks, dirt, and soot to stand me on their shoulders, one after the other, to reach the surface and climb out? I wait for your reply."

And there was that moment again. It took my breath away, because I saw Mon and Con breathe heavily, like this was an affront to their professionalism. But this time they were tired of it. And being worn out, they had no edge, so they had to give me the bottom line. Putting on my tongue the intelligence I was learning there and swallowing it, I began to think they came that close to locking me up for flushing out the fifth man on the block. OK, I knew what the silence meant. It just wasn't on the record.

"You better keep the coffee and donuts on your side of the car," I said. "I can feel it kicking again. There must be a good side to this." And I moved away from leaning over their seat to opening the door again to attack the neighborhood. I was a chip up, because of my confrontation with Smith. And with my wife counting the money back home, I was free to terrorize him for picking on us. I got the door open. They knew what I was about to do, and I knew they didn't like it. So just when my feet were about to hit the pavement, Mon backed up and then hit the brakes hard. The door slammed back shut. I had to bring my feet in to keep them from being sliced!

And then there was more of the stinging silence, but Mon finally broke the ice, and it spilled all over the road, waiting for the next spinning tire that ate it up and got buzzed.

"You see, there's some very good ideas with you, Ben, and we both like them," said Mon. He looked over to Con, and it was unanimous, at least the nodding part. But Con smiled, and Mon said more. "We know you're adventuresome." He looked at Con again, and he nodded and smiled reciprocally. "Both of us wish you well." More smiles and nods. "We needed proof, and we got it from the last experience." They had held back, because it was the first time they defended me. I was keeping Smith from them. I wanted them to deserve it.

"Yes," said Con. "You deserve a blue ribbon for your last performance, and we'd like to deputize you." He looked at Mon, both smiled, and then Mon said what I braced myself for. I didn't lose hope. But first he high-fived Con.

"We don't have the power by law to do that," and both of them kind of looked the other direction from themselves. I could take it. Then they fist bumped. "You'd have to lose the gun."

"Wow! Anything but the gun," I said.

"Yes, you could run with us, but you couldn't shoot," said Con, and they looked at themselves again and smiled, turning quickly away.

"Hot dog!" I exclaimed. "I needed that, guys. I'm telling you the hairy-awful truth. Is that the way to become a real policeman?"

"Yeah," said Mon. "We're listening. Enough of this, and you'd be accepted in the police academy without a test."

"We're ready for the Twenty First Century," they chorused, high-fived and fist-bumped again. "You listening?"

"Great, guys. I've got to dig in the donut bag. I think one or two will go down good." There was a way they could fully deputize me on down the road, but they kept this to them-selves. I might never know, and the job was wired to be dangerous. I couldn't shoot back if shot at. But I could buy a derringer. Having two guns in the family, I'd have reservations from the world for Loro and I to be a duo. Screw Mon and Con. They took too long to decide. And we had the other car, of course, but it counted. We'd make time with twice as many on stakeout. Maybe I could slack up on the job and make Loro think we were parking like kids do. The longer the stakeout, the better. Crime could hit a climax, and we wouldn't be far behind.

Then they pinned a badge on me. I didn't see it coming, but my chest couldn't stick out enough to equal their graciousness. Sharing air with them made the sun smile. And if it was a rainy day? The badge would reflect the light. Wow!

"We trust you, now you're a partial deputy. You have to get rid of your gun by the honor system," said Mon.

"Yes, we're honorable." And they belly-laughed off the rest of the conversation, or was it a bookend to what they were forced to say? It was time to concentrate back on the neighborhood.

"I'll get rid of it as soon as I can," I said, honestly and honorably, laughing along side of them. I was a good man, and they were good cops, weren't they? I was listening. I was placing every excuse I had in my private eardrum, but to make it legal, I had to tell the cops. The exception was the honor system. Wasn't it great?

Chapter 14

Thanks to a little philosophy on the road—usually those times don't produce as many chances, since the price of oil went up—but it worked, and we three were watching and listening on another great stakeout. I had brought Tod's pet parrot with me. He had forgotten I had it, but it did prove there was a time we were on a high mountain pass and weren't butting heads. I was also thinking since the night had come down hard upon us, that there had to be cracks in the ground that showed pieces of light coming from the sunshine on the bright side below us, but the odds weren't good.

The earth was pretty thick. So I looked for lawn mowers with their own headlights, and Mon and Con got ready for strange movements—anything that pulled a suspect out of the deck. There could be related rustling noises or people sightings that looked suspicious, like the sound of bullets firing or a scream from one of the telltale houses. Nobody I knew thought this was a haunted neighborhood, but they could be wrong.

It was confusing to see absolutely nothing going on, so I decided to tell them about man number four, Mister Smith. I began by saying he was a psychiatrist, and he wasn't back at his home after observation, like we were told from the beginning. I had enough to say he was the one who temporarily locked all of his neighbors up, because they were his suspects for murder, and he had the holy power to do it. If this didn't work, would he pull up four foundations from under his neighborhood— four suspected ones and not his own house to conceal his intentions? A crane could lift four cement-poured concrete square basement-sized pieces into the air and toss them. Not much scared him. He was gifted in talking away fears.

"You mean you believed him?" Mon asked.

"How could we be so enamored to stakeout the head psychiatrist of the mental hospital?" Con asked.

"Your new word is enamored!" said Mon.

"Let's have a donut, Ben," said Con, and we chewed for a while. "Smith's ability to lock everybody up would come in handy if he needed a victim to be silenced—like after he shot it out with somebody." That was a donut each. Both picked up another.

"Well, you know what else?" I asked. I took a bite. I was still grinding on the first one though. "I saw the fifth man, who we thought was dead, come to life again, making time in his house with some ladies."

"Oh, no," said Mon.

"I see what you mean, Mon," said Con. "Done could have had his nerves in check looking forward to banging one of his girlfriends, but the bullet forced them to stand on end, once again why he was mad at us and so nervous. He thought by playing dead, we would go away." Then Con smiled like he was right, took three small donuts, and stuffed them ail in his mouth at once.

"Guys, you know how to inspect an innocent or guilty bug on a blade of grass in a meadow?" I asked. "Each of the bugs has a cow coming closer to chew it up. So the answer is, quickly. Decide as quickly as you can. Done has as many problems as what starts with the second girlfriend—while still having the first. He seems to multiply, and in time he could take us for a ride. Let's not dwell on him. Nip it in the bud, and we'll have a better grip on the rest of them."

"You'll catch on soon," said Con. With his mouth so full we could barely decipher what he said.

"You know what that means, Ben?" asked Mon. "He's back on the list of suspects."

"But all bugs are the same, and there's a whole field of cows. Let's quickly take knock him off the list, before he gets us devoured. Of course, we'll be sorry if he does die. You know the short span of life for these criminals. I also saw Bill," I said.

"Who's Bill?" asked Mon and Con. The donuts about took over their faces.

"He ran out of his comfy home and chased down some puke that hit the grass near his property line," I said. "It wasn't on his side so he ran back in."

"That's all you saw?"

"Yes."

"Well, that means he's either got a big nose, or he can't have anybody near him for fear of finding some secret his place is full of. A dead body? Or queer instruments of destruction? Heck, if we only had a search warrant!"

"A dead body, Mon," said Con. "He loves the smell of deterioration so much that puke mixed in takes the pure stink out of the corruption he wants to sniff."

"Well, eat up, Con," Mon said. "We've got to upchuck in his yard." And they stuffed in a whole bag of donuts between the two passed until they were ready to be sick. "Proud of us, aren't you, Ben? Let's this be your inspiration. We're going outside the car!"

It was only one of the three bags I had, so we still had the endurance to last all night. They each bent over his yard, discarded the contents of their stomachs, and ran back into the car.

"You should have your own cooking show," I said. "My name would be listed in the credits. I don't think I'd want to show my face, though."

"Great, Ben! You still have your gun? We can't count this night against you: we have the right to carry a gun, so you should, too. You didn't accept being a deputy, did you? We'll find that badge somewhere—I know it's nearby." They actually pretended to hunt. "We'll have you officially as one of us next time. Tonight, all we have to know is if you can tell the difference between the good guys and the bad guys. I'm sure we can trust you for that much."

"Now be quiet so we can tell when he's coming," said Mon.

Then it hit me again. I was in another world. I was going in that house if it killed me. I took off my shirt and ran out of the car.

"Where are you going?" asked Mon.

"I'm going, going, gone!" I said. "Hold my bird for me."

"We need to do this thing together!" Mon yelled in my direction. "I'm too sick to go after him."

"I feel a little off balance, myself," said Con. "But he's running in the red—two strikes are against him."

"A true trooper," said Mon, and then he sat back with a moan. "I need some milk."

"Or some Pepto," and Con sat back holding his stomach.

I didn't remember if I had heard their warnings or not. First I smeared some vomit on my shirt, and then I was at the door—the third man's, and knocked on it. He was going to see one way or the other the vomit Mon and Con had spit out. The door opened. Was he already on his way? I couldn't tell, but he was exceptionally clean, I noticed, and the whiff I caught in my nose when the door swung clear was one not unlike a hospital's.

"I need to wash this," I said, and brushed past him.

"Uh, the washing machine is in the basement, but you can't

go down there," he said. "What's on that shirt? Germs and crawling things? Regurgitation?" He was emphatically step-ping down the stairs after me, and I blew out the donut I was too full to chew.

"I can find it," I said, while he spied out the cavity of his front yard through a basement window. He even opened it out a foot breathing through his nose, whatever he smelled had just breezed past him. The lawn could wait, but eyes of our cops and our suspect met for a second; and Mon and Con curtly waved with happy smiles, beating their temporary sicknesses. Bill brutishly slammed the window shut and went after me. I was as surprised as the needle had been when it stuck my rear end only to find that instead of making me wide-eyed in pain it sent my eyes straight to the back of my head.

There, high up on the wall were five more shirts straight from my closet at home with vomit stains just like the one I had in my arms. OK, maybe not from my home. I wondered if he had tried a spot remover or bleach. "How come those are still dirty?" I asked him, on his way down the stairs coming toward me. I was curious to see if we could keep some conversation off the record, but he could shoot me. And I could shoot back. Then I could tell Loro something! I had bagged a vomit-smelling hospital doctor, and I was the only one who thought he was a criminal.

Then I saw the sharks! Big ones—all over the four walls! Big deal, so he had some giant dead predator fish. But a skeleton was hanging out of each mouth. What beat all was his life-sized picture of himself without an arm, and an upside down shark hanging from a hook—half swallowing the missing arm. I wasn't through looking, but then he grabbed me. He tightened a grip around me like cops do, before the handcuffs go on around the back. But the thing about this was that he used both arms! So I came to. It was another mental breakdown, and it wasn't him wrestling me to submission. It was men in white, dressed like they were from the mental hospital. How could I clear my mind enough to know if the guy had one arm or two? It was critical to know.

"Who are you?" I asked.

"Your mama!" one said.

"We shoot sharks, stakeout man," Bill said. "Don't we, guys?" My gun was in reach. Oops. It fell on the floor. They picked it up. "Shoot him with his own gun! Now! He's a shark."

I looked again at the wall, and there were sailing ships, pictures of millions of tropical fish over a reef, and all kinds of scuba gear fastened up like they had a place to dry out. My shirt was in the washing machine. But there were no sharks. Why would I have to die in a set instead of the real thing? Maybe I needed a psychiatrist, but the only one I knew was a suspect. And if I trusted him, wouldn't there be a conflict of interest with the fact that I knew his part of a corrupt game of breaking up families?

I think we'd get along fine for five minutes flat, while I rested nicely next to him with all that trust being a perfect target for the old butcher-knife hook he sported in the name of Bill. According to Mon and Con he wouldn't change one iota, if he had given me the twenty thousand. I kept most of the information surrounding the money to myself, even though it might prove he was on the trail to innocence. But that was Smith. This was a better fisherman, and he owned the boat. We weren't friends, and Bill was the one who called the mental hospital, I guessed.

What else was going wrong? Was my family breaking up, and my wife on her way to the Caribbean? One of them had the schedule, and it could be moved up. Everything was going wrong now that I lost my chance to shoot the white coat. I would always regret that. Bill would take our picture, and we'd have the best postcard in town. But I reminded myself of reality. I should do that more often. Thoughts become more baseless, and we all need a few to live—another theory of mine.

"I don't know why you came after me," Bill said. "You ought to grill James, like Smith said. He knows everything. I just take my neighbors out on fishing excursions near the Keys. That's all I do. Who's missing—if there's a murder investigation? The only way I'd be guilty is if I was so angry at my wife for leaving me, I'd kill her. But I'm very depressed, and you'd know it if you knew me. I was labeled as a schizophrenic while I was in the mental hospital, and she got scared and ran. Game, set, and match me up in the Caribbean. I wanted somebody after I paid twenty thousand dollars, believing a new wife would wash the hurt aside. But the date turned out to be Mary, my ex-wife! She blamed me for murder, if you want to believe her; but I had nothing but sadness, and now it's worse."

The white coats patiently waited for his speech to end be-fore they brought me out of the house. "Go ahead and ask her about it." They were removing the bubble gum from the bottom of their shoes. "She's down there on some island, where multi-millionaires have bought protection from Smith." They stretched it to see if it recoiled into my hair, but it didn't. "They drink salt water as crazy as a mule with a turtle shell, but will never be forced into a mental hospital—world-wide. That's how powerful Smith is."

I interrupted. "You know chefs don't spit in the soup any-more. They throw in a big piece of chewed-up bubble gum." They wanted to know if I was kidding. "I'm positive."

"If you're about to inherit a piece of a continent, you'll have to settle with him, or you won't be a leader or owner for long. And your whole family being in brain-to-brain combat could be institutionalized. You want to go, right?"

"Not really," I said.

"See ya."

And I was off to the mental hospital. I had to be glad he didn't order the white coat to shoot me more than once.

The Court Blamed Me

Now I can be the shark. I passed the test. Where is the nearest ocean? Surely Bill wouldn't catch me again as I swam all over. How-ever I did want to know the odds.

Chapter 15

There was a knock on the door to our apartment, and it congealed at a sofa chair across the carpet from where Loro sat. He took off his hat and introduced himself as Smith, on a happy journey to produce a pie-filling grin that made his ears wiggle; he was telling her in his most serious manner that I was a schizophrenic. He was the psychiatrist.

"Yeah, I already know," Loro said.

"And how long have you known this—a day or two?"

"Yes, maybe a week," she said. "He's been gone about that long."

"Do you want to go somewhere? Do you want to get away?" he asked. "I can tell you schizophrenia is incurable. The scares and nightmares will only continue to get worse. They don't know what they're doing. They see things that aren't there. It gets very frustrating. They know they're going back and forth from reality. But they're convinced they're lucid. If you question them they know all the answers. Love becomes a four-letter word. Being in an unreal world, which nobody believes but themselves, they become violent. There is no doubt brewing. They turn on their closest people—and this is you. Has he ever hit you or shaken you?"

"No."

"He will."

"When?"

"Just let me say there are about twenty schizophrenics locked up at the penitentiary right now for trying to kill their wives," the psychiatrist said. "You look shocked!" The hairdo hadn't come off, yet, and wasn't through doing her favors.

"Well, I'm somewhat shocked," she said.

"Don't be," he said. "It happens more than you think. I'm glad we've reached you before something happened. I remember he calling you ugly—are you the same one?"

"Yes."

"You must be hurt. He almost killed me! He had a gun. You don't have a wound on you that you're not telling me about?"

"No."

"He could be beginning the hunt or planning out the murder so he gets clear away. It looks like he was on the verge of letting you go the last time I saw him," he said. "Leaving is the best thing for you. Do you help him through his sickness? You know, we really don't want another reason to lock some-body up. It's best if we catch it before it catches us. Do you know what I mean? Some of them place objects around the room to beef up their luck."

"I don't help him at all," Loro said. "I poke fun at him."

"You're as good as dead," the psych said.

"No, we're like that. We didn't like each other from the very beginning. We've always been at each other's throats. We like it that way," she said. "So we're strangers when we make love. For example, I'm going to do something to him for calling me ugly."

"You're as good as dead!" he said, again. "Leave him and come to the Caribbean with me. We have a whole staff that will pamper you with anything you want. And we'll fly in multi-millionaires who want to marry you to start over. You'll die with

Ben. Has he lost a good job recently?"

"You need to know this, you scoundrel," Loro said. "My husband is on trial at the Federal Courthouse of these United States to decide if he's a schizophrenic or not. It's not for you or me to decide. The jurors will determine it with a pile of evidence. And I know perfectly well every doggone schizophrenic isn't a violent man. If it becomes law that he's a sick man, he'll accept it like a gentleman along with a life sentence for killing his dad. If anything, he's doing his dead-level best not to turn the judicial crank the wrong way." I was a stranger at this point. I was bending the truth of the system, but this only led to making some fun plans for the bedroom.

"He's innocent, and I won't have any knock on the door try to tell me he's not!" Bucking the system was the only way to get at Tod. We'll discuss this one night. If I could hear her, I'd be over very soon.

"Well, it's been good to know you. I'll put my feet down and leave. Do something with that hair." And he prepared to go.

"On second thought..." He rushed back to her side, and she continued. "Why don't we trick the stupid jerk? You got a few pictures of the potential husbands?"

"Sure I do," he said. "I'll mail you an assortment."

"If we trick him just enough, and he gives up on me, and I hear about it, I'll go through with the main plan to remarry in the Caribbean. Would that be icing on your cake?"

"Sure, that's how I make my money—one fork at a time. Your lips to mine," and he kind of grinned in hope there'd be more than silence. But there wasn't. "You'll find the choice is tantalizing." Then he left.

Loro wasn't stupid. This gold-tooth excursion would be strong enough to get me back for everything I had ever done to her and then some. And it would challenge my intelligence— something she dreamed of from the beginning but always ended up with something else that made her look sick. I was pretty smart, and I always wanted to see if she could cut deeper—with mercy of course. From that short visit she concocted a whole scenario coming from the penitentiary on through the court case and ending up on Green Street where I was sup-posed to be. Or what? She picked up the phone and called the cops. How was I doing on stakeout? She wanted to know.

I had been driven to the mental hospital and dropped into a padded cell. This is where I'd end up for years before jail, itself, when I was written down and they were ready. The psychs had a couple visits in their records, which would help them out with the court case against me; but the reasons wouldn't survive cross-examination. The first time I had my smoke, and then they let me go free. What a joke on them—or was it jail? I forgot. No skin off my brain. But I hadn't made friends with Jon, and in him hung the balance. Maybe he wasn't a big shot. I hoped nothing would go past the hairline. I'd heard horror stories. And being there locked up gave me the idea that the executive board of the mental hospital, stripped of its name because of present litigation, laughed its guts out the day I arrived. But I had Tod's bird with me. She was under my arm, not in view of anybody. If they knew, they'd hold the bird's psychological condition against me as toxic and try to put it out the window. No attendant would see its pretty yellow and blue feathers anymore, even if they both raced one by human traffic and the other by natural wing. The bird's flight was to South America straight from there, but the attendants had connections that slowed them down. Now if I had a hawk or a ten-foot condor, the nurses and their help would run for cover before they opened their windows to them. The usual new client would bring in logs to go in the fireplace or hay for the horses or shovels to tunnel out. It was all going toward help for the new wing, of course. Every time they were committed, there was a new wing going up.

However, I didn't predict how far Tod would go to get rid of the parrot—even death. It was evidence, and I knew it, and

Murph Donnan

he did, too—when it was too late. If I got back to court, I had a fool-proof genuine meticulous plan. To equal their indulgence of putting me on the stand every darn day, I was glad I had Saturdays and Sundays off. By the way, what is the bail amount for schizophrenia? Crazy, I'd soon discover.

There were tentacles Tod had within the long arm of the law (and lawless) that triggered one little glasses-worn man, Jon, the bastard son of Smith, who held and esteemed himself in his recently appointed job. He would crack a case, if that's what you'd call it. Concoct a medication was another name for it, and he'd try his best. He had a promotion coming if he landed right out of an experience the Air Force offered him. If he sat in one of those military jets, as it scratched skyward, making those hemispheric-white trails, the military would open its doors to catching more weak people they didn't know what to do with. Once they were worked over, they'd leave the protective shell of psychiatry. I didn't know what the military side would do. Maybe it was the same group, and they were hiding, shaking in their boots.

But Jon baled out at the very top of the sky blue, releasing the bubble the pilot was under, which also included the driver's seat and the flight instruments. As anybody knows or can figure out, the wind was so strong that the captain at the wheel couldn't put the top back down, so he had to bale out, too. There went the aimless jet worth more than a few millions of dollars to the ground below to blow up and send trash toward the crater it opened, all to the delight of the waiting ears and eyes of the Unidentified Flying Object club members. They were watching, so how did they know?

"I just wanted to see who was in charge," Jon said across the air to the pilot, as they both fell by parachute into the Satcher River, swam upstream twenty miles, hiked up the nearest hill, waded in a swamp, and through the mud to the waiting arms of towels the psychiatrists held up to dry them off, as a gesture of

The Court Blamed Me

warmth. They were dripping with sweat and river water.

"Is this a mental hospital?" the captain asked.

"Yes, this is where I work," said Jon. "I'll keep you away from harm."

But there were only two psychiatrists who held the towels out to them. Ten or twenty patients with more psychs came out slowly with the daze holding them all together, as a group, looking like a leper colony in their hospital gowns. They were walking in their sleep, but wanted to see what the commotion was all about. I was watching them head out the door, seeing through one of my windows; this made me wonder why the heck I was left behind. I gave the bird one word to chew on through my shirt and planned a punch in the face to whoever stole it from my possession.

But that aviation engineer, the so-called friend of Jon, didn't want any part of it. "I'm not going in there," he said. He went over to the mud flat, the swamp, the hill, and back down the Satcher River with freedom oozing from all his pores. Why make a friend of someone who forced him to lose his jet? It took more work, but he was there by the river, ready to be picked up or be fed tea and oranges that came all the way from China. That's a song. I needed inspirational stories like his to feel better about myself. I saw him turn around, but I didn't know why. I hadn't done any wrong, as my buddies, Mon and Con, would testify, despite the things I imagined. So I concluded I'd decide for myself, apologize for pushing my way into Bill's house, and leave as soon as possible.

Patiently, Mon and Con, snatched a late-night dinner with Bill, which would go on and on for over a couple hours. He was glad to spend some time with them. They saw sharks, too, but in color photographs, and wallet sized. The shirts were blood stained, not puke stained, and there were so many alike, because he did have his arm torn from him. He kept changing the T-shirts to keep an unstained one ready for his wife to see he was bearing his own pain. He wasn't a criminal displaying his own blood, exactly. He had shown his wife how much he sacrificed to go fishing, and there was no dirty trick gouging me with insanity. Who wouldn't want to see his fishing museum down in the basement? And he hadn't called the mental hospital. Smith did, as soon as he spied my shirtless body force its way into Bill's house. The fastest revenge can depend on time to gather power to back it up. He'd been talking to his ex, and she was channeling her anger at me. It was a multiple surprise she had a conversation with her husband.

My eye had blown up Bill's photographs like an eagle sees food to capture with the prey-part of its brain. One look and pounce—that's what my eyes did. I was just starting to be interested, but the man in white was all over me. Anything passed this was shut down. Sometimes your mind can play the worst trick. I had permission by law that stated I had the right to shoot the white-uniformed man, but I was glad I didn't. If I knew what I was about to see—the insides of the mental hospital exposed like grains of sand to me, I had bought the farm, and by my thinking, things were crazy enough to have blood on my hands.

Chapter 16

Jon was given charge over me, but I didn't know anything except he'd tell the judge all kinds of stuff, including a psychiatric slant on me. There was nothing left but to rely on my own mind. I knew from my farming-help days a bird folded up by putting its head under its wing; it'd play dead and wouldn't move a muscle. So there it was under my shirt at the armpit—a witness to hair and deodorant. I'd be released and leave out of there in time to give it more room to flap about. I was sure of it. I had cops on my side, and more I didn't know of. Maybe a stakeout was in the parking lot. I graduated with and because of optimism, and my mind slipped in many thoughts like that—all the time. But this didn't mean I wasn't worried some-times. I'd have a bad scenario and sink right into it, waiting as the crochet ball did to be hit—and it always was. Maybe I'd go through the hoop.

Jon came in with a flutter, and after a short rendezvous with the nurse, he interpreted what his dad meant as his case for the night. He opened my door and came inside.

"Hi ya fellow! How ya doing?" He opened up his heart, and I saw its blackness that the spectacles couldn't erase.

"Fine," I said. "Who are you?"

"Your mama!" he exclaimed. "No, I'm just kidding. I'm here to help you. You know you're in a padded cell."

"I understand that, but why? I'll never commit suicide."

"You know that now, but haven't you been in and out of reality?" he asked.

"Clearly forgetting something is like being out of reality, and all of us are guilty of that," I said.

"You can have forgotten your mind, as it was?"

"You can say that," I said. "Catching up on the latest gossip about my mind tells me you weren't so privileged with the others."

"Then you don't have a mind, you could say?" He wasn't making any sense at all, now. Who was this jerk? He looked more important than ever.

"You have the right to say that, but it isn't true. Everybody has a mind no matter what they do. I'm hoping to become a policeman. All I have to do is work hard," I said. "My mind is well taken care of."

"We don't want you as a policeman."

"You don't?" To me he was just expressing his opinion.

"Ask anybody. Have you asked around? Nobody wants you on the force."

"According to the universe, which is biased toward all living things, a man is the sole owner of his work, and no other, right?" I asked.

"Right." He didn't know.

"OK, it would be unjust to take it away from him," I said. "Right?"

"Well, I, uh, am not going to take your job away from you. I'm seriously concerned about your—"

"Life? Please listen," I said. "On the one hand justice means for him to keep his work. He is not going to take it away from himself, right?"

"OK, I don't see your point." Now he's thinking, but not very well.

"So on the other hand of the unjust person, he's the opposite. He's a just person, and takes nothing away from anybody. I have my own work, feeding donuts and coffee and helping the cops on stakeout, and I don't steal; so I'm a just person. According to your own rules you have to be a danger to your-self or to others to be committed to a mental hospital. I'm neither, so you should let me go home," I said. "I'm sorry for the inconvenience."

"You're a schizophrenic, and I've heard of a couple of your delusions," he said. "There are four small windows in this room. Look at the first one." And he pointed at one.

There was a man stretched out horizontally as in a medical hospital. He was undergoing an operation. About four men in paper hospital gowns were holding sharp instruments. They had cut into his scull, spraying something on the exposed brain, and piece-by-piece had flung the bone out onto the floor. Dogs barked outside their door, but the doctors weren't done.

It was soup and sandwich time, so the head doctor dared anybody to eat their soup off the body, while the doctor probed the brain for the one connection to a muscle that would twitch; thereby spilling the soup. If it spilled, the head doctor would win. The loser had to pay the patient's cab fare back to his home. He was in an outpatient basis. If it didn't spill, of course, the doctor had to pay.

"You see him. He's getting the scull swap, an operation we've developed ourselves. He was a schizophrenic. Maybe now he won't continue to be—peaceful, peaceful as a man could be."

I had looked enough, but I had to turn to the second window.

"Now you see a discipline problem. We were trying our best to determine what diagnosis he lived with, and he gave us a lot of trouble. That is a real saw!"

My eyes bulged as I peered at the injured man. It was evident from looking at his face something was very wrong. He hadn't been given anything to knock him out, so he was belted down and screaming in agony. My eyes went down his torso. A saw was cutting off one of his legs! I went to the next window. Each time, each window, I hoped for something good, but as it was, I never had the pen or paper afterwards to write home to grandma, and how could I? Were they all operations? Were they docile now? But so what if they were, you know.

Through the next portal to hell, I saw a worn out stringy-headed girl on her knees hitting the floor with her hands. She was in a four-walled enclosure with clear glass all around and twenty people staring. This was bad, but one of the clear panes of glass showed the man having the amputation. With blood spurting everywhere the hospital always had trouble keeping a clean-up crew. Their reputation stuck with the humble people, and the whole town eventually knew it. They'd gone to court, but the judges were corrupt; and since it was easy to be paid off, my judge had learned of its rewards. The amputation was over, but the doctors lobbed the cut-off leg to the girl. She was his daughter!

It drove her crazy. What were her problems before? Who knows?

This surely made them worse.

"People will just have to learn I'm not their problem," Jon said.

What did that mean? Was Hitler his great uncle? Some-body inspect this guy for German words.

And then the last one. There was an Air Force captain with a ring in his nose tethered by a rope to the knob on the door. It opened and closed as the night went by, and he'd have to run with it to keep the ring from pulling his nose off.

"What is the purpose of this?" I asked Jon.

"He was a spy who tried to get to know me and my mental hospital," he said. "Nobody can get to know me, and this message will set everybody in the world straight." How many countries had misinterpreted this guy? Better, how many deserted islands? And the ones there had run off.

"Who is listening or cares that much?" I asked. My mind was back on the sharks in Bill's basement. Maybe someday he will stuff and string up Jon. I'd give an arm to see that, and he could have three—maybe a big toe after thinking about it. I shouldn't have to fall into the torture of their kind of humor. But he was a mental hospital hog. I'm sure he thought he was the only sane person in the entire world.

"Shut up!" Had he read my mind? He would chew it up if he could. Maybe he was trying. "You were found to be in contempt of court!" he said. So there was no mind trouble, thank goodness. That would really be weird. What I had to know was that this was a runaway hospital, not like the majority of such. Jon and Smith had to have taken control and run it completely amuck—or else I wouldn't keep my head on straight.

Mon and Con were at the admittance desk, right next to my ward. And they had filled the pages of information, which had wings of its own, off the fruition of their badges. I had one, but I didn't know what I did with it. Interpreting the rules to the letter of this fine institution was a psychiatrist's heaven. Skilled with the ability to get away with anything, they were worse than corrupt lawyers—probably because they hired them from time to time and were given their way of practicing.

Then my partners came in asking for the key. This was the sticking point. If they didn't bargain the key out of the hand of the intern, they'd have to turn around and leave. It got down to paper and scissors, the child's game, but we didn't win. Then it was arm wrestling. After losing that, there was flipping coins. Time was valuable, now.

"We need our coffee and donuts man!" demanded Mon. You see, the intern was a former patient, and his ways weren't our ways. You'd lose up to an eye to understand them all and print it into your memory. Then there was a permanent cut where his skin had been between his nostrils. He had submitted to their punishment, and dealt out his own.

But then my door flew open, not by the cops, but by Jon. He had gone momentarily to instruct the intern. Definitely, he was going to set up something similar to the four patients I saw and would never forget. Then he saw the cops. He had to push my door shut, so they wouldn't know, but I let the bird out. My mind was in that bird. It went directly to Jon and began to work on his eyes. I wanted it to peck out the big right one. Why have a starving bird? After a long minute of what could be seen on the fifty-yard line as a cock fight, he relented and pointed to where I was. I reached for the open door and opened it a little more.

"Ben! Ben! There you are!" Mon said.

"You're outta here," said Con. "We're brothers in the force. We'll catch you if you fall. And let's give a small hallelujah to who deserves it."

"You don't know, guys," I said. "First something clicked in me, then I lost my mind for a half an hour, seeing sharks on the wall, skeletons, a big murderer, vomit all over the place, and a one-armed man that turned into a two-armed man. The man in white woke me up. This place hasn't the right idea, if not, but I mean since not, but all punishments are not alike. I was running a few possibilities through my brain. How did you know?"

"It turns out Bill knows something about this place, and he's friends with Smith, so it's under strained circumstances that he's let somebody know. We had a dinner date with him. It's pretty late now, but we found you. Let's get out of here!" They were lying out their ears. I had thought about this question. The white coats had to have brought me out of Bill's front door, in perfect view of Mon and Con on Green Street. I was an eyewitness, and by the looks of my handler, they could tell where I was going.

"Let me see if the bird will go back with us," I said. "He's done so much, he may want to set up shop." But he jumped on my finger like he had found a good family already. So I was going to fry for a while, huh? Maybe this was better. I was more impulsive than adventuresome. I didn't want to dump on them, so it might help them in the long run.

The wad of Jon's life was to hold his eyes from bleeding too much. So we were heading toward the car. I wasn't sure if I lost part of my mind or gained it in my short stay, but I knew how they wanted me to risk it. I had been given the grand tour, without swapping my brain cells. The bird gave me back the one I lent it. We were bonded forever.

The cops were busy calling the appropriate authorities to clean up those mental hospital woes. There ought to be a song and required listening for younger folk.

"By the way, Jon lived off and on at the first house," said Mon, "but we don't know the guy who lived with him. There's still a mystery to pick up."

"You mean the one painted with pink polka dots and surrounded by a gigantic fence?" I asked, and laughed. We all laughed, as we plumped down in the car. I'd be laughing forever now that I was relieved of that fluorescent dungeon.

"Yes, seems like Jon left the residence when the paint and fence went up. Somebody still lives there," said Con. "But catching him is too easy. He works in the eye of society as a bug you can't rub out, meaning he explains everything to somebody all the time. I'm not sure if he murdered anybody or what?"

"James is next," I said.

"No, don't you get your sights set on going it alone. OK? We do it together. All three of us," said Con.

"You're talking to me, you know," I said. "I had the opportunity to shoot that attendant that took me in. I'm for the battle! How could a mind go head to head with a murderer and lose?"

"But you're not destined to be in the lead," said Con.

"Your new word is destined!" said Mon.

"You haven't the authority," said Con. "Give us the time to conduct an investigation the way a real one is done. You know, we have worked some teeny-tiny jobs before."

Murph Donnan

"All right."

"Here we are." We pulled up behind my car on the same angle as we parked from the conception of what was their idea. At the top there was human traffic up by the Done Shotit location, but I wasn't prepared to go over there alone. I was beginning to learn cop strategy. What I didn't understand for sure was why we didn't invade Smith's house, but after some lengthy conversation with Mon and Con (two against one) I learned a stakeout was meant for us to remain outside of the houses. A stakeout was staying in the car. Why this was so hard for me was the question of all my delusions or preemptive strikes, as Mon and Con called it.

A couple hours went by, and a fellow came out of the first house through a hole in the fence we hadn't been there to witness being built. We fought over the spotlight, because it was too dark to recognize anybody for mug shots. And I al-most won getting it turned on. But then I got cussed out. We had revealed our intentions, and they blamed it on me. And they were right. But the man didn't seem to notice much. He took the mail out of the mailbox just ten feet from us. We all squinted, but we still couldn't make out his face. Then he pulled out his mailbox from the dirt and threw it to the ground!

We went, "Ahhhh!" scared it was hurled our way. But he shoved it end on end toward the fence. Then he took the few loose boards to the side, climbed back in, and we heard the door slam.

Chapter 17

Trying to hold me down from jumping up and engaging myself with the neighborhood, Mon and Con told me to eat donuts and drink coffee. You see, the pencil pushers at the police station were calling up the suspects themselves. We were the foot soldiers, and they were the generals. They knew the right touch when obviously I didn't—and I took in that responsibility. But it didn't look like I had screwed up any-thing.

For them, I left the first house alone. I figured if we were to go in, it would have to coincide with the captain's orders. He knew what the suspect's name was, and he told us. It was Sam, the middle name of my brother, Tod. A truly valiant effort would have been to call his name when he picked up his mail, and reveal ourselves in a conversation with him. But they didn't do it.

There was a black cloud getting darker as each house was consecutively wrapped in night-color gradations. The change in atmosphere inspired a little bit of blurry hugging and clinging, while Sam's house was as dark as a pin-striped suit dipped in a can of ebony—making it the last one we'd want to explore.

But like an explosion of ash from a nearby volcano with an

unsuspecting scuba diver taking pictures of a reef thirty feet below, the projection of our rich view, before we knew it, was pitch-black visualization. And then his air went out, taking with it the bubbles that would lead him up to the top. He'd drop his tank and weight belt to float to the surface only to gag on the scalding-hot expulsion that covered most of the day-light. How dark could it be? And how did Sam live in such?

    A couple days went by as we entered the weekend, and it was still dark, when a city bus rode by and parked at Sam's house. I recognized it as the one that ran over my dad. The driver climbed out, and a car pulling along side sucked him in to its back seat, heading then to the city. Was there another criminal who helped Tod kill Dad—the bus driver, himself? I was so antsy I turned our car into a padded Fourteenth Century church bell. They were big back then. But anyway, I was the clapper hitting one end of the car to the other end. I bounced around so much, Mon and Con thought I might hurt myself. "We're not letting you out, no matter what!" they said, and kept the automatic door locks off manual.

    But then Sam appeared! He came out into the yard and saw a green three-story target painted on his house. He made some violent gesture and went back inside. I guessed he'd come back out to take a gander at the bus, but I didn't know. I knew with my pushiness there was something to gain from him, but the cops told me I had used strength against strength. I knew better than that. Approach with intelligence, and I'd have the back of the suspect against the wall. Sam, Sam, Sam. What did you do? What have you done? Have you not done it alone?

    Sam, you deserved to be in a courtroom made of wood and refinished with new varnish, so you got so sick sniffing it in your lungs, you'd stay in the hospital for a month—when it didn't happen to anybody else. Then the doctor would convince you to confess, when he had never had succeeded that before. And the jail they would put you in would flood from a nearby dam break, and you'd died by drowning, something else that had never happened before. A million to one—you'd die with a lot of pain, but I'm sure it would happen.

A bunch of kids were next.

"Are we witnessing a delusion, Ben?" asked Mon.

"No, I see the same thing you do," I said, "unless we give them free rides around and around Sam's house with donuts and coffee to munch on. That would be a delusion. For now I'm scared for their lives."

"No funny business, Ben," said Con.

"OK, guys," I said.

But the kids had to have practiced for the occasion. They all had the same flowery dresses on except for the boys. They were coming to the curb and held small songbooks as if they couldn't memorize the few lines they were assigned. I checked reality again around me. It wasn't my imagination. They sang.

"Little selves"

"For little shells"

"If your cell's an oyster"

"I've a million miles"

"From lots of whiles"

"To get here to bless you"

"We know who you are"

"And who you're for"

"When the court convicts you, from guess who?"

Then they all chorused at once, saying, not singing, "Your mama!"

All five of the windows of Green Street across from the suspects were lit. The children sang their song and marched back to one of the doors where the light went out, as they were invited back inside with bored looks and giggles and everything in between. They were completely undaunted. Then all the window lights went out. But one of the kids had a hammer and nailed shut Sam's makeshift door in the fence. He was a brave little guy with aspirations I sympathized with. Then he caught up with his friends wiggling through the door. Every-body went for the donuts at the same time, and we sighed with relief. The little guy wasn't attacked!

If James had heard the pure children's voices from the depths of his house, he was sure Sam heard it, so he came running up to us and got the driver's window to come down.

"This is your last chance," he said. "I don't know how long the neighborhood will hold him. Come with me, and I'll show you where the body's buried."

That set the pins and needles to pricking. I was out and in a bulldog's mood. But they wouldn't let me go. "Just kidding, just kidding," they said, and pushed a switch unlocking my door. I grabbed a donut for retribution and hoped it was the last one, but it wasn't. I gave one of them a dirty look, but he took it to mean I was his mother and wanted him to clean his plate. I think he told me earlier he grew up on coffee and donuts instead of the bottle. And when vegetables were introduced, he decided to become a cop.

We followed James to Sam's backyard, and he pointed to a piece of ground resembling a garden plot. Bill mysteriously showed up in a tux.

"I'm dressing up for this momentous occasion."

Smith came over, too! "I'm rounding up the crew for Bill, but I'm not leaving until this sailor has a last look on the land."

There came Done to round out the neighborhood. He had a girl on each side of his arms. Everyone was watching us as Mon found a shovel and commenced digging. All of them gathered around, squeezing closer.

"Ow!"

Something was down there, and it was alive! While this caucus was celebrating their victory with whistles, claps, and cheers—maybe Sam hadn't killed anybody—Mon and Con prepared to hear the speech that would make utter fools of everybody. In the meantime, Sam went out the front door with a body on one of his shoulders and the mailbox on the other. He had knocked the flimsy door back open, and he was heading for a new real estate acquisition next to Done. Sam had moved! And he kicked the bus as he made his way in the dark. James admitted he had organized the paint, the fence, and the bus. He didn't know it, but this was too much for Sam to live with. He was on the lookout and knew his day would come, but Sam was escaping right from under his nose.

The person in the shallow grave wasn't dead yet, apparently. It was Bill's ex-wife! Sam had buried her alive with just enough dirt to keep her underground, but without enough weight to stop her breathing. She would die in a matter of days. We saved her on the second or third day, and she was very angry; throwing her shoes off with worms in each and tearing her clothes, as if the itches had spread unchecked.

"What's your name, ma'am?" I asked, but she had something else in mind.

"You did this, Bill!" she said. "Bill knows me. Tell them my name. Go ahead. Say it out loud."

"I didn't do this to you," Bill said. And I believed him. I had a doubt going that he killed her, when he told me she was in the Caribbean.

"C'mon, let us brush you off. Stand up if you can," I said. "You must need food and water."

"Bill will get it. You love me, don't you?" she asked.

"How long have you heard of this?" Mon asked the group. "I know James has only learned recently. How about the rest of you? Done? Smith? Bill? Is she right?"

"Will you give us immunity?" asked Smith.

Con knew what to do. The entire force had underlined it in their manual, "Pulling-people-out-of-graves." And the gist of it was not to get too involved. He went over to the back door and knocked on it. Nothing. He knocked louder and said, "Police!

Open up!" Whoever came to the door, he'd accept it. Surprise didn't enter the picture. This was the moment for an arrest. Finally, after all the thousands of stakeouts and the leaching of yours truly, which was more trouble than they admitted, a large reward was coming our way—if someone opened the door. More knocks. Con was getting ready to break the door down.

Then it opened. What came out and put its feet over the threshold was the pivotal Jon who wasn't comfortable outside his mental hospital. He had one foot inside his day job, and the other was off the "court." This guy could play ball. He didn't want to speak, but he had to say something, or he'd be hand-cuffed and sent directly to jail among familiar strangers, near and dear to him; because they were the type to be plucked from their sorry environments to be tortured, until their schizophrenic heads came off from the pain. He'd fit in that crowd. Oh, yeah.

"Oh," after Jon took a quick look around with his one good eye and a patch on the other. "I see you've unearthed his last victim. Nobody else spilled the beans? I don't live in this neighborhood."

Mon and I were continuing to prepare Bill's ex-wife, Mary, to drink some water.

"Why should I give you immunity?" Mon asked.

"Well, I have a questionable business," Smith said.

"You did it, Bill," Mary said.

"She thinks I did it," Bill said. Everybody nodded.

"That's a good reason," said James. "And as to myself, I guess I had the common sense to investigate a notch sooner. Maybe I talked myself out of it. OK, so I have one of Done's girls over every now and then. Give me immunity."

"I have my own immunity, don't I, snookums?" asked Done, as he kissed one girl and then the other. And they all moved in closer. They were circled around Mon, me, and the girl scraping the gunk off her clothes.

"I could pull the plug on every last one of us," said Done, "as

The Court Blamed Me

long as I'm not dead. Have I ever been dead? Anybody? Promise you won't kill me?"

"We need immunity," said Bill.

"I'll give you immunity," said Mary. She raised her fist.

I got to speak. "What we've got here is only attempted murder. This isn't the one he killed. Someone is dead and won't come back to life. Who did he kill?"

Sam was halfway up the street with every step getting harder because of the hill. He dropped the mailbox. Trying to pick it up again, he dropped the dead body. Then he took a break, but he couldn't take long, because the body was stinking. A dog began to bark until all the neighborhood dogs joined in. The truth might work. It was a last-ditch effort, but sometimes it wraps up a wound and shows some care in the middle of everything.

"That's all right," he said, to whoever was listening at that hour of the night. "It's just my mailbox and my wife." (the truth) he said. "She's a little cold." Then as the stench reached his nose he slapped her cheeks on one side and then the other, over and over again. He had gotten to the crazy part of his mind; she may come alive again, being warmed up with the slaps. The dogs barked louder when the slapping crushed their ears.

"Stop that slapping!" said an interested lady neighbor. "Here, use this." A wheelbarrow was presented to the scene.

He put his wife in the wheelbarrow, and the generous person went back inside. On her way she muttered, "Most people have cars," and, "Pew, something stinks."

"It's the weather," he said. "She'll be inside soon." And it was much easier with wheels. Some of the dogs had courage to box him in, but he kept going. They woke up the neighbor-hood, but it consisted of people who knew him.

The mold was being pressed at the gravesite. They were all talking as if the pyramids were right behind them, and they were discussing a royal body with the family.

"If it weren't for you, Smith, we'd never have pretended

schizophrenia!" said Bill. So there was one disgruntled person. Remind him we get his share of the ten ton blocks on Monday.

"You wanted a new wife without the complications," said Smith.

"You made it so effortless," said James.

"You could be Smith's wife or Bill's next wife, couldn't you, snaky ladies?" to the women on Done's arms. They giggled.

"I'll probably never marry, because of you, Bill," said James. "I never heard of Smith until you enlightened me." And the Sphinx had the tail of a mouse under its paw, until the blowing sand eroded it.

"Smith has got his own underground railroad," said Bill, spoken like a true rebel.

"You guys are going to jail, aren't you?" asked Done. Where's that? Where pushing and pulling those big blocks was punishment enough, and the only clock was the sun.

"You're still a customer of mine," said Smith. "You better remember that!"

"You causing us to remember, Smith?" asked Bill. "She remembers!" And he pointed at Mary. She came a dime a dozen. Put her on the spit. Open that flue. Ben, did you leave room for a chimney in that big diamond-shaped rock pile?

"They don't get immunity, do they, cop?" asked Mary.

"If they get immunity, then I get immunity," said Jon. "It has something to do with the judge, doesn't it, Smith?" I started to like Mon more than Con, since he had probably convinced Mon to look the other way when I came out of Bill's house on my way to the mental hospital.

"What I want to know is what do you know of Sam's first murder?" I asked. But they all walked away extracting themselves from what was the first grave and going to their own homes. Jon closed the door to Sam's house, but the cops weren't through asking him questions. Talk, talk, talk, and we've only got sixty five years to get the work done—maybe one hundred and

The Court Blamed Me

sixty five years to be exact. Take it from your Pharaoh. They'll travel hundreds of miles to vacation here one day.

"Guys, don't leave me," said Mary. "Don't go!" Then she turned to us. "All you cops are alike. Get your hands off me." She twisted and flung us off.

But then it hit me. At three o'clock in the morning and surely settling down too much for anybody to take, I witnessed about four or five square holes in the ground we hadn't seen before. They were all in a circumference of the broadened-out circle to the shallow grave we had seen. First Bill fell in. He was down in the dirt six feet deep. Then James yelled. He was caught by the obvious trap. It was dark as an insulated bell with bats hovering now that the noise was gone. Smith's big body fell in, and he was knocked out like on a pillow filled with sawdust in a fight. Done was kicking and screaming. His women fled and got away flailing their hands and running. But a hand clenched his ankle and pulled him in.

It was a skeleton that devised the grip. There was a skeleton in each of the square holes six feet deep. They were alive enough to clasp shackles around the wrists of our spectacular suspects—Sam's revenge against his own neighbors. But were there that many tempers to douse? Why would they be mad at him for his own murder? Or murders? Usually skeletons meant foul play, especially ones dragging people into a grave. Done's two scared girls hadn't regained their wits as they ran away, so two more sets of meatless skinless bones jumped out of two holes and went after them. We could hear their screams megaphone louder, among all the joints and rattles a bag of bones would have.

"Click, click, click," locked the skeleton's shackles on everybody who fell in the graves, so they'd never climb out. What makes a skeleton afraid? What makes them run away? If I shot at them, the bullet would go right through. I could call the fire department to turn their hoses on them. But I knew what made bones run. My mind was sharpening up. And I was certain of it. And it wasn't dogs, which had unlikely been in the annuls of history. Canines liked bones, but mostly with a little meat on them, not like this case. The skeletons looked bleached and completely clean as if prepared for a show, maybe in a doc-tor's office.

I got my hands on a knife, walked over to the closest scull, grabbed it, secured my one arm and carved with the other. I cut a hole in the scull and took the hamster out by the hind legs—then the wheel. I let it go, and the skeleton fell to the earth. I did this to all of them, until there were unworked free little-furry things going in circles around us—and the skeletons all laying there motionless.

Smith got out of his pit first, and said, "You won't get me to help you anymore."

"Tod didn't even do it," said Bill, a little slower than Smith to climb out, but he thought he was being unfairly tricked. "Maybe I'm wrong in telling you, but Tod is a schizophrenic. His wife is in the Caribbean like the rest of them."

"It's all your fault, Smith!" said Done. "You were the first schizophrenic."

"I got it from Tod," said Smith. Why were they talking about Tod? I didn't understand.

"No, you didn't," said Bill. "You got it from me, because my wife left me depressed."

"Tod was the one," said Smith. "He's got the judge on his side."

"Tod got it from me," Bill said. "Now what do you have to say?"

"If you must know, I diagnosed you randomly," said Smith. "If you took it seriously, there's something wrong with you."

"Tod told us to dwell on it to see for sure, and then we went to the mental hospital," said Bill.

"Tod didn't want to be the only one," said Smith. "Have you

The Court Blamed Me

seen him in court? He was acquitted for killing his good-old dad. Now he wants to pin it on his brother, a true schizophrenic, and no more than a very remote idea. I think Tod's idea is to say, if he does convict him, that he's still the equal to any other schizophrenic. But you didn't get it from me!"

"Or from me," said Bill.

"I'm not saying anything, unless I get immunity," said Done.

"In fact we're gone. Contact our lawyers," said Smith.

"Yeah," said the rest. "We know who did it, but we're not telling you." And they all went home.

"You're not putting me in any stinky hole anymore," somebody said. And they all spread out like a tarantula on roller skates.

This was after the live bones shoveled dirt over the guys who fell in the graves, thereby trying to kill more. Man, this was a dangerous neighborhood to live in. Lots more clean live bones were the responsibility of Sam, but where was he?

The fire trucks arrived. "I called them," said Mon.

And then I came to. Did Mon see me take the hamsters out? He couldn't have missed that, but he did. And it took a long while to go from one bag of bones to the other. I put in some work! Then he told me.

"We can flood the entire bulk of the backyard here and see by the yard's soil where another grave is." I said this knowing I was wrong. Mon had only seen one grave the entire time, and definitely no bones. Bottom line—I had just had another break from reality. I looked around for sure. No, there weren't a bunch of nervous, squeaking little animals anywhere to be seen. And certainly there were no graves dug up and covered up in the last few minutes. I gave myself credence. I had solved the problem! The backyard was the same. But if Mon found one with the fire trucks, I would know exactly what to do.

Chapter 18

The court case was wearing me thin because I didn't get any sleep. There were always ruinous atmospheres to fight to keep my head out of the clouds, where it didn't belong. Serious situations shoved it up there. These were in the afternoon when I'd put them in dreams to catch some shut-eye. When it worked I could settle down on a dime. But the excitement of being on the witness stand kept me awake for hours. And not getting any true rest I was afraid to death they'd start asking me questions about my breaks with reality and begin to pull actual sweet droplets from my body. I felt scared and run-down. What if this proved I was a schizophrenic? Did this mean the judge would put me in jail on the high chance, and maybe some odds or two, to scare my wife away? I depended on the United States Justice System. The court wouldn't cut some corners and pull some stops just to expedite my wife's packing for the Caribbean. These were pretty sharp statements for my mind made of glue. Putting her in that finger-shock hairdo was an indication that the ones against us were pretty sharp. And sometimes my mind was like a lava lamp with my slow reactions.

The papers could already be signed to meet some multi-millionaire Smith set up for her. All I had a hope for was a small death for both of us. And not being afraid of such, she'd have her teeth free to bite and tear into its reality. She'd weed out the temptation enough to wipe off the evil face of it, learn more about hard times, and even swallow the fact that I had called her ugly only in jest. She had so wanted to get me back, and I knew it. So why would she want to do all that for me? It didn't sound like her.

Oh, well, I rang that bell up and then down. I was up against the rafters. They were the first to hear her noisy solo. After the acoustics bounced around for a while up there, they got in line for the normal ear, but they were still the first to hit the roof. I didn't tell Mon or Con about my imagination as it opened up to how Loro sounded in our wishy-washy world, so I could depend on something—anything as it landed on my personal life. Instead, I hung my head. I was due in court in a few hours. If I didn't fight with energy on the stand, the scales of justice had no other way to go but down. What was in that gamut of pounds and ounces for Tod? Gold and silver? My brother probably picked up what fell out of the grasp of the homeless, and slept in garbage bins to further take advantage of mankind. This was true even though he had a perfectly good house—oops, it used to be a house. He had lots of good neighbors. He never invited me over, but as a real infant he could have predicted this childish court, knowing to this day that it was unnecessary.

What I did tell Mon and Con was that I was nodding off while I stood. Their answer was they'd let me sleep in the back seat until the sun came up, when they had to leave. What do you call a parrot when its sleep is interrupted? Talkative. The bird was in my car sound asleep. Who knows what birds do or feel, but they all had sharp talons, and I wondered if I respected that. What if he had a nightmare and thought I was Jon? I found out, and I saw there was nothing to be afraid of. The parrot liked me. I was through dozing off somewhere in the morning and made it on time to the witness stand. I took Tod's parrot with me. Seeing me walk over to my seat next to the judge with the parrot on my finger, the crowd broke out into a sparse moment of laughter. Watch out! It might mimic that.

"What are you doing with that bird?" the judge asked.

"It's my brother, the prosecutor's bird," I said. "Listen." I kissed it lightly on the beak. Then it ruffled its feathers, and said in a clear-cold voice.

"Why don't you kill me like you killed your wife?"

"That's my voice!" said Bill's ex-wife, Mary. She had blurted out the exclamation right in the middle of court! And she stood up! "Listen to me....why don't you kill me like you killed your wife?" It was an exact copy of what the parrot had said. There were murmurs, so she sat down.

"Objection!" said Tod. "This is highly unusual. The defense didn't warn me of having a dumb bird as a witness."

"I didn't know it," said my lawyer.

"Approach the, uh, bench—no, not you: just Tod." This was unusual, too, but the defense had no law, and he and his assistant were looking.

Tod leaned up to the judge. I couldn't hear them, but I began thinking he was actually the one whose neighbors had all but trashed his mansion. Maybe he had a sleeping bag.

"Is that your bird?" the judge asked Tod.

"Yes."

"Well, you've got to, uh, kill it. If there's enough, uh, tampering on your acquittal of your murder case, uh, we all could be found holding the noose. Why did you, uh, handle the papers in the first place?"

"It wasn't up to me. I was accused of murder," said Tod.

"Oh, yeah, uh, well, you know, uh, I can't do anything but the occasional contempt of court against this guy. He knows my contact at the penitentiary."

"C'mon now. You've sent plenty of innocent derelicts to jail

The Court Blamed Me

for being schizophrenics," said Tod.

"Yes, but, uh, quietly," the judge answered.

"You don't have to send him up," said Tod. "Indict him. We'll convene another court for the punishment. And it'll be a long sentence for murdering my dad." He chuckled. "How are people to know I blinded him with the light, so I magnanimously had the responsibility of leading him through traffic? And that same bus that ran over our dad is parked at my house, along with pink polka dots on the front face of the mansion. And a gigantic target is painted on to show beetles and worms themselves the fact that everyone within miles knows I did it."

When Tod stepped back a foot from the judge's bench, I kissed the bird again.

"How are people to know I blinded him with light, so I magnanimously had the responsibility of leading him through traffic? And that same bus that ran over our dad is parked at my house along with pink polka dots on the front face of the mansion." It said more. "And a gigantic target is painted on to arrest beetles and worms themselves to the fact that everyone within miles knows I did it." The parrot said all this, and the entire courtroom heard it and gasped! And clapped a little. And some of them were smiling, like what would happen next?

"Back to your seat," said the judge. "Who, uh, do you think you are?" turning to me. "Dash that bird to the floor and, uh, step on it, or you'll be in contempt of court!"

"I can't kill Myrtle," I said, and held her in my arms a little closer. Sam was Tod? The neighborhood might whack him before the justice system did. I worried about it, even at this moment, cause I daydreamed so much. The news was out! Tod would be known around the world. "This means you're corrupt, too, say, judge." I just spoke my mind, sometimes. I wouldn't be on the stand alone anymore, but I was probably the last one to find out.

Then the judge's phone rang. "Is that you or me? Excuse me,

Ben."

"I don't have a cell phone," said Tod. He was staring me down like a rock falling in an abandoned well—and I him, with the fleshly part of my twitching eye-lids closing in on the blackest parts—and him, me. The last years had meant the most. And me, him. He never gave me birthday cards. I knew it would add up and bite him someday.

This was the last place I wanted to be in to finally acknowledge to myself that Sam was Tod. The murderer we were trying to catch on Green Street was actually the same law-breaker I was after on the witness stand. How coincidental! But wasn't I to do more about it than wave the checkered flag between the speeding car and the house it was barrelling toward at two hundred mile per hour? There was a crash in my brain. And law-abiding society was the crowd in the car. Of course, Tod was doing the driving.

But surely, this was the time to feel something lodged in my throat. He was my brother, and murder must have corrupted him. First his wife was killed, and this threw him off track, so he capped off the rest of the violent feelings in his head by killing our dad. He wouldn't kill anymore. But that was what all murderers promised. Even if I skipped that wild hope from people like him, how would I feel if he got to the Caribbean, and I didn't? Life's not that unfair in a country with laws.

Maybe everybody else knew he brutally killed his wife, and the court was a sham. But wasn't it though? There was a funny part. The judge was probably in it up to his neck, and because he had such a boring life with only a Seurot dot of glimmer from his separated married folk, the rush of adrenaline pushed for more. He wanted to move up to murder. Tod got away with it, so the judge would, too. The cops had many cases they hadn't solved.

But Tod was my brother. Maybe if he had only killed one person? But he had killed two! And the whole world was against him. It held the friends, relatives, and neighbors of Tod's wife and our dad. I couldn't condone murder and get elected to office. I couldn't buy a church and be the top religious guy. And I couldn't marry my grieving mother to take my dad's place. I couldn't do anything, since my dad and my sister-in-law had been killed. One of these days it was going to be worse than that—like when I missed them enough for a phone call. It would be just a simple chat. And they wouldn't be there.

I wondered how Tod's voter base was doing. He was probably breaking one promise after the other. Could it be true he sacrificed everything to convict me? I really didn't have enough to hope so. I would eventually cry. Dad was the glue that kept us together. So Tod must have hated me a little knowing, without him, we brothers would go our separate ways. I was accused immediately after the murder, so I didn't have time to console Tod. I so wanted to throw my arms around him while I had my tears. But those miracles don't pop up coincidently anymore for a person to ride smoothly through life. Tod had messed it up. He'd soon be a shell.

"Then it's me," the judge said. He put the phone to his ear.

"Doggone it, I'm in court now," he said over his cell. "You better be quick."

"They're on to us," said Bill. "They can figure out that a snag held up the system, the one you wanted immunity for, so Tod had to kill his wife. They dug up my ex-wife, and she could spill the beans on any one of us. What do we do?"

"Just lay low and don't go out of your house—for any-thing," said the judge, "until I come over. Tell the rest of them." He hung up his phone and put it back in his pocket. It promptly rang again, and he about threw his robe into the air like a disc of pizza dough. He had to get to his phone, which took a moment, because after it fell down, he had to pick his robe back up from his ankles, and the cell phone was near his belt.

"Yes?" The ring tone was "Taps," And it couldn't be more appropriate. He was probably imagining others in a funeral, not him.

"Listen, Judge. I can tell the cops anything," said James. "But I'm blackmailing you. Either give me a million dollars, or I'll say all kinds of stuff about you, you perverse wheel of injustice!"

"James, do you want Jon against you?"

"No."

"Well, he may be knocking on your door any moment now," said the judge. The bird was listening. "And that eye he lost?"

"Yeah."

"He didn't like it," the judge said. "So it had to go. I can call him off, if you send in your regular five thousand. We can't call it a club if we lose you, James. C'mon, buckle up, man. We can stay friends. Just think how excellent the next one will be."

"But it costs too much money," James said.

"There's a secret face out there on Green Street that painted the target on Tod's house. It can be you if I don't see five thousand tomorrow. We all promised to send in cash each month. Call on Done. He has the means and the muscle to give you two instead of one. And you know this is beyond the call of duty, when you see your match in the Caribbean next month." Maybe he was talking about my wife. Oh, she's talked about a cruise before.

"Who is Tod?" asked James. "I thought his name was Sam."

"Sam's his middle name," said the judge. "I may get him to murder the defense attorney—in self defense, of course. You give me a reason, but heavy on the may: I've been against murder all my life. Little deaths like broken bones are just as funny in families. Kidnapping is also an excellent crime, but it doesn't separate itself from murder too much. You see what I'm driving at? I'm going to let you live. Is everything all right now?"

"Yes." He hung up. The judge hung up. But then it rang again.

"Excuse me, folks," said the judge, to the courtroom. He swiveled his chair so he had his back to them. Tod didn't want to say anything. The judge had him on a string. But the defense did, too.

The Court Blamed Me

"I object!" said my lawyer. The judge swung back around.

"For what? One phone call?" the judge asked.

"Yes, you're talking to someone in the gallery. This is untenable." And he pointed at Smith who quickly put his phone down.

"Smith?" the judge asked.

"I have to talk with you," said Smith. I kissed the bird again.

"I have to talk with you," the bird said.

"You're in contempt of court!" the judge said to me. He banged down the gavel.

"You're in contempt of court," the bird said.

"Take him away! Smith, I'll see you, uh, outside," the judge said. "This court reconvenes in four days at ten o'clock." Amidst some muffled laughter and normal-people noise, the bird said, on my shoulder on my way out, something that came from that black house.

"I killed my wife, Myrtle. She's dead now—no trouble to me anymore."

And as the courtroom emptied, all guesses were brightly whitened and highlighted if you said what a licking the judge would give to Smith.

"You want to go back to, uh, jail?" the judge told him.

"After pretending schizophrenia, anything's fair," said Smith. This was wrong. To make matters worse, Smith was only a rich man slumming.

For that, the judge took off his shoe and clubbed Smith over the head with it. It knocked Smith down unconscious, and he later went to the hospital. The crowd was as straight as a razor coming to the side of the judge. "It was self defense!" they said. "The big guy was going for his gun under his jacket. We saw the whole thing."

And others said, "Too many people think they can argue with the judge."

This was a piece of a crowd. How many favors had he done

them? Or else, they were going for employment. And there was room for common sense.

One body said, "He shouldn't have called him while he was on the bench. Why worry a great man? The judge is fighting for us."

And the last one was, "Having a law without a judge would never work." And they gave him pats on the back, as the ambulance moved in.

He was plainly reasserting his dominion, which was given him by the voters. And no one would call him anymore, mainly because he'd keep his phone in his chambers. Obviously, he had just snubbed the parrot and me, but to get him back, the cops tapped the calls from Bill and James. Mon and Con had everything down to the last detail to tell me when I met them that night.

"You know, Myrtle, murder is so easy I could kill again," said the bird. It got in the last word. Some of the people leaving sped up. A parrot was important. They understood that much of the truth.

Chapter 19

"**D**onuts and coffee for everybody, you lonely suckers!" I said. "I also have a few candy bars to pass out. I'm glad to see you two again in the dead of night. The whole courtroom was so spellbound by Tod's parrot, the judge forgot to throw me in jail for contempt!"

"You got the loneliness part right. Nothing's astir down our neighborhood street, and I mean I'm waiting for the dust storm and the tumble weeds to roll in," said Mon.

"We have picked up some evidence concerning that first house with its new fence, polka dotted paint job, and unscrupulous giant target over everything. We found the half-empty paint cans scattered around the other side of the street," said Con. "And that's not all."

"The neighborhood knows more than they tell us. Do you think this is an invitation to visit the right side of the street?" I asked.

"It's up to the captain after we tell him," said Mon. "He'll give them a ring if there's a material witness hiding with them. Who can talk without discussing the present case with Tod in the neighborhood? He already hit the roof when he read of

Tod's acquittal. It was such a small and quick court case, the journalists didn't even have a whole paragraph for the paper," said Con.

"Yeah, we're still trying to figure it out," said Mon. "From what we get off the tapped phones, Smith and Bill put the pressure on Tod to kill his wife. They admit it down to the holes in their shoes. That was the reason for murder." Did they not know about the Caribbean and the draw it had on people like Tod?

"That Tod is my brother! He's the one who lives in that first house!" I was astonished before, and now again.

"Yes, but others are just starting to figure it out. We found out before you did. If the press finally picks it up, the whole wide world will know. The house is the thing. Tod will be up to his neck in scandal, and he will lose his job at least," said Con. "Nobody else wants to blame you, so the court will be dismissed. There's nothing better than good neighbors, and we can tell you right now, Ben, the right side of Green Street worked just as hard against Tod as you did in court against him."

"You deserve a donut," I said, "and I will pour you a cup of coffee—it can be streamlined with cream and no sugar, right? We're messing around with an industrial mass-produced serial criminal with the prize hidden inside. For years now he's had something against everybody. My dad, being faithful to the truth—and I have to take a moment here to choke it all down—must have found out about Tod's murdered wife and was en route to tell the cops. I want to believe him, you know, but when we talk on the phone, the need for truth just doesn't come back and bounce around, like in regular conversations. I fall right in forever and ever. Of course I'm not calling him again; I'm waiting my chance in court. It has to be something like that. Do you think I'm schizophrenic?"

"No, you have the opposite," said Mom "You have dreams that were unfurnished. We gave you a chair and a sofa and some shelves, and you went to work. It was eighty per cent you who opened up this neighborhood. You've been great, and sooner than later you'll be wearing a badge like us, not the deputy's. In the meantime, you're in the lead. Nothing wrong with waiting, now that's true, eh?"

"No," I said, "but what happened with the grave the fire department washed up? Anything?"

"They doused the whole backyard," said Mon, "and we found some old skeletons. They were murdered by the past owners of the house. The sculls were broken into, and little plastic wheels came out," said Con. "There's already been a court case. The last ones who lived there are still paying time and will finish it off when they die. Maybe the house had something to do with it. It happened to both of them. There was some kind of pressure laid on Tod, but exactly what? We have some opinions."

"You didn't find any hamsters?" I asked.

"Hamsters? Are you crazy?" asked Mon.

"I, uh, thought James had some pets," I said. "They could be digging around."

"Well," said Con. "The story we pried out of Jon's mouth was that years after the last couple had been tried and convicted and sent to jail, Tod bought the place. The skeletons, when they had been laying in the ground enough to bleach their bones, rose up and came after Tod and his wife. Smith and Bill may have dug them up and gave them the push. But I think little hamsters ran the wheels in their brains, thereby, running the bones at Tod and his wife." From listening to him, he thought he was smart.

"There's an old story we could believe," I said, of course.

"What old story?" asked Con.

"The one you just told," I said.

"Well, believe it or not, it's midnight, and we need a campfire with a bunch of kids scared to death to make it a good time," said Con.

"Are you sure I didn't imagine this in one of my trances? But I don't remember telling you," I said. It worried me that someday they would think I was off my rocker and pull it down with me in it. What would grandma do for exercise? That would be my reason for it not to happen.

"No, we got it confirmed that Smith and Bill have been messing around with some old bones. Remember, we tapped their phones," said Mon.

"So when they scared Tod and his wife," said Con, "enough to bring out the deadly weapons, Tod killed her by mistake. Innocent before proven guilty?"

"They know you're listening," I said, "or the whole world is in a break from reality. C'mon now, Mon...Con. They want you to think he's innocent." There went the last of my attachments to Tod, no matter how delicately Mon and Con handled it—just because we were related, no doubt.

"He could've been digging around in his backyard and ran into them. If he was slightly unbalanced at the time already, it might have scared him to do something unusual," said Con, "but that's putting the pressure on himself."

He had the brains, so maybe he took home a wheel for a souvenir. They should be mine, but my story was worse than theirs.

"They know you're listening from their phones! I'm sure of it," I said. "The next thing they'll say to each other (am I right?) is that they'll trap the captain in his bathroom stall, while he's drinking his morning cup of coffee. This would be at Tenny's, his favorite breakfast joint?" If I didn't have a point, there'd be a fight over that wheel. It was supernatural!

"They sure did. OK, he picked another restaurant en route to work after they heard the tap," said Mon. "But every time he sees a new customer, he imagines their skeleton. It could drive you to violence. Maybe we got a point, Ben—on your string."

I pulled out a string and tried to imagine a point on it, I made a loop for Jacob's ladder. "They don't even know he eats breakfast," I said. "How about the one where one suspect tells of an impending robbery against another, and by the looks of it says, in other words, he must be warned. Or else some violence was planned. Does the captain pick up the phone to clue in the victim so he won't be killed?" If I was right, my work would coast on pure smooth silk tonight.

"Yes, that's what the captain did," said Mon. I laughed. What an excellent night to feel good!

"Now he's got the captain's soft spot. He can coax him to any part of the city and plan a shoot-out at their own convenience. They have time to practice—time to pretend the captain here and there with men or not with men. If it succeeded, more than one man would be lying dead," I said. "And you began to believe them when those old bones came alive. I hate to say this, but the bones were a temporary prop to help you believe the rest of their schemes. They're laughing their guts out by now, saying, why don't we dump the bones in the judge's chambers? If they convinced him to murder, they'd have a choice on who to look up to."

"Ben, how many times has the judge held you in contempt of court?" asked Con. Whoa, boy. He was getting close.

"Four or five times!" I said, and fudged a little for pride. And both of them broke out in laughter, but they were still acting as one. That irked me. It was like the husband painted polka dots on his kid to trick his wife into thinking the son was two steps away from death. It was that kind of funny. I coughed and laughed.

"Well, you must be getting curious," said Mon, and I was. There was nothing going on, so the conversations were two pinches of tobacco more exciting. "Since we've tapped their phones—and the captain had to be talked into it, and you remember that all of them know about you. They know you being in contempt, and they took some part in it. Thanks to modern conveniences and their big mouths, we're sure they're about to make a move. A big one—against you! Con turned around and gave me a pat on the back. He was proving he was above me in my hour of need. Or was I looking too close? I was looking for some thanks, but I knew it wouldn't happen.

"We're sure about this one, Ben," said Mon, and I was in submission.

"Yeah, we believe Smith has a list of witnesses to your dad's murder, and you could foul it up in one shot. Smith needs the judge to know them to hide them in his special way. If you were out of the picture, Smith could be confident in the names, except for Bill's ex-wife. The list isn't worth using, if they can't put a stop on each and every name. Most of them know their two cents is worth something, but Bill's wife has ten dollars! Smith and the judge may have to kill her, too. The judge is against murder, but it looks like he's warming up to it."

"It sounds like," said Mon, "that Smith is forced to give him the list. He's doing it grudgingly, because she made love to him, and he can't turn on her. Bill wants her to keep talking, so that proves his marriage is back on. The judge is going to have to figure something out."

"What does this mean or lead to?" I asked.

"I don't know," said Mon.

"I don't know," said Con.

"Nobody knows?" I asked. "Don't you know, Con?"

"Nobody knows," said Mon, covering for Con.

"Who's your leader?" asked the parrot. "I can kill at will, when nobody will know."

"Who's your leader, yeah," said Mon.

"The judge is the leader! That's it," said Con.

"Who loves you?" asked the parrot. "I can go to the Caribbean with you, and they'll let me take over, I'm so much a pirate."

"We do," said everybody.

"Wow! Look at that judge go," I exclaimed.

"While the big-boy Smith is pestering the judge, he's more

disturbed by you, Ben. That court case is receiving some attention by the public. And it's getting worse by the minute," said Mon. "They have to hurry it up. The list will prove worthless by the time Bill and Mary open their mouths."

"Way to go, guy," said Con.

"What does this mean?" I asked.

"It means Bill's ex-wife probably had been with the judge, too, in the hot Caribbean, no doubt." They didn't know much about the Caribbean, and it was too late to tell them. "And he buried her or had Jon do it. Mary has already, or will, make amends with Bill, so he's innocent. The judge could be building forces against Tod, because Tod's best friends with Bill and his proud Mary, but only for a moment. Smith knows what will happen when he gives the list to the judge. He'll tell Smith to put all the witnesses in the mental hospital. This would discredit them, but since it's so easy to learn the motive behind it, Smith would be sticking his neck out. He wouldn't want to do it."

"So the judge would put them in prison?" I asked.

"Small victory. You escaped," said Con.

"Can you see twenty people running away from that place?" I asked.

"Since you left, I called in a tighter policy for future runaways," said Con. "You're not running from the law, are you? Then don't worry about it."

"You and me are getting a little rough, aren't we?" I asked.

"Listen to me!" said Con.

"Your new word is listen, Con," said Mon.

"Hey, we don't know this guy from an Adam's apple. And ever since he's been with us, he's been to prison, the mental hospital, and trespassed a number of suspect's houses—completely against our usual policy. I think we should step outside!"

"You got it. Let's go!" I said, and I opened the door and got out. Con was out the same time I was. He came over to me.

"OK," he said. "Mon can't hear us. You're gay, aren't you?"

"No, I'm not gay." I predicted a fist fight, so I wouldn't have to bare my soul when there was no need—which I had obviously been doing too much already.

"Yes, you are! You want me, or else you have an attitude to take me down."

"I'll take you down and step on the remains," I said. "Put 'em up."

"You are gay."

"No, I'm not"

"The fact is I'm the biggest, and you're about half my size."

"You're gay?" I asked.

"Do you dispute my advantage?" he asked.

"I don't rank in the gay world," I said. "I noticed you watching me on my way to the psychiatric ward. You saw me coming out of Bill's house. Why didn't you step out of the car and save me?"

"So I'm the biggest?" he asked, again.

"I'd rather fight you than live with the doubt I'm not on the up and up."

"OK, I'm the biggest around here, get it? A little respect, OK?"

"Yeah, fine," I said.

"Great! The reason we did nothing when Jon took you out of Bill's house was because he goes everywhere, it seems. We want to track him a little. We think Smith is going to kill him, once he makes a home in the Caribbean with enough cash to last forever. He doesn't want anybody to tie up loose ends by grilling Jon. Bill is made of money, but he wants to keep every penny for himself. He'd rather kill Jon himself than pay some-one to do it. So we want to coordinate all his moves to intercept the gun or the knife or the thud on top of his head."

"We can go back now," I said.

"Yes, problem solved," he said.

And the conversation picked up where Mon and Con left it.

"James has to be the one who rounds them all up, but he's

dragging his feet. Done doesn't, uh, like to work. He's already made his millions. And Tod? They, uh, all want to blame him inside their club and leave, uh, the law out of it. Murder wasn't necessary to keep the multi-millionaires breaking up marriages. Tod gave it a bad, uh, name, and he scares the rest for holding onto his prosecutor's job. He'll have to duck that corner of a career and round it off, so he can protect, uh, his buddies. Right now they may not believe he's their friend, all the better for the judge," said Con, without a blink of an eye or a twitch of an eyebrow, but his tongue wet his lips a little, so he could say, "You're not in their club, Ben, so he could hit you—before Tod. Smith is probably going along with the judge, but he'd want to take on Tod before the judge did."

"We have no bite without knowing their Big Move," said Mon. "Whatever it is, we haven't picked it up on the tapped phones. "You want to try? Have at it, Ben. And, uh, Con! Are you well? You sound like the judge all of a sudden. I want you to button your jacket and never see Ben out there again. You're the best con man I know." Then Con gave me a look. It was almost a smile.

"You got it," I said. I thought of Loro. And I waited a second for my trance to take shape, but it didn't. Where was my schizophrenia when I needed it? I wasn't taking any medication, and I was stepping my feet way out there. Anyway, I headed out the door with half a donut in my mouth. I also had my gun to my side, ready for anything. I was still honest. And Con handed me a cell phone.

"If you get into any trouble, call me up." So that's what they wanted me to do. I couldn't talk a good case, so I'd have to work one. It was time for me to mature and slow down a little, but would they respect that? "Mon has a cell phone. Here's the number. We think you can do it, Ben. Calm the monster and slay the dragon. Make it an historic battle, better than anything you've ever done. Get your picture in the paper. We'll wait right here. We don't want to get in your way." They smiled at each other! I remembered they were honest cops, and I was an honest fledgling—and gullible? You don't know how much. I hadn't been a cop before. Now it looked like it was pretty important. I had hopes—tremendous determination.

"Great! I couldn't have better pals in the entire world. I won't let you down," I said. And so I was on my way into the darkness, however blinding it was.

All the windows were lit up on the side of the street owned by the jurors. They were giving what they could without discussing the case. And you never saw any of their eyes, always peeping down the street and up a little to the houses in question. I was convinced they knew everything down to the growth of a blade of grass. Only if their eyes had brains. Tod's did. If he saw a gesture or a flinch in the jury that only looked askew, he'd try to remove the man or woman from the court case. His sightings were biased of course, so he didn't always get his way.

Tod thought he had predicted the votes of everybody there by a shrug of a shoulder or a lean this way or that or a blink of an eye or the finger one juror gave to him and his stares. And he believed they all talked to each other, while they were home, or they had no reason to tear apart his house as a group. Let's hear it for good neighbors. It was easier than he thought to lose a residence.

Imagine how frustrated the jurors were, because Tod wasn't on trial. They'd eventually tear one board after the other from his house down to pulp for paper. Then they'd burn that. For now, they put their hope in little old me and those two warts sitting in an unmarked car—who didn't allow anybody to freeze them off. Maybe Tod's wife was related to or friends with one of them, but we didn't hear any dishes crashing or people screaming. Resiliency bedded together with patience, and the pain of a dead friend would last a lifetime. Isn't that what you wanted? It made quite a lucky horseshoe for the wrong side if the amount of death was "created" as opposed to "just happened," which it

The Court Blamed Me

wasn't.

My dad like to throw horseshoes. There were people who toured the country in sanctioned tournaments. But he was more like the family ringer. Each time he and our loved ones got together, he'd set up the familiar equipment and try to buy us kids a position with candy or the odd unjustifiable fifty cent piece. You could tell there were oodles of us getting in line. The family was together! He had good aim toward us and the stake in the ground miles away, as we called it. And even if he didn't know all of our names, he kept the score, moving us to the semi-finals and then the finals—until there was only one next to him, going for the main prize: a real horseshoe coming from a real horse. He'd show the winner (of course my dad lost) how to hang it to hold good luck.

And it was a traumatic experience to lose the game he loved best. He'd pretend a heart attack, laying down twitching and turning. He'd do this every year, so some of us older ones had doubts it was really happening. But all the others would jump on him and take orders to keep him alive.

"Hit me in the chest! Move my arms up and down! Give me a shot! Step on my toes! My head is in the clouds! Pull me down!" And then he'd stop everything by telling them all to go look for a casket. They'd actually try, and be constantly surprised he was alive the rest of the time we were together.

If Tod was a stake in the ground, we could hit him with cold steel, taking turns. I lost all other definitions. I didn't know he was such an outcast. I was fighting the world to get to him, and getting tricked, since he was in between two streets I already knew—not continent upon continent as the globe suggests. My mind was obsessed and lost some bar-gains. I didn't put it on anybody else. Now, who could ignore the whole neighborhood? Then it sounded like the whole world again. Did the population ebb and flow, until a catastrophic event made the bulk of them jump into one little block? Where he was? I irrigated his desert with my one drop of water accusing him. But my effort was futile unless an extra-rainy heaven heard my plea for my sisters and brothers up there to hose us off and meet me to beat the desert into the ground.

I did feel better knowing I wasn't alone. If my mind were made of the ruins of Rome, one fallen pillar would be eternally missed. And the other would never be, though I could see the pieces laying there in the dirt and grass.

Chapter 20

I didn't know what the judge meant by a recess of four days. Maybe he thought I'd vacation a day or so with my storm club. We wanted to know why the Parthenon hadn't been hit by a tornado for hundreds of years. Weren't there trails of current ones circling the mount it was perched on? Or did he run those cogs in his head to think I'd be committed to the mental hospital for that long, or in prison until court began another priceless session? It was obvious the judge wanted to imprison me somewhere. Maybe someone would. But you don't make a life enjoying someone who went to jail or was under observation. You'd lose your endurance. You should look forward to your courtroom expertise, your record, or pleasing a higher being. Accruing blessings you'd enjoy would propel your life, unless you lost your case and went spiraling downward. But the judge didn't lose. He was the host of the shebang, not on one side or the other. And he had a voice. He set up the sentences. That's a rewarding end to any ginger-bread story.

What happened to me? Being on the stand every day court was in session turned my stomach, as if I ate a whole half gallon of ice cream at once. My brother was the murderer, and he'd be giving the orders if I let him, shaking the judge to the core for weeks. With an idling mixture of fascination, caring for those in similar situations, and the common but intuitive release of your soul to the universe, with only yourself to meet it described the heart of the case: feeling your whole life from the beginning to the end. It was exhausting!

I spaced out and then collected myself. I was an open heart on a stage, and anybody knows there's a protracted recovery situation that lasts forever, if you don't know the audience. Tod only had one bird to help. And it didn't do anything! I'm sorry. Maybe it turned one juror's head. In my opinion, and I was thinking very hard, the judge thought he found something glittering in the wood and varnish the day he recessed the court without putting me in jail. I had looked at him and thought he had lost his concentration, but it was a reaction he could translate to thought by combining the expressions on the faces of the regular jury and the attentive courtroom.

Maybe it was the reflected sparkle off a flute that the owner held, until it and many more resumed play. A silent orchestra didn't offend him. He was thinking murderers had a place in society, over the drug-addicted musicians, and they all sweated to be caught, despite their intentions. Anyway, there were girls all of a sudden; none you'd meet in church, of course. People were here and there, and empty spots were filled under the judge's gaze, as afraid their habit of murderers and women got cut. There were more killers to build on as the orchestra thinned out, and some girls loved the danger. Actually, the criminals only forced them out of their seats—not exactly a crime— and ran them out of the room. There was no crime there either, especially before a court; and if it weren't for the presiding judge, the orchestra would play, and the criminals would be sent out of the room. It was life to the judge, and he was hooked! Don't you guess what the judge was doing be-tween appearances that looked like he wasn't even the least bit interested in the people

The Court Blamed Me

there to watch? He had a little spyglass no one could see, and it even recorded every little thing that happened before he came onto the bench.

The judge's job was a lifetime endeavor, but would he be brought down with Tod as I persevered? The judge had to keep his job to be corrupt. Maybe that's why I was set free. He couldn't bet against himself this time and win a lot of money.

Something merged into women with a man who killed. He became a lion, a basic animal, and women loved to be "babies"— you know, "Hi, baby. You're a good girl." They loved to be patronized and pawed. So the lion took over to have his pride. He got anything he wanted and would ever stay in the lead, if only psychologically. He had to, or he'd be sorry for killing. But as it was, he only killed to "survive," and his whole life was an internal worry that he wasn't a match for his girl. Working men were always in the lead with their job and its importance, a little more complicated and challenging—believe it or not— something that gave arms and legs to a mind.

I guess the judge thought he was the lord of his kingdom with all the people his subjects. Nobody saw the peddles under the bench that controlled the invisible wire, the trap door, and the sandbags, which would violate some. I've never seen them. There was a lot of power to deal with. Appreciation was the name of the game, but everybody who consistently visited his court wanted to knock him off. He never got killed, so he grew stronger. It was a wonder his courtroom was this peaceful. It usually wasn't, compared to other judges.

There was an overwhelming sense of cockiness needed to get away with something as if your life depended on it. You'd be pretending you were the boss, but the judge was the boss. Pay attention to him getting away with murder. A judge was right there at the top. If he killed something, it would be compounded with interest. If his brother killed a few more, after his first, a precursor to Tod, and then was rushed into death, the judge would have to escape the avalanche on the mountain of evidence. So he didn't make it a habit of siding with violent achievers.

In order to be a leader you've got to know you can only get away with so much. If you went too far, there were caves with holes in the ground that went for bargain prices—much better than jail.

He did change a little, burying from prying eyes his talent for destroying marriages. He'd make the women scared of their husbands who presently, suddenly, and maybe with only a slight chance would doggedly come up with a form of schizophrenia. The multi-millionaires weren't hard to find once they knew they had the vine-ripened power to buy anybody they liked. There was no murder there, and this was what the judge was proud of. He knew the bottom line after supervising all those questionable chain-and-ball castings. Criminals killed, and the judge didn't. If he changed, he'd have to accept that he beat the world of non-violent crime and glowed enough at the top to his satisfaction.

The judge actually agonized over my court case. It took so long to adjudicate. He knew I had opportunities to cut the propeller off his new innovative race-equipped sailboat. He owned that thing, figuratively, and tacked away from the binocular store so nobody looked at him. And he was good at crashes, because he was quick on his feet. I, a true schizophrenic, (I usurped the power if I was one or not) had come his way and would cause his boat to wreck. For one thing, he wouldn't get to murder Mary. He was dwelling on her and the blood that would come. The Big Move was planned whether Mary talked or not. Nobody knew it, but I was the one they were against from the beginning, wanting to topple Tod. This was the gem glittering in the faces of the judge's courtroom people. The room proved it to him like the other times had. He knew his subjects and how to rise above them. It was the hub of his life. He better know all

The Court Blamed Me

about it. That's how he got his money. So was it murder—Mary next after me?

So the Big Move was planned to make up for and agree with the blinding glint in the eye he knew was coming. It would take all Smith's efforts along with the judge's own, but soon one night I would be hog-tied and ready to meet my fate—never to come back to another stakeout at Green Street, the judge's own backyard. Yes, he knew of us and exactly what we were doing. The Big Move would clear the road ahead for more murders, a change of his judgeship that wasn't agreeable to Bill or Smith. But he had Tod on his side, when the natural-born leader of all criminals needed some help. With all of the judge's political weight transferred to the prosecutor, it would be an easy coup for the judge to take all the power and hold on to it.

But could he go any further? Men wanted to be real, and Tod could teach the judge this, while women were brain-washed by centuries of planned-out evolution. Tod might not know that. The judge wanted four days off to think. Obviously, he checked our schedule when we were out there. Had I run him into the ground? I wasn't scared of his gavel and where it put me. I had friends and a sense of truth. He had goons, and he didn't trust them. He'd tie up Mon and Con and take their clothes for his and Smith's, and stakeout in the same car while I came driving by. He'd test the sharpness of my hopeless reality. Of course I'd think it was Mon and Con in the same place I left them. They would look a little different, but like schizophrenia, I'd think I was just seeing things and hop into the car in the back where they wanted me.

They'd give me a couple donuts, and then as the truth came to light, I'd be boxed in and driven to jail, or worse, proving the mental illness finally sunk in. The judge would accuse me of murder with a clear conscience, and I'd break down and cry or something. And the door made of rolled steel stood a fair chance of being shut till the day I died. This would be the Big Move, but

I didn't know it. I did have a clue I upset the judge a little. But Americans accept Americans. He didn't even know me.

So when he left the bench for his street clothes, the orchestra, as always at the end of a court session, picked up their instruments and played "The William Tell Overture," more for masked men than for posterity. Everybody and their cousin was waving their arms and directing. I was in the lead standing up and swiping every note, because we were happy court was over, before I was whisked off—usually anyway. This was the one time they didn't do it.

We cut the audience in half. Some of us wanted to stay until they finished, and the others had to go to remain serious. At least the criminals left. They hated symphonic music, even if only half the musicians were there. The bailiff was caught between worlds, and his face was getting so red, he had to toss us out. I put my arms down and left. The strings were last to go, the clarinet was caught between measures, the horns didn't quit together, and you could tell; and other reeds sounded like they bumped into the flutes. You know it took another fifteen minutes for every one to pick up the sheet music and pack up the music makers into their cases. They never practiced at it, so the first shuffled out, leaving the bulk forming a line. The last ones walked and half-way ran to keep up, and pushed the lagging criminal ahead.

"Get out of here, criminal!" the musician said.

"No, you get out," said the offender.

"OK, I will get out," he said, and the musician walked ahead out of reach.

"Wait! You tricked me!" And he took off after him, but never caught up.

There was a traffic jam at the door when the bailiff shut the lights off. So everybody's page-turner lit up the flashlights, and happiness took hold of their normal positive frame of mind.

But back to the stakeout.

The Court Blamed Me

We were there at the spot on Green Street that the judge may have just as well handpicked for our own vehicle to be compromised. I took off into the blackness of night with a swagger and noticed the lighted windows were all on. Clear vision was only about ten feet. Now I knew why Mon and Con had given me the baton. They couldn't turn on their own headlights to see what was going on, or they'd reveal themselves. And heat seeking binoculars weren't covered by the budget. In fact we were the only stakeout present hook or white-collar crook in the town. It didn't happen that often.

Tailgating was similar to stakeouts, and more often than not, they called in making the captain think they were on some back-bay road spying on suspects. The captain called in for reports, and they told him the truth. The criminals were at the game! It didn't work every time for the original goof-off.

So I had some dirt in my eye; it wasn't smoke, was it? I had the afternoon off after dancing to the music of the orchestra, so I did have some shut-eye. Maybe it was a piece of the sandman. But I'd never seen so much murkiness. A couple steps forward, and I thought I was going blind; but then I saw something: a male—fifty-pound overweight man in a dark suit? I wasn't sure of the suit. I thought of yelling out to him, "Hey, pal. Take it easy. Wear plaid next time, will you?" But then, maybe he couldn't see me. He was at Smith's house knocking at the door. "Why don't you call him?" I thought about asking him that question, too. The lines were bugged, and the ultra-sharp investigators who manned the phones had to depend on little-old me up for bat. He kept on knocking, and nobody was coming to the door. "Break the glass and climb inside," I threatened to say. Then we'd take his con-tempt-of-court glute to jail for burglary. "Here, I'll help you," I didn't say. It was the judge looking for Smith; by then it was obvious to me. I picked up a rock and hurled it toward the biggest pane of glass on the front side of the house. If it broke the darn thing, he'd take the wrap, everybody thinking his outrageous temper in the courtroom was comparable to the one in the community. You began to think he was on the edge of doing anything, especially after a few hardened criminals passed his bench on the way to a future that even wild rats wouldn't want.

"Take that, you imposter," I so wanted to say, as the rock hit the steps and bounced off. He turned around, and I felt like each of my pores had a lit Christmas-tree light in it. How visible was that? I lunged forward with quick steps squealing like a frightened mouse, which hurried on up, as if the mouse-trap clicked after me but missed. If I became a cat, I could be mistaken for a mountain lion or a tiger. Don't they go after judges? Something was holding me back from a face-to-face meeting. I was sure he hadn't forgotten to load his gun. And he knew it was so dark outside that the danger was he had the option to shoot me for protection and would go home no worse for wear. Who'd blame a judge? Then the cats would come out to play, turning it all back over to the wild.

Well then, don't you know it: the five lighted windows went out. I cussed to myself. I wanted to verify the face I saw. Then four of them came back on! I didn't know many cuss words anyway. Evidently, we were communicating. I began to depend on them, as if they cared. And then I saw. It was the judge. Then on a top floor, Smith's window light went on and off. He didn't want the judge to come in! It was just like Mon and Con had said. He followed the judge grudgingly.

I'd tell Mon and Con all about it when I came back. Right now I was determined to make it up the whole block. I had my gun out in case I'd have to shoot any turncoat critter between the buttons of his robe. I wasn't kidding, and I had to take a second look over my shoulder as I hurried along. He did have his judge's robe on; now the thought came back to me.

This inspired a lot of imagination.

Was he adjudicating a black-market court case? Did he

The Court Blamed Me

have his own courtroom in the underground community—a haven for pickpockets, a handful of low-lying pimps, small-time fences, and egomaniac pirates and gamblers? If so, for a fee, he seized the moment and solved the arguments criminals had no brains for. One way or another, this guy was having fun, and I was running away. I couldn't take on the leader of all the crooks in town? One word, and I'd pick up the contract I found in my box, which may as well have a space for my signature. I might not sign it, and then surely die—a human event. The devil didn't do anything to you until after signing. Nowhere does it say he hurts you when you don't sign. But whoever depended on his integrity found the way to ignore him.

So I was kinda looking forward to the corner of the block where shelter presented itself, the curtains parted, the speaker of ceremonies stepped out, and this singular over-weight lady sang a tune. Yes, I wanted the fat lady to sing, but I was going to finish my work—maybe tune her in to the Walkman when it was available.

It was the adjoining street. We weren't contracted to go that way, but I would. I got to the top of the Green Street block, looked, and turned left. The first thing I saw was the river down below and then a row of houses up the hill from it. One of the houses, in fact the very closest one, stood a mail-box with my name on it—Packin. That was my name: Ben Packin. And my brother's name was Packin: Tod Sam Packin. And I was Packin it up! I had to lay the King down and get out of there. The chess game was over. By the way, he had guard dogs on his front lawn, so I thought I should go on home. There were donuts and coffee waiting on me along with a good conversation.

So as not to despair, I had some good items to bring to the table. I actually had a winning hand. I did my job, but when I passed by Smith's house without incident, I realized the judge's timing was way off, if he was to come after me. And if it was more than that, it wouldn't happen. I beat the wrap both Mon and Con were talking about. If they had a Big Move, I didn't see it. And knowing them, they were probably laughing it up, having made a bet against me.

"Is that you, judge?" Nobody was over there but the judge. Maybe Smith had been asleep—simple as that, and now he was meekly asking questions. How would you like it if some-one knocked on your door right before sunrise? I was soon to be home, and I'd turn on every light there was, until I dropped off to sleep. I'd be in bed the usual length of time, because there was no court in the morning! Ten o'clock would come and go. My mind may have been calm and clear at the moment, away from fear, but I leapt the last ten feet toward Mon and Con. I actually jumped! That far!

I was miscellaneously entering the car, but inside after the door closed, I was very particular.

Chapter 21

What I wanted to prove to the world as a human being was that I wasn't a schizophrenic, but I didn't know how to fight it economically if someone tagged me. I knew one hundred per cent of normal people set themselves up from time to time to pretend they aren't so normal. They play with the idea. Like, "How is your grandma?"

"She's great now that she's taken a turn for the worse."

If you were serious when your lie was in jest, and it had nothing to do with joking, and you weren't trying to tell the truth, people got confused, thinking you had insulted their intelligence. You were talking life when the subject was death. You were in the fault, and if you didn't care and didn't clean up your tongue, you'd end up labeled a schizophrenic.

I kept myself clear from lying outright. So the tape over the hole I was worried about was that I may have lied without knowing about it. Take my "trances" on my stakeout job, for instance. It hit me, and without gravity holding my head down, that I was in an entirely different world, believing my imagination. Thereby, I was accepting the lies of my surroundings. I wanted so much to believe in anybody but myself, a symptom of something worse. But any guy, defined as a person, can live with a set of different opinions and philosophies. Actors do. Until it caused grave suffering for the incautious person or the people around him, I didn't worry about it.

Life to me was to catch the criminals, not to overheat my intentions concerning the two blips on the screen that zapped a hundred inside-brain connections. Three or four well-insulated cerebral stems out of the hundred were probably at odds against each other from the law of averages, and meant I was only three or four percent off the wall. The doctor who figured this out was a brain-transplant revered specialist from one of the old scary movies in black and white. I could take my three or four impulse reacting mind twisters, depend on them primarily, and I'd be better off than he was. So I was generally normal. Call me schizophrenic, and I'd kill you—well, not kill exactly. I was actually so unoccupied or absent from the charges and the direction of the present case, I wasn't worried about my mind and its moving parts at all. But ask me again when I got home or about what I said in the past. Maybe I was getting better. Maybe I was getting worse, and I had just tricked myself.

The proceedings were a symptom moldy enough for me to prove Tod had killed our dad—the sick truth. It was slapped with two pieces of bread on either end to sandwich him in, no matter what anybody or the judge was saying. He was my hoagie, and I thought he enjoyed me taking a bite. Hiding it also must drain him, except for the people directly or indirectly involved.

I did know my brother was free from anymore blame, since he won his court case. I also knew it was dangerous not to have a razor-sharp edge moving against the charges. My dad was a good-old cork, not represented by the injustice of blaming the wrong person. You wouldn't see his earthly finger pointing from his blessed last word or breath. He didn't build up hating any of us. So I was breathing for him, and being alive, I owned, documented, and bought stock in my finger, which pointed the

The Court Blamed Me

one place I wanted.

But once was enough. The judge would get me if I tried that again. Maybe that one time in the beginning was too many, but wouldn't he have done something already? Maybe it was mixed in with all the other anger. And it was so dark in the neighborhood, who could do anything? The stars them-selves must not have dared come out.

"Give me a donut," I said. "Please hurry up. Now! OK, great." I took a large bite. "Oh, that feels good. All right, that hits the spot." I swallowed. "Now the coffee. Oh, yeah. I knew there was some left.

"Do I have a story to tell you! First, I have to wash the soot stuck in my mouth. My throat sucked in that thick air. Is there a helicopter dropping gallons of syrup on Green Street? I'm sorry. There had to be hundreds of them it's so dark out there."

All of us looked. One of us stuck his tongue out for a taste. It was either Mon, Con, or me, and I'm not telling.

"Needs a little butter," he said. I think the mystery man's favorite meal was pancakes.

"What did you find out?" asked Con.

"The judge is looking for Smith," I said. "He may not have been looking for the others. They've left, and Smith won't open his door." Then all the windows on the juror side of the street went dark. "The neighbors have sort-of won. They have successfully kicked out the scum, while new ones moved in." We all looked for a real estate sign on Tod's old yard, and there was one! "I think it was planted before he moved out. He was ready. He's up at the next block, now. I read his mailbox. I told you Tod's move was to give the judge and the neighbor-hood the slip. But I didn't know the judge would knock on all the doors. That's what I figured before he hit on Smith."

"The judge is losing it," said Mon.

I swallowed and chewed.

"Yeah, we've got people who overheard a conversation between him and Smith right on the courthouse steps," said Con. "He didn't know what to do with your court case. He's scared if you win, it'll bring down his kingdom, full of schizophrenics and their wives scared of staying married to their men, just something he accidentally fell into. Well, he manipulated the whole scene, and that's illegal! They say if he can't handle one measly little sick guy with the whole world against him, he's lost his touch. It's only a matter of time before the judge pulls everybody down with him. They'll have to leave town."

This was the time to call in my cards. I'd said enough.

"I didn't realize I was winning," I said. I didn't count the friendly atmosphere, but how much was I to trust these guys?

"It's better than that," said Mon. "If they all get caught, you'll be honored with a badge, better than being a deputy. This is the real thing. Mind you, it'll only be a discretionary decoration, but within two weeks if you don't kill any innocent thing or abuse somebody, you'll be voted in officially." Con got Mon ready for a fist bump, but Mon recoiled in anger.

"Don't you shove that handful of knuckles at me! You're best at violence, I know. I've always known."

I had to keep up the peace. "But I don't know how to expedite your hopes before skepticism sets in. It's still a hundred to one shot, isn't it?" I asked. I kept the celebration of myself quiet for now. This threw all my brains cells into what happened on the Asian Express. And if it got that complicated, I'd give the case to Mon and Con, the veterans.

"You can't improve by pulling the short straw? You know we're trying everything we can to put you in the lion's mouth, your best suit. The judge didn't shoot at you or chase you, or anything?" asked Con.

And I had to answer questions. "He saw me, what was the third time off the record. I must be all over him, and it must hurt. I'm the little guy he throws around in court, but also the

The Court Blamed Me

detective in his own back junkyard. Maybe I scared him, if I've been ahead like you say."

"There's a law that says it comes back on you," said Con. "Opposite, but equal?"

"You know, some criminals throw the olive branch, because they're so tortured inside," Mon said, "and want it to quit."

"Well, you're free to ask the blanket if it helps you catch some good sleep. You'll enjoy your bed tonight," said Con. "You deserve that much, and those are fighting words. We expected an attack that began against us, and then ended with you serving a lifetime in jail. I'm glad it didn't happen. What would happen to my faith in the justice system?"

"You only have faith in good old number one—yourself," said Mon.

"I do not."

"Yes, you do."

"How about a high five? Will you give me one of them?"

"No."

"There could be a phone call, if you're still listening—Ben?" asked Con.

"Yes, I am." I tried for peace, but there was something more important, and you couldn't turn off the eye. It was brewing.

"Tod calls up Smith and thanks him for putting off the judge. After a few details, Tod regains his leadership and turns the whole lot of them into hard-core murderers. They won't know when to stop."

"As if I had the choice of staying away from jail or the mental hospital," I said. "Anyway, good night. I find myself so insensitive to the feelings of criminals at the end of my day. I could've scared him. Maybe I did. Maybe I didn't. I love you. I love you not." I threw away the rest of the plant.

Before I grabbed the last donut and switched cars to speed on home where my glass of milk was waiting, as long as the refrigerator had gas and was working, I thought about how much Mon and Con had changed since my first day. They had depended on me for so much. But they hadn't changed a bit! So that stopped the issue, at least in my mind.

Con took out his gun to our great surprise and broke out of the passenger seat. He also pounded his breast like a monkey once he got outside. He grabbed a brush and dipped it in one of the confiscated cans of paint with the darkness as a camouflage. I didn't know it, but Con felt guilty for wanting me to battle everything with teeth, even though I didn't have any-thing but guts to put up against it.

Con was all fired up into action like a broken but flaming-gas line going straight down Green Street. He took the brush and painted a stripe on the houses to the right, where the lights in the windows pressed against the darkness, which was a tad less now that they had come back on. He didn't see it coming. Two flying Omdinda circus men from the mental hospital grabbed him and proceeded to belt him in a straight jacket. Their talons had him secure. Now, if they were parrots, they wouldn't have to call in air cover. But all loose parrots primarily returned to South America, where they came from.

"Who are you?" Con asked. So he was disturbed, but this was on the record. Somebody roughed up a cop!

"Your mama!" they said. And understanding Con was only half the way down the block, Mon sensed the trouble. He turned his car on and backed up until he was on the next street. Then he floored it and opened his window. For the next ten minutes he circled the block, yelling things like, "I can roll circles around you!" or, "Don't think I can't surround your under-arm pits!" And the best one was, "I step on toes, too," as he barely missed their feet with the car tires driving by. It took two minutes flat to circle and have another chance. He was aiming at them.

The judge showed up. "Where's Smith?" he asked. Then he turned to Con. "I know you're nothing but a dirty-little

THE COURT BLAMED ME

schizophrenic, and I've given you nothing, uh, but mercy from the get-go. This will change. Your brother told me he watched in horror, uh, when you guided your dad into the path of the bus. You've hidden behind that clinical definition of paranoia long enough. I'm, uh, throwing out the jury and, uh, making the decision myself. You're going to be locked up for a very long time."

"So why didn't his brother say something?" asked Con. "He could have told his dad to stay back."

"Well, there, uh, was, uh, all, uh, that noise, and uh... you know..." said the judge.

"You're under arrest!" said Con, and he splattered the judge with what was left in his paint brush, while fighting the jacket. And Mon was driving around and around and around. He aimed for some juicy toes, but they all moved.

"Oh, you're not Ben," the judge said. "I know you. You're Con Riley from the fifth district." Then he wiped his hands on his robe, which only made a smear. "I'm sorry. Let him loose, gentlemen. He's, uh, not the right one!" And right at that moment Mon drove by and aimed at everybody!

"Get out of the way, Con!"

They all scattered except for the judge who faced the headlights from where they came. He was sure he had the time to give Con a kick in the pants. It hurled Con straight to Mon, and the neighbors behind the Green Street windows stopped gathering their sawing and painting apparatus and generally listened to the tires screeching. The car stopped, and Mon came immediately over to Con to help him face his accusers-something at least to divest them of their power.

"Take this straight jacket off of me, Mon," said Con. "We should run these guys all in, and that includes the judge."

"Your mama!" they both chorused, against that. Jon must have had younger brothers. They didn't know their mama.

Mon tore at the jacket and backed up the small crowd.

"Where is Ben?" the attendants asked. I had been gently sliding out of reach of the controversy, knowing who my boss was. It wasn't the judge or the jerks from the mental hospital. So I quietly turned my engine on and drove off the premises for home plate. It was safe over there, I hoped. My gun had a central-holster location, and my apartment was so small, the gun and the bullets would be very accessible.

Mon took the jacket off Con.

"We take orders from him," the attendants said of the judge. The offenders were still talking! "We don't know who you are, if you're not Ben."

"And it's so dark," the judge said. He took his wet hands and chased the rest around in circles.

"We see you over there," said one, in a throng of passers by. They were interrupting the judge's fun, though. They were also crossing the street from the jury side with hammers, toilet paper, chainsaws, and more paint on the way to Tod's old house. "You can't stop us," thinking their half of the street was against Tod's side of the street, and they didn't forget the court case. The vigilantes didn't risk a conversation. They just exercised a scripted demolition, since Con had them all riled up.

"What is this, Con?" asked Mon, as he threw the white cloth to the ground.

"Simple. I slapped paint on their houses like it came from Tod, in his efforts to redress them for what they did to his house. So there they are—in turn, acting against what he just did. I just wanted to see how much of the neighborhood was on our side." And he laughed.

"They didn't know Tod had moved," said Mon. He also laughed. "They're definitely on your side!"

And the jury group proceeded to string all objects with toilet paper, sawed down trees, and hammered out the windows. Then they used fluorescent paint over the tops of everything. The crowd stood there admiring their work in silence, and smiles

The Court Blamed Me

took them back home.

Somebody called the local news station, and a picture of it hit the papers the next day.

"Who is Tod, the prosecutor?" asked the news. "Is he corrupt, or what? Is he in a court case nobody wanted? Is he a criminal? Had he hurt someone and used his high office to get away?" The press was interested, and this was all I needed to reclaim my freedom in fair play.

Chapter 22

Wow! That was close. The man in the straight jacket was Con, and it wasn't me. If I were out there in the darkness where he was, I'd be picked up and moved much faster. With the steel-belted van parked nearby I'd have no choice but to be driven away before any conversation. The cops had the power. I was only the coffee and donuts man—still. Officially, I didn't have a voice; I didn't carry much weight. Who can eat and get more important at the same time? Donuts didn't cut it, but don't tell Mon or Con.

The judge and his sidekicks had a piece of their plan. They had captured Con. All they had to do to complete the picture was to take out Mon. Then they'd take their clothes, set up in the car, and wait for me to show up.

It wouldn't happen, of course. Maybe the judge knew this, even though Jon could help. The judge must have been thinking about killing him, instead of counting the favors Jon had saved up. But servants like him kept the big man, Smith, friendly—a very important maneuver.

So I made it back to Loro as she was waking up. I came in the door immediately pulling socks out of their drawers, putting

The Court Blamed Me

something under the lamp so it was tilted, moving the dinner-table chairs an inch here and there. I also needed the coffee to spill each piece microscopically from its bag to the shelf. And then my milk glass had to be halfway filled sitting on the counter. My wife was looking at me the entire time, and the faster I was urgently adjusting everything to my satisfaction, the quicker Loro was making notches in her regimen to be fully awake—enough to talk with me.

"You're strange!" she said. Thar she blows!

"Material life is fickle," I said, "and we don't have much to go around, so I have to tweak this and scrape that to take full advantage."

"I don't think the spilled coffee or the milk glass or any of those things know what you're doing," she said.

"Well, they ought to if they have a mind," I said.

"They don't have minds."

Beat that, I told myself, and I did.

"I said if," I rebutted. "What if they do? They may be hibernating, and if I interrupted their sleep, they'd never come alive and work for us. It's like ice. It sleeps inside the cooler, but once you take out a tray, you check for sure if the water has frozen. A nasty trick would happen to us if it wasn't. That doesn't scare you? " Now, that was true enough to put it in the Bible.

"So bring the tray out and let it sit for a while," she said.

"I can also bring the frozen meat out, or I can just give it a nudge, since I know I'll take it out soon," I said.

"That's what I mean. What earthly good would that do?"

"I'll show you," I said. So I went over to the freezer and gave the meat a tug. "Now I'm on my way, and if it has brains, it'll know that and get ready, too. Have you ever had a piece of meat that wasn't ready? You know it looks like brains to me to have something thaw out."

"No."

"Then somebody must have touched it," I said, "for it to be

available to you."

There was a pause in the conversation.

"Everything has brains?" she asked.

"Yes, to basic levels and below," I said. "There aren't many in ice, say, but don't you react impulsively and kick a cube if it fell to the floor when you needed it? You automatically thought it had feelings, kicking it like that"

"I'll try forevermore not to kick an ice cube again, when it's down," she said.

"Don't kick anything when it's down," I said.

"You mean you?" she asked.

"Yes, I'm tired. I had a hard night." I put up my jacket and saw my blanket.

"You can sleep soon. I made the bed," she said. "But one more question."

"Yes." I hoped every inanimate object was my friend, because I was afraid she was about to destroy a piece of me.

"You've given those small brains a lot to think about. Moving objects about, however little, they're burdened by the step one molecular brain can take. The leap is way too high. What I think is you have unburdened yourself to get them going. They were doing great as they were, calculating dust particles and the changing of the light and so forth. You get them overworked if they do have brains. They'll burn out and never do you a service. There's a slight chance a fire will break out, and the whole place burn down."

"What?" She was going to burn the whole apartment down and blame it on the few items in the refrigerator? C'mon!

"Yes, you probably think I'm throwing sand in your eyes just to play around, but I know your ritual here has been a proponent of schizophrenia for some time," she said. Loro rose out of her position and moved about a few objects of her own. Three pounds of gold bars were smudged, her double string of pearls were stretched, an authentic signature of George Washington

The Court Blamed Me

was moved perilously close to falling off the shelf, and keys to the safe deposit box, which held a mil-lion dollars worth of stock, were hanging on the lampshade—I didn't know she was kidding. I was paying her no attention, as she announced the gold bars being moved and so forth. She was mocking me, and I was already intimidated. She had described those things in so many words to me, and I had no way of not listening. The bargain of her living to her old age with me was beginning to cost again. I had to think of some-thing.

I went over to the chest of drawers and pulled out her underwear, threw it to the floor, and stepped on it, like it was a live bug that wouldn't be killed no matter how much I stomped.

"You know what this means?" I asked. I answered my own question. "It means the game is over! Everybody is born rich, knowing the first second is life itself, having no room whatsoever to move around in the womb. So don't complain over the few bucks I have in my pocket."

"Do what you want," she said. "We'll have clear skies when we grow older. Until then nothing matters."

I went over to my chair and got comfortable. I leaned back, draping one leg over the arm rest. I had to make it up to her, since I was so sure.

"Do you want me to explain schizophrenia?" I asked. Now that'll do everything. Some discussions are as good as money.

"Please do," she said.

"OK, take one head, and it has a train of thought, doesn't it?" This was fun to me, following the lead of Socrates, like I was him. OK, so what?

"Yes."

"OK, take a singer's head, and it has a train of thought, right?"

"Yes."

"And that singer will have a train of thought going on even when he or she is singing—not much of one, but it's there, right?"

"Yes."

"There's no telling how separate the singing is compared to the train of thought, depending on how well the singer knows the music, right?"

"Right."

"There would be another kind of train of thought if the singer knows the music so well he or she can daydream at the same time, OK?"

"OK"

She was such a bright young lady.

"In fact if you know the music so well, you could day-dream about anything, just singing away. You can make plans, solve problems, or happily decide what to eat the rest of the day. So far, do I have your attention?" Socrates must have thought this way of argument up in the womb. His ma asking questions he had no chance of answering—you know how mamas do when they're pregnant. Some even try music.

"Yes."

"The problem arises when the singer, now quite high over himself, thinks he can have a conversation with the singer next to him—while he is singing! This is schizophrenia. He thinks he can, but we all know he can't, and so he disturbs the group. He doesn't know why. And if the choir director admonishes him for trying it, he'll probably deny everything. It will happen over and over again, until he needs some sort of clinical attention. Still listening? Remember, you just got up, and you must be rested."

"Yes." And she halfway yawned.

"Well, take me, for instance," I said. "I put little things here and there for my satisfaction, and you think I have a hole in my head, don't you?"

"Yes." I was glad she wasn't laughing.

"Well, does this hole come in the door expressing itself, once I came inside, or is there one in my head throughout the day?"

The Court Blamed Me

"I haven't heard of your strange habits outside of the apartment except for one or two, but for the general argument, you do have a hole in your head no matter where you go. I'm especially concerned you work with a gun and might not come back home—you know, because of that hole," she said.

That meat was ready to come out, if we should let it thaw before the meal, I noticed. And I don't believe she did. I wasn't smarter than her about the cooking, was I? If my "trance" hit, I would be supercharged!

"Well, I've surprised you, so far, with the weight of my career, haven't I?"

"Yes, and no further comment," she said.

"Well, I'm here to tell you I received an accommodation for my work, and I should be a policeman in the near future."

"Great." There was a hidden clench of the teeth made known.

"And wives of all policemen worry about their husbands throughout the day, holes or no holes in their head. But you knew this?"

"Yes."

"And it is common?"

"Yes." She was telling the truth.

"All I have to do is simplify," I said. "If I can do serious work, enough to worry you, with my gun or my singing, and still get ahead in the meanwhile with a hole in my head, I must not be schizophrenic. For according to you, that is strange. And you're against me in my court case, something else strange. If I am weird in your sight, you're the one who needs to change. And you can do it. You can accept me a little more. We're already set up to have more fun. I can't remember the last time I squealed with pleasure, but it's near, and I can feel it coming whether you like it or not!"

"I was going on the tenet that we treat each other however we want until we've grown old," she said. "And I take your schizophrenia to be a dig against me. I have to shovel constantly."

"Add a little age then," I said. "I admit tenderness has to come from both of us, but if it gets us up there a little faster—and you know how time flies—old age will have some practice. I've been wondering if we will flail about, not being used to it, when the autumn of our lives takes the stage."

"You have?"

"Yes, there's nothing wrong with thinking about it. Don't you look ahead?" I asked.

"Not much."

"Then this is a lesson for both of us," I said. "I'll be the piece of meat this time. You can touch it to get ready." And we both laughed. You know what this meant. We were really getting along. And the meat could last another day.

Chapter 23

OK, our marriage was getting better, and I thought twice before I rearranged the whole apartment. We were a real pair, and this was the first time we fought to eventually agree on something important. We weren't meant to be free and loosened up to the sharp point of danger. Tenderness would take its place instead of scaring each other just to get a laugh. It was a very long way from depending on excellence—love, secrets, and favors. But tenderness was one of those fine qualities available that took root in the hearts of men and women. Sometimes it was the hands and feet involved that shook the building. A fly on the wall might give a buzz that said we weren't doing our best, but the walls would shake it off. The results from our battles were sketchy, but we could have a breakthrough as long as we agreed our brains were higher than all the material objects of our household. Simple? I had to think about it. I believe she knew the edge of our marriage, and it just about cut me during her performances.

That's the beauty of it. Being comfortable was paramount. We wouldn't have a marriage if we constantly focused on the other person. So we argued for and against our marriage every time there was trouble—just like pros. After a while there was no tighter union, and it would be at our own pace.

Two days passed.

"Somebody called you last night," Loro said, while the commercials were on.

"Why has this come up?" I asked. I had just caught on to the story, and I didn't want to be disturbed. It was a single man's Utopia when she wasn't talking. And that's how I met Loro. She had a friend that talked more and made a point of it. For months we didn't say anything to each other.

"They did call last week, too," she said.

"When were you going to tell me—next month?" All right! Time out. Try not to blame anybody. There must be mercy, I thought. Who knows what guided her if I didn't?

"How about never?" she asked. "They didn't promise any money."

"Money from what? Is this a business deal like with the cops?"

"No, it's not about the cops," she said, and I was beginning to feel the fear that had enterprises with a street full of suspects. The law might have long arms, but the gangs owned the fingers. They reached your throat. By the way, if fighting is the way, why the insults? You should be pleased the opponent agreed with you for a fight. That's what you wanted.

"Criminals?" I asked. I grimaced, hating to ask the question.

"No," she said, and I laughed inside and saw a "sigh" building its fort, a kind of expression that had a "whew" in the middle of it.

"You don't want to tell me, do you?" I asked. "Don't, if that's your pleasure. I hear a knock. Somebody's at the door." I folded my arms and set the chair back. I was going out for a drive, maybe hunt Smith down. The judge wasn't going to quit looking for him, and I didn't know if he already hooked up. Maybe I'd get lucky and have an epiphany of where he was. And there could

The Court Blamed Me

She must have seen the picture before, and registered it as a warning.

"About that I'm not."

"Well, I should call them off," she said.

"We're here," somebody said.

"Call who off?" I asked. "The press?"

Then there was certainly a knock on the door.

Another pause in the conversation. I stared at her blinking eyes and shaky head. She looked guilty of something.

"But you told me you had claws, etc."

"I tricked you." She flashed the dumbest smile.

"How long has it been a trick?"

"Oh, a few conversations ago. Are you going to let them in, or will you wait for them to break the door down?" she asked.

"I'm getting the gun," I said. Her fun, and our wonderful marriage allowed it, was to hurt me.

"You won't find it," she said. "It's in a safe place right now where you'll never get your dirty-little hands on it." I was sick according to her and should live in the mental hospital.

I wanted to open the door for them, but I sat down befuddled and immovable. She thought this was fun, and it wouldn't hurt anything.

Worse, I'd have to understand. I'd have to share the laugh she got out of this and take all the pain, too. Yet to have happened, my mirth would look down and not find the bottom.

She opened the door. "He's been schizophrenic more than I can handle," Loro told the two men, as her rosy cheeks proved how well I took care of her.

"What do you want?" I asked of them.

"Your mama!" Jon said. If she were here, I'd gladly let her take my place. Questions would go crazy in their heads if they thought of killing her. An impulsive spirit would make them sick. But I knew when I was out-gunned, so I let them put the straight jacket on me, and we all rolled down to the mental hospital in peace. They had a receptionist, too, so I checked in with her.

Jon didn't remember me as far as I could tell, and I wasn't in the mood to remind him. Something was wrong with that patch on his eye. It didn't come with a funny black hat, a foot-wide belt with a silver buckle, a dark waistcoat with a million buttons, and boots brushing against a swashbuckling sword every now and then. He was a pirate, and I knew it. But he was a walking dead man according to his bosses ahead of him, so my judgment was not to bother him and hope he got saved from his dreams.

"Mister...?"

"Mouse," I said.

"What's your first name?"

"Hickey."

"Well, Hickey Mouse, who is the President?"

"Grover Cleveland," I said.

"What year is this?"

"Fourteen ninety two. Columbus sailed the ocean blue," I said.

"Why should people living in glass houses not throw stones?"

I was still in my straight jacket, but she had reached across her desk and was fiddling with it and almost freed one arm. In a moment the other one was free—enough for me to get rid of the entire thing. I pounded on the desk!

"Because the boomerang hit Africa, and Europe was removed by the spatula!" I emphatically said.

"Do you actually want me to believe that?" she asked.

"What else do you have to go on?" I asked. "You don't know me."

"True. Very true," she said. "Sign here, and then go through those doors." I imagined a door-sized valve where you could go in, but you couldn't go back out. I was in for a hanging, and since it had enough effort behind it, I gambled against myself, preparing to win. I didn't want anybody's help: we all go alone when we die.

The Court Blamed Me

"Thank you, gentlemen. That will be all," she said to Jon and his helper.

Now how would I get out of there? Maybe I wouldn't want to. My wife was my world, and the world put me out. And it was all for a laugh, or pieces of it, because she just did what she wanted to do, and it would become a reason, though not enough, to split us apart. Our old-age goals made this stuff nothing but silly. This was quite a surprise for obvious reasons, but if I missed a court date, they'd have no mercy, and by presidential decree they'd find me in permanent contempt. I'd never present my side of the story, and Tod looking down the barrel of my gun (where I believed I had him so far) would turn it around and unload the pellets inside to blow me away! I had to have permission to load the shotgun, aim it at him, and fire, metaphorically speaking. I didn't have a shotgun in reality, and if I did, it wouldn't work. I was toast with loose dentures.

And then I saw my savior, the Lord Jesus Christ! He was in the form of James. At least it wasn't Tod who had just begun a campaign of visiting the hospitals in our rambling city. This is why I didn't hate Loro to kingdom come, because she didn't make the request where I was. The pictures would be in the newspaper, and him and I wouldn't be smiling with some sick kid feeding on our power. For now he had the prestige.

Chapter 24

James had turned over a new leaf. He hadn't always cooperated with the police. He had been in the "gang" back when Tod's wife was killed, but things scared him when the cops started showing up. He wasn't the perfect replica of innocent appearance like all the rest, though he was honest. His scheming neighbors completely missed the signs, believing everything to be in jest.

James was only having a hard time. How do you work a dead body out of the picture when you're trying to be an informant? Everything didn't fit in place, so the corpse was his ace in the hole. The crummy friends he made were pushing and pulling him out of service. He didn't want the fight they planned for him to stick his neck out, freeing up the others for a boat to the Caribbean. They wanted him to go later on. But there was something fishy about this, and he knew it. Believing how dangerous they could be on a moment's notice, he committed himself to the safety of the mental hospital. And consigned he was, right over there! He was having fun with the other patients. And he had enough sense not to fall into the cracks.

"Hi, James!" I said.

"Oh... hi... Ben!" He said.

The Court Blamed Me

"How come you're here?" I asked, innocent of the consequences of wanting to pry into someone's private life.

"One thing led to another. How are you doing?"

"Actually, I was sent down the river by my wife."

"Muddy waters clean up when they hit the sea," he said.

"How do you know that? My record is getting worse. I have an idea I'll be in jail before all this clears up. At the sea? Isn't that where they fish for crab? I wouldn't like the bait, but I may see those traps and fall into one." I laughed. I wasn't a crab.

"Shhhh," he said. "I've been instructing my good buddies to head out to sea. We've got nothing left. Don't ruin it. No-body is a crab." He didn't laugh.

"Can you introduce them to me?" I asked.

"Sure. This is Rod. This is Dod, and this is God."

"Hi, guys. I'm Ben," I said, and then I put my head down next to James' in secret. "One of them is God? How fateful is this? It's an outrage."

"Weil, he has an imagination. All of us do, but being in here settles down the creative side of things. I see him making it up inside with God being friends with him, even if only by name," said James.

"Well, I'll keep from calling on him. Oh, it mixes you right up!" I said, and we both looked at each other.

"I can hear you," said God. Then we laughed.

"No, it's the other way around. The patron hears the booming voice from above, not what comes from out of a mouth," I said, and laughed, but the joking was over. I was the one out of place.

"You're new, aren't you?" asked Rod. "We're getting out of here as soon as that door yonder cracks. Shakespeare says she'll appear being the sun, and its warmth put the cold-blooded edge of the sword against our reunion, not yet under a million times I've seen her plainly in my heart. She has to be very skilled holding the medicine and the door at the same time."

"I want my medicine," said Dod.

"I want mine, too," said God. "Here she comes! Pretend nothing happened."

"Nothing has happened," said James.

"Then there's a chance to revolt," said Rod, "When she believes nothing is going on."

"You recruit the rest of the ward?" asked James.

"No, don't worry. It's just us," said Rod.

"Do we have enough to overpower the guards, once we make it past the first door?" I asked.

"The medicine gives you super-human powers," said Dod.

"Meds!" the nurse yelled. She had come through the door, but it closed and locked behind her. There was no crack in the door yonder.

All of us reached the line-up for whatever ailed us. Then the place went into a frenzy. Ten other patients broke out of line and circled around the meds lady. They were tearing the floor apart and spiritually pumping gas into the inner fires of the copious rejection of having a mental hospital at all. They didn't want to be in it, and the opposite looked impossible. So they were going round and round, building up the steam that might lead to the violence we needed to break out. This had to be the way. I knew what went on in here. They covered you with bricks from the inside out.

The nurse took it to the cleaners where nothing came back ripped, as if she was our star instead of the sun. For some weird reason the ten swashbucklers needed her to believe them in order to push forward in life, so when she had the door open, they just kept on circling and didn't try anything. They fizzled. Nobody believed in them. Of course if someone did, they'd know the patients were busting out, and would subdue them enough to stop it. By accident they were sharp enough to keep it a secret. Believing in them meant everything, and except for this once, from no fault of their own, they had to be up front and transparent in life. The training wasn't there to show them what was appropriate. There should be a breakout where the best of protocol and its formality was in its representatives. If you asked me, they all needed suits and ties.

Heck, if they had jammed the door open, we'd put wings to our feet and run right out. The law of averages determined only a couple of us would be caught, and I'd have time to meet my court date. How do you make a mental patient dead serious about anything? My alternative was to talk with James. I clung to a hope, maybe a starved one, since I had busted out of other places like this. But my luck was picking one rice kernel at a time for harvesting. Of course, isn't that the normal method, anyway? Maybe I could trick hope itself. That'll do. I got James' attention.

"What if we tell these guys God believes in them enough to have a train parked outside? It'll take them to the fair or something just as good," I said. "If we had the numbers we could break out of here, them being on our side."

"Those men circle around anything, pretending to get ready for ants to invade, birds to fly in, or a truck to squeeze past the door. They can't be organized," James said. But I did like the ants and the bird that I thought he spoke of. If he didn't, I did, but I wasn't in touch. That was more than fifteen seconds ago, the time when my bet against myself came due. These men weren't approachable. So I bet they were. I disagreed. I went right over to them, and as long as they weren't born growing up with another language, I'd have a chance.

I said, "Hey, guys. Ben speaking. You guys interested in crime? Like murder? I know something that you don't. I know that guy over there can tell you all about dead bodies. We both know of one, but he's seen it. Come with me!" And they did.

All ten of them were curious, some of them strayed, but most of them walked over to our table and wanted to hear about it.

I said, "James, they want to hear about the murder on Green Street. Can you throw in a dead body?"

"Can I?" he said. "I sure can. She was killed because her

husband wanted a quick divorce, and she wasn't about to agree. His neighbors pressed him hard, because the trip to the Caribbean, where new girls were primed and ready, was on the calendar and couldn't be erased. He had to go with them if he went at all." James was enjoying his moment in the sun. "I heard it through the walls. They were screaming at each other."

"Where's the dead body?" Dod asking this made him nervous.

"I'll get to it," James said, and he kept going. He chose the Caribbean to pick up another girl for himself and thought he was tired of the old one. So he killed her! He'd seen pictures of how beautiful the girls were down there. So he buried his in the backyard. So this, so that, so what, he thought."

'That's disgusting!" one of them said, but not for me.

"That's downright evil," said another.

"It's true," I said. "I saw the hole he dug to put her in." I didn't tell them he was my brother—much less that he was the one prosecuting me. Everything was supposed to work outside the mental hospital.

"Ugly and unseemly," said another.

"You saw the hole?" James asked me.

"Yeah, I snoop around enough. He dug her up and moved the body," I said. "I didn't see that part, though."

"Heinous!" said somebody else.

"I did!" said James.

"You did? When?" I asked. I so passionately wanted the murder not to have happened. But now that it did, the kitty was coming my way; they were interested!

"Late one night when it was so dark that only your two front teeth reflected, I heard him digging; and it was on my side of the property line. I leaned out my window seeing him catch on his fly, first the two legs—"

"Gross!" said one out of the ten.

"First, the two legs—so he grabbed them by the ankles. The

skin came loose in his hands. He discarded it by flinging his wrists. He about slipped on the dead skin that made it under his feet. Then he pulled with all of his might the rest of the body and didn't even take the time to fill in the shallow grave. Maybe it was her subconscious pissing that kept him moving forward."

"No way!"

"No more candy for you."

"Time to move on!" But they didn't. They were awestruck and wanted as many details as possible. They were eating it up, like they were the inventors of the knife and fork. I'd take a meal outside of this place.

"God says not to tell anymore."

"No, I didn't," said God, "but I should go and pray about it." He got up and left.

"Rod says."

"No, Rod doesn't," said Rod.

"Dod says."

"No, Dod doesn't," said Dod.

"What about you?" one of the ten asked me.

"I brought you over here," I said. "I'm as spaced out as you are. But that doesn't mean to quit. You owe me money, now. I didn't think you'd be interested."

"Oh, yeah, now the story changes a few things." This man's intelligence surprised me mute. I was related, you know, and vulnerable.

James stuck to his story, even though they may be drooling on him in the short future. "After he dug her whole body up, he put her on his shoulder rubbing sour blood on blood. Taking the mailbox on the other shoulder, he walked on down the street to his new residence a block away. He wanted a view for his wife, so she could understand his quest for the Caribbean. They were in sight of the river."

"That's where she is?" asked one.

"She may be in here. James is, and I am. We saw her as we

came in, I think. We could find out if the Caribbean was worth her life."

Then there was a knock on the door.

"Nobody knocks on that door!" the patients said.

"Give me your money, now, while we still have our spines. The door is going to open. I'll keep her away from you." They fished in their pockets and gave me a total of six dollars. "They want their dead body back!" I said. They gave me two more dollars.

"God says we better leave," said God. "I prayed, and our best foot forward is our left or right."

"And he means it," said James. "It's time to go!"

"C'mon, guys, let's go!" I said. And when James got up, Rod, Dod, and God followed suit. The rest of the ten were afraid of us.

"Come in," they said to the knock, as it rapped another time. The ones who knocked believed in whoever said, "Come in." The door opened, and all of us were a scramble to get out! We had been given the proverbial second chance. A couple of them didn't make it, but the rest did, including me. I had no reason to believe why there was a waiting cab outside, but six of us fit in that couch on wheels, and we were off! A couple more didn't make it, because there was no room to spare, but I didn't think all of us were concerned about that. We were heading to the city, and I to my court case. And I had cab fare!

There was a man who ran out and stood near the doorway of the hospital, and he was waving his arms in the air as I looked back. It must have been his cab. Oh, it was the judge! "Uh, wait!" he yelled. I'd recognize him anywhere. I slinked down in my seat hoping he hadn't spotted me. What a good place to look for Smith, though.

James was unsure about leaving, but he let his instincts take over and promised himself he'd work it out later. He had an idea to talk to the cops about all he knew, in order to give him more police presence. I was a happy man looking forward to my thirty seconds of testimony, once we left the hospital grounds. Smith... the judge—I was in too deep to change.

Was it a bad omen to have escaped so many "cages?" It didn't mean my whole life in one or the other, so that's life! And was it opening up doors to where the majority was locked up or free? I had a point. The majority of most countries was free—even their butler, most of the time anyway. I was comparable to any of them.

Chapter 25

I had these repetitive court cases, and I had to fish so hard to make my case. It was reliving an arrow of a murder straight to my heart, and it was getting impossible to face all those people again. It drained me having to go to jail for contempt of court every lousy tick of the clock. Meeting Tod's cold stare told him how I meant to destroy him while he looked into my soul. And now I had dirt on the judge, he was as bad as my wife.

They must have talked about it with my wife. Still, I didn't turn either of them in. My tired self said the judge had charge over so many people, I was only pretending if I thought I could let others know. They'd be hurt by my whistle blowing, and furthermore—what was his crime exactly? He was breaking up marriages and putting schizophrenic criminals in jail, but he had the clout to write off these instances as mistakes. He'd promise to do better. Who knows what would happen to me after the charges went in the books. I'd get the shaft, of course, starting with the pointy end.

So the deadly stinger, left over to paralyze the judge's ego-filled world, was the murder they all knew about on the left side of Green Street. It shouldn't end with only Tod going to prison.

They all either had a story to tell with their "friend" in jail (if he went) or had a kick out of knowing he wasn't in jail and spun the yarn propagating the lighter side of murder to innocent ears— or told this from jail where they'd all been scooped up at once. Which plot would you want your parents to hear? Ask their kids. They run from danger. They always have. If they just stood there dazed with the pit of evil inching closer, then their parents had already nudged them the wrong way. And what about the evil pit coming closer to the grown adult? The jury should hear this. Choose to put the prosecutor in jail, by running away from evil, and hope all of his cohorts also gotten the brown grill-mark suntan. They'd have less to say about how good murder was. It was crazy Tod still had a job.

So we'd take a little evidence here and a little evidence there to bring down the judge. We were trying. We couldn't count a number of cases consecutively, because he'd see this coming and steer as many as possible the wrong way. We'd have to do it with stealth.

Right then, as the court opened its session, and we had stood up and sat down, I remembered: I wasn't supposed to be there. It hadn't been four days. But soon I found out why. The judge I was all concerned with wasn't there at the bench. Bill was! This was lunacy. Had the judge caught himself before the ceiling came down upon him, like he was sitting on a sink-hole—before the scare was too late? I was hoping.

The prosecutor wasn't there either, but I refused to think he got scared. I knew Tod all my life, and his best qualities were never to give up and never to fear anything. Of course, that was before he murdered. Being a criminal brings a string of new responsibilities to your doorstep. Not worrying about them hatched a crate that was balancing on their head. I never understood how criminals on television shows didn't get their neck rung, just once, to see if oranges or apples would fall from the "basket" perched up there. They should get dumb and make mistakes, like real criminals. I was searching for any-thing that would rub our contemporary smart-and-sassy lock-pickers to exposure.

In reality, as I watched the local news—you'll notice too—a good percentage of new criminals turn themselves in. Many more go peaceably when the police show up. Either these guys were too old to change, when the crime pumped fresh blood into them, or this wasn't very new at all. Maybe they'd been in and out of lawlessness since before they knew the difference, and they just ran out of gas to live in mansions in a fine section of town. This is when they made up the Caribbean scheme. They were safe at this juncture, but still didn't know the value of money. It travels through the hands of good people, too, and they're attentive. And responsible. And more ingenious. Crime has a small glory.

So I was ushered to the witness stand, agreed with the swearing in, and gave the judge a look that said he was only an alien with a robe on. I truly expected him not to know the English language. The prosecutor was a wave in absentia, so my defense council, Buck, was first. The case opened up with him paired to be the one stuck by the thermometer. He pulled it out, ready to begin. Buck walked over to me, and I had a breakdown right then and there. A slew of the crowd sitting in the prosecutor's side all put rifles to their shoulders and aimed at the attorney, Buck, my money man. If we won, we'd capture a sizeable settlement from the government. I wanted that? You better believe it! Sometimes I believe I didn't, though.

I yelled, "Don't shoot!" Everybody thought I was crazy, and the prosecutor's helpers (now in charge) carved a notch in their notes.

But then a shot fired! It was true. It really happened. My imagination had only gotten ahead of reality. What were the odds of that? I could trust myself much more, instead of thinking I got close to a humbling disease. I guess I had never been sure.

The Court Blamed Me

My woman was. However, she was too objective, or was I too subjective? Now I knew how my trances sneaked in—I'd be daydreaming, like now! Wasn't there a shooting? Wake up, man. I was an easy shot perched there on the wall.

My defense-man, Buck, ducked, but he was already down on his knees from my warning. There was a commotion, wouldn't you know it, behind the plaintiff's pew concerning a gun. Some patriotic men were wrestling with the assassin, until they had his business out of commission. There had been a real shooting, what I imagined in my trance. If it weren't for a few good men on the lookout, the bullets would have kept coming toward the only man in town who would take on my case pro bono.

Then I came to, but I didn't notice the difference. My defenseman got up from the floor, dusted himself off, and continued. I had an eagle eye. If I had seen the barrel of the gun pointed at me, I would have jumped clear to the floor, a distance of about ten feet; and if it was aimed at the judge, I'd have grabbed his robe and brought him to the floor with me. But the gunman didn't know what sort of imaginary world I was part of—a kind that protected me in the strangest of circumstances. Why would people shoot at me? They should have mercy. I hadn't done anything.

So what was he thinking about in the time allotted before he squeezed the trigger and met his jail time or escape? It must have been in the milliseconds. He wasn't much of a thinker. And I didn't let him know, as he was led off to jail, awfully sad I didn't, I suppose. He gave me a fowl look, and with one hand, he carefully engineered a countdown aimed at me as if something else was planned.

So this meant it might not be over. Then I saw about ten or fifteen prison escapees sitting further back on the plaintiff's side of the room. I went back into my trance and felt like what I almost was—a policeman. And you know, before there was any issue, we had to fill up with the famous, powerful, and stimulating ingredients.

"You got any donuts and coffee?" I asked the judge.

"Are you, uh, in contempt of court, yet?" Bill asked. He didn't know. All he did in the presence of a serious society was to mimic the judge's speech.

"No."

"Then, uh, wait for the court to be over," he said.

"But there are convicts over there who need neutralizing," I said, "before they rip us up."

However, since the press had reach of our case and knew it was a bombshell, a reporter went over there and stuck his microphone in one's face.

"Do you have any plans against the state of affairs in this court case?" the reporter asked. He crossed eyes with the judge, he knowing Bill could shut him down.

"Yes, he does!" I yelled. The crowd murmured. I seemed to know everything.

"Order, uh, in the court!" Bill said, as he banged his gavel.

"No, I don't!" the criminal said.

"Yes, you do!" I said. Bill picked up his gavel, and it looked like he was about to throw it at me.

"Yes, I do," he admitted. Whew! That would have hurt, and he wasn't more than three feet from me. I've had teachers that did the same with pencils.

"Well, what?" the reporter asked.

"This!" he said. "I was tried and convicted of schizophrenia, and I've been jailed for over ten years without any medication or anything." (Just think how much tail the judge got from this one transaction.) "No council, or I mean nobody to draw me out of my inner conflict. I've managed to determine it's all about forgetting and being inappropriate." (So the bars embarrassed him.) "I've had ten years to think about it. But my buddies were on death row." (Our state didn't have the death penalty, so imagine how this trick went down) "I've brought them along, and I think they're schizophrenics. So time served should be enough. Ten years is just fine, right? But I'm going to vote this man on the stand is innocent of all mental illness." (He was fighting for me? What a heart.) "Who deserves being locked up for forgetting your mama hit you over the head to get you out of the kitchen or inappropriate action throwing the silverware out into the grass, so she won't pick up a knife and stab you with it? We get to vote, don't we?" A vote? He should get a car and a house to park it in. But this guy had initiative. He wanted Bill's house, except for the dead bodies all around. Of course he wouldn't say that.

"What are you planning to do if you don't get what you want?" the reporter asked. But things were looking up, weren't they? Those diagnosed with schizophrenia were out of jail. If we were looking for a few mud holes in the jail system, they were already drained and on their way to the beauty parlor for facials.

"Ask my buddies," the convict said.

The reporter took the bait and waved the microphone over their heads. They didn't want to reveal anything. He looked at Bill again but got nothing.

"Uh," one said.

"Ahhya," went another. They were pure cavemen.

"Something," was the clearest note of the ten.

"You know." I think this person was brushing his teeth with a portable kit.

"Golamatic."

"Censure," got close to a real answer.

"Dockta." This may be a word somewhere.

"You better believe it."

"I do," said the last, and he meant it.

"Back to the news desk," the reporter said. "This has been

channel WXBO. Remember to use deodorant. Bye."

Bill didn't want to escort these men out of his court, because he was afraid the one-gun security man wasn't enough for ten hardened schizophrenics. But he did something. He ordered the bailiff to get down to the nearest thrift shop to bring them clothes to use over their striped prison uniforms. One of them had on an orange jump suit. He'd take advantage of the good-natured charity of the judge, too, and stay away from the prison's chapel where he looked like the devil.

"Well," Bill continued. "Is, uh, this now an end to your schizophrenia? You seem, uh, to know more about what's going on than I do. Maybe you're, uh, not mentally ill. How about, uh, you, jurors?" They looked around and pretended he didn't do that.

I was coming out of my shift with reality. It only took a good eye to see those convicts, so exactly what was it good for? Maybe my reality caught up with my hazardous imagination, humming it more each time I was hit by one. I wanted to control these powers of my existence in the sun. Then I could have less and less of an affection toward thinking a hundred miles out of the box. I didn't see how I could get rid of them anyway. But then, shouldn't I imagine all their nurses taking pains to make sure the convicts were healthy, wealthy, and wise? We could make a videotape. Oh, they didn't have nurses? Maybe a spotlight on how nurses worked up here in different places—they could be from the Caribbean. Who wouldn't want to plug in that one!

But the answer to his question, are you still schizophrenic, was something like, "You saith it. Onto this end I came into the world." What more traumatic stretch of moments was comparable to my otherwise normal life? Then the double doors swung wide open, and a base drum with its player marched inside and on down the aisle.

"Boom, boom, boom."

Next were two clowns dressed for the circus. A big fat

The Court Blamed Me

guy on a unicycle came after, and he had a treasure trove of tambourines and harmonicas in a bag to toss to the audience. Then there were girls with hoops and streamers, tumblers, and handsome guys juggling flaming swords.

"This has to be a trance," I said. "I'm in my imaginary trance world."

"No, it's real," he said. "What's the matter with you?"

"We're schizophrenics! We're schizophrenics!" they chanted—all of them with gladness and fanfare. It was overwhelming and glorious. Everybody caught their point. And something squeaked like a child's toy, but I think it was thrown in their path from a kid in the gallery, and got run over or stepped on.

"We're not kidding," said the leader. "And we'll be appearing at the fair grounds tonight for our show. All of us have been diagnosed clinically as paranoid this or paranoid that."

"I've got something to say," I said.

"Do you have anything to say?" asked the defense. He was supposed to be first to ask questions. Then the circus chanted again before my answer, but the whole audience copied them.

"Say it! Say it! Say it! We did."

The judge pushed his gear in, revved up, and said, "Say it! Say it!

This guy, uh, isn't mentally ill. This guy isn't mentally ill. Cha, cha, cha!" And he got up and shook his booty, revealing the large paint stain on the robe he had borrowed from the real judge.

Everybody laughed! Some of the audience started doing it.

"Objection!" said the plaintiff's helpers.

"I object over you," said the defense.

"No, over you," said the plaintiff.

"My objection is bigger than yours," said the defense. They probably objected to the same thing—the judge. He was still dancing on his bench. And his big belly was doing the hula.

The clothes were given to the convicts, and they were changing in front of everybody. Some in the courtroom got to their feet to find a better look. All of the female sex in the jury box sat back and wondered in silence. The men of the jury chanted, "I object! I object! Say it! Say it! We're schizophrenics, too!" But this turned a wild hair off the girls out of the jury box. The prison men must have been that good looking, or something. You know, all that good nutrition from Gomez's cooking.

"I don't object," said the plaintiff. She was female. The whole team of Tod's were female. He must have been distracted from time to time. But why was this different from other times in our country? America was famous for its sexuality.

"Say it! Say it! Say it!" the whole audience opened their mouths to the flood of things to come. They all must have been disappointed. The convicts put their new clothes over the old ones. And I only rose to the occasion. In fact I wanted my shy life back.

"What would you like to say?" Buck asked me.

"What if (I'll ask a question) a house in a normal neighborhood was painted with pink polka dots, a fence was added so you couldn't come and go, a twenty foot target was thrown in the mix, the trees were cut down to fall into and tear the roof apart, more splotches of paint slapped on, and toilet paper was hung from the demolition? Wouldn't you come to the conclusion there was something strange about the inhabitant? Maybe even worse—a violent individual, somebody you wished would move?'

"Are you saying in this house lives a murderer?" asked Buck.

"Yes, I am." Well, he had moved, but it was still his house.

"And who lives there?"

"Tod, the prosecutor!" I said. "My bosses, both policemen, have conducted surveillance for a long length of time, knowing one of the five houses in a row on Green Street had a murderer in it. Tod's house is the only one that has been targeted by the neighbors, the ones living with his day-to-day life. I saw them running towards it with paint, saws, and toilet paper."

"This, uh, case is not about, uh, murder," Bill said. "Do I find you, uh, in contempt of court?"

"No." I shook my head to help convince him. He was al-most a soft touch.

"Then proceed," Bill said.

"Tod came over to my apartment and convinced my wife to leave me," I said. It wasn't Tod, but I wasn't far off. I was opinionated, so why not take a dig at Tod, my favorite target. Maybe I could arrest him, myself, if the case lasted that long. "He did this by proving to her I was nuts, and needed to go to the hospital. I don't know how to do that. I can't commit my-self. I'm as sorry as I can be and maybe worse, but I lost the only job I loved, and the whole scene of rejection falling from heaven into hopelessness, because I didn't understand what was happening—I might have picked up a few paranoid feelings of insecurity. But that's all." My opinion is mental hospitals should be nothing but banquets laid out for patients to freely come and go. Psychs would be there to socialize. If you're not hungry, you don't participate. The world was welcome, the entity that gave us the problem. Loro would never go.

"I'm not saying my wife is part of this vengeance, but she didn't like the job I landed, supplying my donuts and coffee to policemen on stakeouts. It's just natural for her to disagree, because the last job had real money attached to it. The job I have now has little real money, but I'll be packing a better wallet once I get promoted—and this is soon. My ballooned-out chest will have a badge pinned on it in a matter of weeks."

"Are you homeless?" asked the defense. There was only Buck in charge—nobody else.

"Yes. I'll try to convince my wife at home one more time I'm not but labeled with psychological terms, but I don't have any false hopes. My brother killed someone, and his life hugely improved after he won his court case. If I had an inappropriate mind, and he's a murderer—why is his life better than mine? Except for his house, of course." Everybody laughed. They remembered my description.

"Do you have proof your brother, Tod, murdered your dad?"

"I was an eye witness," I said. "As I made it to the other side of the street when the bus came by, I saw my brother's hands beckoning to my dad as he gave signals. He kept saying, "A little more...come...a little more," until my dad was right into the path of the bus, which had no way of stopping. I clearly saw and heard Tod—and then the awful crunch under the city bus. But he's going to say I didn't remember, and I'm just making up stuff. How he tricked the state into exonerating him, I'll never know." And that took so much fortitude to say (I wasn't the most honest person) it was finished baking in the oven, and by the crank of my knees knocking together I pulled its door open, felt the heat, tasted the food, and sat down to eat; I finally got out my side of the story! I wasn't sure it would ever happen.

"We saw the whole thing," said the clowns of the circus, "And it was from the big tent, the one in the middle of the world. It wasn't a city bus. It was an elephant. It's sad." My face changed shape. What? "Can you bear the fact that his foot had to be cleaned up?" They said they were schizophrenics. It was all too possible to forget the circus was just the circus, and instead they were out of their scalding minds!

But this spaced out our suspect, Bill, the new judge, obviously only a substitute, while the usual judge was off some-where.

"Are you, uh, in jeopardy of contempt of court?" he asked me.

"No." I got tired of his questions. They didn't look easy.

"Well, proceed then," and Bill's face was beginning to turn red, again. We were trying to convict somebody, and Bill was in the line of fire—or did he not know that?

"Why would your brother kill someone?" asked the defense.

The Court Blamed Me

"To cover up his first murder, his wife," I said. I was on cloud ten or eleven—further up from cloud nine. Somebody was interested.

"How would you feel if you found out your wife was the daughter of your dad?" The defense asked that. I told myself there was another important angle. Surprise!

"I wouldn't feel right. I'd probably get sick," I said.

"That's the true news," said the defense. "Now we've said it, it's out, never to be said again."

"My sister-in-law is actually my sister?" I asked. "Tod married his sister?"

"That's what I'm saying. Tod is missing to get his head together. That's why we don't see him today. The judge probably thinks he can help, not you, Bill."

"She probably knew," I said.

"And your dad. That's why he killed both of them," Buck said.

No objection was heard from the prosecutor's mobile office.

"We have to cut for commercial here," said the reporter.

"OK, fine," said the judge. He was off the hook. Pressure was not suspected. It was all Tod's fault. But Bill had to towel off the droplets from his eyes and throat, like he was a cham-pion tennis player. But once that was over, he let out a sigh of relief that would power sewage at twice the speed down to the tank. Man, somebody was plunging. Judging wasn't as easy as the real judge had told him.

There was no pressure that he, the real judge, Done, Smith, and James had against Tod that made the lifeboats deploy. They were free, it seemed, from the touch Tod needed to put the bloody finger on his wife. They were honest when society demanded it. And America was like a backyard roast and bar-be-cue for everyone. If you got past the prying looks in the small town, you'd find a sharp reusable favor for yourself in the sisterhood or brotherhood of your friends. They would test you, but didn't you do this to yourself? Come together!

"We're now inside the court case of Ben Packin who is accused of being a schizophrenic," said the reporter. "Ben has told me—come over here, Ben. He said his wife pulled a joke on him getting him committed. Ben, can you explain?"

I reached the mike. "Hi, Loro. I hope you see me. I'm coming home. Somebody by the name of God and his friends sprang me from that awful mental hospital in more than one way. See you soon."

"Thank you, Ben," she said, from a computer at the apartment. "I'm glad you found religion, but stay away from coins with two sides. Those still watching us on television of the court case against schizophrenia will also want to know the circus showed up over here at our place, too—like they aren't one unit? Don't they know schizophrenia? I'm not saying I do. See you! By the way, I won't be here, when you come home."

Chapter 26

What about that bunch of inmates who had obviously fled from prison? The judge hadn't done anything about this, and he didn't know Bill had—in his appeal for clothing. Were we about to have a violent response by Sled? Someone had already unarmed one shooter from the gallery. Was this a sign the court was a blood-and-guts issue? Was I, the defendant, the worst schizophrenic alive? Was my presence a rift in the fabric of our society that dressed us up in preservatives? Either I had a can opener to rip into it to supply another gun with the bullet Bill needed to become true to the jury—or, the twelve had prejudged me and had an idea schizophrenics were the worst of all people, so they wanted to put my head in a vice and pop it by cranking. The case was unfolding its way to jail or freedom, but I didn't seem to defend myself much in front of Tod. Was I just going to ignore the charges, like my plan set up—I knew I did it that way. But was I really going through with it? Would they believe what I said? Would there be no appeal attached to my word that that was that?

"WXBO blowhards signing off temporarily." The reporter laughed. "How about that? I'm a schizophrenic. It was time to come on, and I just dialed us off."

That wasn't funny. The circus was next to be interviewed, but after they overheard that and the one where the elephant had something to do with my mental health (from their own ranks) they had second thoughts. Isn't a courtroom somewhere to be as serious as possible? The court was concerned with people's lives and certainly their futures. I mistrusted all of the antics of the courtroom and felt sorry for the escapees in order to look deeper, knowing we were all a scandal inspected to a certain degree. But the jury needed a reason why I went after Tod instead of defending myself. There really was no sure win, because I didn't know about schizophrenia anyway. Watch that one small argument about the bus and lots of people downtown that saw it, where I only had my word against his—would my bones crackle when the jury squeezed them or wouldn't they? That's what they wanted, I gave it to them, and they would judge. I might have to kill Tod myself.

"Let me take the lead here, Buck Price," I asked the defense attorney. It may have been better if we switched places, but Bill would've grabbed me.

"Sure," he said.

"We're in a trial here, aren't we?" I asked.

"Yes," said the lawyer.

"And I'm the defendant, right?"

"Yes."

"And I've been accused of schizophrenia, yes?" Bill didn't complain at all. What was happening was backwards to the usual proceedings.

"Yes."

"And the schizophrenia was manifested when I didn't remember which side of the bus I was when it hit my dad, right?"

"Right. He accused you when you didn't find it in your memory."

"My crummy mind had protected itself by blocking out

The Court Blamed Me

the memory, since my brother, Tod, had testified. If I was with him the entire time, I wouldn't let him kill my dad. Obviously, I wouldn't, right?"

"You're right, and he said you were with him. And if he was with you, why didn't he stop you?"

"But now I remembered, I propose to you, I always had a good mind; and it protected me from seeing my brother say and do things detrimental to the safety of our dad. Who wants to see all that lead to murder? And then my memory returned as if to say it had given me a chance of healing—some any-way."

"OK"

"But did this win over my accusers?"

"No." Buck gave the jury a sideways glance as if all negatives weren't entrenched, and he didn't want to offend the good ones.

"It's my word against theirs, and he has already been deemed innocent, right?"

"Right."

"So what is he scared of?"

"I see your point—nothing."

"Unless his words are gold, and his tongue like silver, he has nothing to go on but hate for me. He could have kept it under wraps and love his brother. I loved him."

"Right."

"Except schizophrenia. If he proves this, I had really forgotten, when I know I didn't; and he had a vendetta against any of my reasons and a personal beef against bad memories."

"Right."

"But if he hadn't dragged me into court, there would be no case against him."

"He can tell what you remembered, more than you can."

"And if this is true, any normal person can disagree with a schizophrenic and win."

"Right."

"But this isn't the gist of the case I have fashioned, right?"

The clowns and jugglers were passing out donuts and coffee. Bill wanted some, no matter what he previously told me. Maybe I was discriminated upon from the first threat I may have been a schizophrenic. It happened.

"No."

"So obviously, I'm taking the chance of losing the court case in my effort to prove Tod killed somebody."

"Right, and you're making me a little nervous," he said.

"Don't worry. I've come to the meat of my questions," I said. "This would be schizophrenic of me if I completely ignored the charges. I'd be giving Tod the advantage of his proof, and the jury would vote against me. They have by law to stick to the case at hand, no matter what the conditions."

"Yes, but you remembered, which was important to that side of the argument."

"I'm thinking in broader terms, but let's do count what you said."

"OK"

"So, are court cases above life, or do they try to persuade, including life?"

"They include life," he said. He straightened his tie.

"And to always include life, we always have life, right?"

"Yes, life is everywhere," The plaintiff's women were helping themselves to some lipstick with those tiny mirrors.

"It is very important, right?"

"Right." Nobody was scratching themselves.

"And if I take life from something, it's stealing, isn't it?"

"Yes."

"So if I plead not guilty, if I won, I could take it to the bank, right?"

"Right."

"But this would be stealing. I would be taking something to add to my mind that I didn't need at all; I already knew I was not guilty. And I would surely be taking from my brother who didn't want to give it to me in the first place, right?"

"Right."

"On the other hand, if I won, by accusing Tod of murder, I would be taking what my brother had plenty of—his guiltiness of killing his wife and our dad. Only killing one and proving it would be justice, right?"

"Right."

"So which one is it that pits me directly against the prosecutor, my brother, since he's a murderer? Is it proving I'm not a schizophrenic, or is it proving he murdered?"

"Proving he murdered."

"Right, and isn't that more a real gut-wrenching court case having one against the other?"

"It happens all the time."

"So there, I'd rather be real than a wimp who doesn't accept life and responsibility," I said, "and I don't want to steal."

"I saw that dead body across Tod's shoulders!" one of the jurors said.

"There, we now have proof," I said. I was glad the real judge wasn't presiding. This outburst put chills down my spine!

"Is that lawful to have a juror belch out like that?" the judge, Bill, asked me. He took a bite out of a donut a clown had given him.

"It sure is," I said, "as much as donuts and coffee." He sipped a little coffee, too. There was a quiet roar throughout the courtroom. Some of them said, "Rock on!" or "Thanks," or "I'm on your side, Ben." Some of the jury licked their lips and eyed the extravagance. The others treated the court with such holiness they wanted to get down on their knees.

But with the tambourines and harmonicas given out, the crowd was banging and blowing. The varnish was striking a beat. The whole place was leaning to the left and to the right. Singing wasn't outlawed when Bill was at the head, and he liked it as he pushed his way into this new attitude. But his friends had sampled it for so long, nobody knew if it would change anything.

After the "party" slowed down, the circus people integrated the convicts and promised them jobs at the circus. Was there an escaping act? Maybe there was one at the magician's booth. How to escape a jail sentence? The magician wouldn't reveal his secrets. But for now, they were all in a line shaking hands with the judge on their way out. Bill was handing out one bottle of wine to each of them, as if nobody was looking. There wasn't even a boat to christen, but they all looked nervous twisting their heads and turning like there should be one somewhere.

"Yes, sir. Yes, sir," they said. "We won't do it again."

But I wanted to take that juror to dinner! At least donuts and coffee on a stakeout. But which house was her lit-up window on Green Street? I wanted to know! If Tod knew of his dead wife and some of the others living in the same neighborhood did, shouldn't they have come, even through a subpoena, to say they knew of the couple arguing? Did he abuse her or express his desire of divorcing? Was he killing off her friends one by one? They had to have reasons they tore his house to bits. The dinner date would tell me all about it. Like who was the last person she was with? The cops hadn't answered this question. With the digging up of the body, James perceived he had set himself up for scrutiny. But why was he scared of Tod in general? Others also knew he buried the body there. Now that they all knew what the argument was about, who would survive?

None of them would escape even a small jail term. The game of Tod's life had turned into a dead ringer of what I was proposing, and let the chips fall as they may. I had a lot to talk about, burning the court case down, not fitting in, but striking the match for all of them to blow up. Innocent by court or not, he had killed his wife and his dad! How did the saying go? This was nothing to sneeze at.

"I'm not going to give up," I said, "until he gets so mad he attacks me physically on the stand in a courtroom where decorum reigns with dignity and cooperation between parties of opposite sides. We'll prove the guilty person here is staining the carpet, even though people like me have to clean it every night when the place is empty."

"No more questions, your honor," said my defense team, the solitary lawyer.

But I had another problem. The judge, whether he was the former apprehensive jerk or friendly Bill, he had one more thing to say.

"Ben Packin, you're in contempt of court! The judge, the author of our Big Move, told me to say that. Oops!" He had to rewind a little, collect himself from that last blurt, and continue. "The court case is over, isn't it? I need, uh, it to, uh, be over now."

"No," I said. "The court is never over until you know the difference, by testimony, between an innocent man and a guilty one. What's your Big Move about?" Spilling his guts about the name of his friend's strategy, he thought he had said enough.

"Either way, the court will convene at ten o'clock tomorrow," and he banged down the gavel. He was looking as red as any man's face painted with lipstick—the kind that leaves an extra bright stain. Obviously, he didn't know how to adjudicate anything with the friends he had; and being among devils, the Caribbean sang his song.

The bailiff led me away, and the band began to play. They'd go for five or six minutes, before they were roughed up and forced to leave. The court case was over for now, but the prosecutor's office was still present. While everybody was filing out, they said, "Don't you want us to say something?"

"What?" asked Bill. "Please proceed. He almost caught his robe on the bench and tripped. But he did bang his knee.

"We have no questions for this witness, your honor." That

was it.

"OK, great," said Bill. "Now we can go home," if appropriate. Bill was handed a napkin from a clown that had red lipstick stain on it and a sultry look from one of Tod's lady soldiers taking her sweet time to leave. He did nothing at first, as he tripped and fell off the bench. And since the stain on his robe was still not dry, it stuck to the varnish on the floor, and he couldn't get up! Then his cell phone rang! He couldn't reach it! The phone rang forever and ever until the orchestra picked it up. They hadn't left. It was "Uncle Albert" by the Beatles, a rainy-day song. With the building not being so high and dry, a small puddle came from the edge and headed with a one-inch tide straight for Bill. This reminded him of the ocean, and there were sharks with teeth down there. Let me tell you, if there was a race set up at the Olympics, Bill would beat the pants off (which was approximately what this chore instilled) the million preliminary events to take first place, because he knew how to do it. He got to his car before anybody saw him and did away with that stupid robe. Once in court was enough! The puddle had stained the phone number to the kiss on the paper, so when she left, the words, "Call me," went nowhere but back to one of the other girls. There were about three of them who had kisses and numbers.

Chapter 27

So it looked like the Big Move against us was the precedent to follow. The mean ones, the judge and Tod, were in some back room of a dirty-smelling dive making up some down-right evil plans for me. They were coming in on a dark cloud and getting closer. Were the criminals doing all the predicting? We would have to be there, too, you know. If it was soon, I'd be languishing in jail, so there had to be something permanent about it to last past my sentence. Respectively, this time I was put on Green Row, which was the long-term branch. I might as well get a hold of my relatives to bring me a television set, a radio, and endless sweets. I may as well get them to supply me with tobacco, so I could get cancer and die. Who called living in jail a life? But I was innocent and thereby had courage to try to get by, knowing things were certain to improve. I had quit smoking, but I had withdrawals, and that wasn't good. You could buy smokes in jail, though they were too rich for my blood.

Somebody came to the prison and walked down the corridor to the elevators, turned left and went through the double doors, came to the purple stripe and kicked their heels around the chapel, found the other elevator, and went up one floor—

making it to the last turn, which told them to swerve right on the fork to land successfully at Green Row. She knew she had made a wrong turn or two and had to backtrack.

That was my wife. She came over to my cell to say goodbye forever and bunted out a laugh, I guessed. She didn't look perfectly serious, so I played along. For it to be funny, her appearance had to be something businesslike. Thus, the wit would be hard to catch. She wasn't going to be the only one who could tell jokes. Maybe she was being satirical. I didn't know. She was so unreal like this. And then I put my hands on the bars, ready for her.

"So this is how it works," I said. "You contract a disease of being in close proximity of schizophrenia, you leave him, and then fly to the Caribbean to pick up your new multi-millionaire husband. Right?" So far that seemed believable, but so odd at the same time. She always hated planes. She'd never take a helicopter, either, or die—come back to life as a bird, fly there, die—and repeat herself to come back. But funerals were cumbersome, and the only bird should have winged it with some more. And how would she recruit birds prepared to die? She also had to fly straight back if the match didn't hold.

"Well—" she tried to say.

"You didn't even wait for my promotion to come through. It was only in two weeks." I said.

"I was never going to throw myself at the feet of a policeman. I made sure you weren't one the day we were engaged. Anyhow, the neighbors were against it," she said.

"Half the neighborhood, and all of a sudden we've moved near those crooks?" I kept it going without a smile.

"They know insanity when they see it," she said.

"They don't know their own souls then, " I said. "You may have lost yours. You're not afraid of me. What you're scared of is another scramble if I lose the job I have now. I don't blame you. It's a free country. Why don't you leave and never have to face fear again? Money does help. I hope you find a real soul mate, somebody you won't have to try to make it to old age with before your happiness shows."

Let her go. There's still room for the breeze of love be-tween us. But this was what we were depending on. It was obvious to me. The whole thing was a monster joke.

"Say, Loro," and I turned the volume to low. "I know about the Big Move. You'll help, won't you?"

"Here's your socks," she said, and gave them to me through the bars. And then she left, making it out after the labyrinth. She never came back.

But she gave me the all-important socks! I needed them. Holding them like gold and silver with my shaking hands and arms, I turned away, trying to decide in which position to nestle them. After a short while I decided on one of the bars in the corner next to the wall. One was tugged a stitch longer on the ledge than the other one. Every morning I would adjust them to my satisfaction. I had no mind unless I spied them draped there, and I didn't know how many peeks time would allow me to enjoy their survival. Each day they would be there for me, though, I felt sure.

"Hey, guys, I'm like you, now—exactly," I said, to my neighbors behind bars. "She left. She was my wife."

"She looked the same way my wife did when she left," one said.

Gomez wasn't around. "What if the only wife we had was the one who just took off? And all of us here on Green Row had shared the same girl until she left us one by one?"

"That would mean," I said, "that she used intelligence for the first ten or fifteen breakups, but made a big mistake with the last one. Surely, you'd think she'd stay with me, or else lose every single one of us. She has no brains."

"But what if she broke up with the first, flew to the Caribbean, and hooked up with a multi-millionaire enough to divorce and take his money?" my neighbor asked. "Then she'd plan to bang all of us. Can you imagine how rich with money her purse would be? But we wouldn't want the money…"

"You know about the Caribbean?" I asked. "Man, that beach must have a hundred dollar bill in each sea shell."

"Yeah, it started with the prosecutor killing his wife, but I don't know who that was. You want to kill your wife or husband? Go to the Caribbean."

"We actually have something in common," I said.

"How do you know we all aren't rich, and she's been with fifteen millionaires? There you go," Co said. "I gotcha!" He eventually told me his name. "Our wives are worthless. Who goes on vacation in the hotbed of the world and says she'll be back directly? Saying the world needs more love, particularly the Caribbean—no, I'll go there, no, I'll go there, back and forth, until she stalks out with your credit card and a ticket paid in advance."

"That's my wife's way of joking," I said. "As soon as we get out of here, we can fly multi-millionaire women over from who knows where to marry us again. We'd laugh in the face of the one who we were going to drop in the long run." I didn't mean that. I wasn't telling the truth. I hid in my own heart, because it was hurting. But I saw through her silly ways. I would wait and translate her English to mine.

"And whose to say they'll quickly find the other half in the Caribbean?" I asked. "Was it possible in a normal length of time they put all their past relationships with us to a reasonable lighter side of conversation that would attract someone? After all, they only knew us. So we'd have to be painted with the positive side of the brush. Like the marriage we had, it'd take a whole lot of inward research. It could even change their minds."

"It didn't change my wife," Co said. "Nothing changed here, either. We've been at Green Row a number of years." Where were the convicts who got clothes from Bill? They must have "graduated" from Green Row, when they blended with the "normal" crowd.

"Everything was all right there at the end," I said. "I even convinced her I wasn't schizophrenic. It was just the deep end of the lake, and I could swim."

"That's the wrong thing to do," said Co. "Then she'd be able to pick out your reasons you were over tinkered up there, like a crow circling an eye ball, and refute them to pass the time. She'd have ammunition to put a halt to anything you said. Has she seen any of your enemies using this method?"

"She saw Smith and the judge," and I had them in my mind facing each other. "They both wrote the book on what was real and what wasn't. Their self-deprecating humor was to see me try to take the cement blocks off underwater—because I knew them, or knew them enough to know they didn't really mean anything. They thought all their opponents should love them back, nothing personal, you see." Then I just broke down and cried. "With all the evil in this world, I took her with me on stakeout that one time." I started sniffing and coughing. I was handed the toilet tissue and blew my nose. There were more tears, but they were quickly wiped away. "She better get a good laugh out of this island, preliminary to our old age, or I'll die before we make it—I mean it! But miracles do hap-pen."

Take Green Row, for example. Gomez was missing, and someone who looked exactly like him shook Bill's hand, thanking him for his freedom, and at the same time he looked directly at me—eye to eye. If that was Gomez, he had a story to tell.

The guard, Telly, was doing his rounds, and we were next. I was apprehensive about some authority given the job of looking into my private habitat. But I was just an animal, not being able to live independently from the boss. Being in jail now, there was a state full of bosses—no chance to save up some money to strike out on my own. Free, I'd make it about two hundred miles before I blew my wallet on who knows what. Sounds like a poem? Or an anthem? Maybe somebody would try and do this. As long as he was received by an audience to take up a collection at the trip's end, he'd see his way to do it again! How far or not so far—that was most of the question. End on end, then do it again. Somebody talented could go a thousand miles.

I was able to improvise by daydreaming (I'll just "be" somewhere else) to make that crucial difference I needed to stay ahead in my world. I had greatly exaggerated my importance that meant well but didn't fit in a confined place for any length of time. Talent was not using your star power. Talent was getting your fingers wet, your hand wet, and then your body wet. Being unimportant made a contrast if you could crawl into thin air.

I was sort of forced to socialize. There was the eternal yelling you had to deal with eventually. When Telly came around the inmates went a little less crazy. In fact, they settled down; he always administered a discussion.

"Hi, Telly!"

"Boy, you've been missed!"

"Hunker down, honey!"

"Telly! Give me five!"

"Telly! The number one rouge!"

"Telly! Shake my hand!"

"Telly! How's the family?"

Telly this, Telly that. Who was this character?

"Telly, did you say hi to your better half for me?"

"I don't care for none of you guys. You know that," he said, and everybody laughed. He had a big head, strong shoulders, and gigantic hands that if wrapped around your neck, you'd have no chance of living. He had a worried look on his face, due to old age, but his personality was happy and chip-per. He had a nerdy way about him from high school and many jobs to prove it, like setting up farms to the computer. But he quit all that to take the job near the first rung of the ladder. He didn't want to think and think and think anymore. The only cerebral effort he had to concentrate on here was not to let these males behind bars take advantage. He even lost arguments, but they never hurt him, as long as the bars didn't come loose.

"Hey, man!" Telly spread his interest. "Hey, guy," to an-other one. "Hey, Co. Wife still gone?"

"What did I tell you last time?" asked Co, "and two years before that?"

Telly laughed. "She'll come back." Then he retraced his steps to the middle of our group, saying, "They'll come back. They miss you. And if they see me, they'll never leave again." He laughed even more. I didn't want any part of Loro after his speech making. Not just any serious thing was funny, but she seemed to think so.

"You know, Telly, hell will drop a degree when you fall into it," said one of the inmates.

"I'm cold, huh? Not as cold as that bar over there, and over there, and over there. Let's try to tell which bar of all of them is the strongest." He was pointing at different bars, reminding them. "You know if I had the keys, I'd let you go. You're my buddies and friends."

"Yeah, right!"

"Prove it!"

"Who is this over here?" asked Telly, looking at me.

"I'm Ben," sitting on my bed and getting ready to lie down.

"Well, I'm Telly."

"I heard," and I was out like a light.

"Will your wife be coming back?" He had a hope? For the others he did. But I thought he was just being agreeable.

I barely heard him, but after a while his voice would spark my neurons to interpret the words. I was almost sick and needed help to concentrate. I was laying down hoping the last time I saw somebody throw up was between Smith's and Bill's yard. I was so tired. Something clicked in my mind when I was on the stand that said everything was too hard to continue; I should give up, knowing I had done my best. The court had it handled anyway with the press coming around, and I'd be free soon. I let my arms dangle, got the small fan in the corner to aim at me (probably left there from something procedural) and tried to pass the exhaustion in every pore from my skin to the floor. I closed my eyes and dreamed.

"You are guilty!" said the judge.

"No, I'm not!" I defended.

The prosecution put a gun to my head. "Say you're wrong!" There were no clues to find under each action I took or wanted to—nothing that hinted a motive I'd turn around to shove into the face of the accuser. I looked for the truth, but I couldn't find it.

"I'm dead enough already. I didn't do it! I didn't!"

The room began to swoon and spin and turn upside down.

"You're getting sleepy...we know you're tired...give us just a smidgen of respect...we have your good-old dad right here with us...dream of his goodness and simplicity."

"Dad?" He was right there with me, wasn't he?

"Now, get him to pick a successful upstanding man in the community. Or the guy who couldn't keep his job."

"Dad, can you pick?" I asked.

"Yes."

I rolled over and felt the energy return. I was so dead to the world around me, I was finally getting the rest I deserved. Being on the stand with no sleep cut me in half. I was surprised I had done what I did. And there was more, no doubt.

"Who do you pick, Dad?"

"I pick you!" And he took out a gun and blew my head to pieces.

"Ahhhhh!" I woke and sat up, but not as tired as I was before. With beads of sweat all over me, Telly watched as I slept. It wasn't long, but then I remembered. "What were you asking?"

"Will your wife be coming back?"

"No, she died in wife-land. Now she's going for the money," I said. I kept the lie going—nothing personal. She was really probably buying up a handful of postcards to send me anytime now. "Got my mail?"

"That's exactly what the others say they want," Telly said. "Why are you all so similar?"

"There is no reason," I said.

"He's right—no reason at all," said another.

"I had a reason, but she used it," said one.

"They hide their intuition. Their reasons are much smaller—we have no chance."

"My wife sued the judge for wanting a reason for the divorce," said someone near Co.

"All in all," said Telly, "they don't argue so convincingly, because they don't have reasons. We may as well admit it, guys, and face it for the rest of our lives—reasons were in-vented by man. I don't know how to get out of it, but that's how she stands. And if our love uses the smallest of them for a point in argument, they're just mocking us. They knew it before we did. Chalk it up to experience, and keep going round and round. It'll improve your balance."

"Which side are you on? They'll come back, or we'll find somebody new. Which is it?" asked one inmate.

"And why should I go round and round?" asked the client on the end. "Why did I get married in the first place? To lose her, and then to be shot out a cannon into the air? I'm not fireworks set on exploding all on one night. I think higher of myself than that. I was not wrong marrying!"

"And I'm not wrong thinking my wife will come back. She was my wife, man!" Thank goodness he spoke up, or I'd have to. I did not think this was the time to reveal my true place in life. We should learn to trust ourselves first. Telly was smacking around like he'd played hockey too long.

"Whoa! What is that?" He was interested in my cell.

"What?" I asked.

"Those two socks over there. They'll have to come to me," he said.

"You can't have them!" I said. "They don't bother any-body."

"They bother me. Take my word for it," and he opened my cell door and stepped over to them.

But I saw my chance, slipped out, and closed the door firmly. It had an automatic lock, and if you had keys from inside the cell, you'd almost break your wrist angling them in the lock from the inside. Besides, he said he had no keys.

I was a diesel locomotive going down the hill, turning away from the green stripe, heading for the first elevators, going down three floors, passing the chapel, walking on the back of an elephant since the rope bridge was broken, turning right, walking through the double doors, and making my way past the receptionist, a giant African guerrilla. Right left, right left, right left. It was easy as pie. Nobody suspected anything. I was free! I would make it to the stakeout to watch out for the Big Move. Nothing lower was higher. I was back to the bottom—of the free world, of course. If there was some edgy off-the-wall imagination dropped by accident on my way down, I apologize for feeling somewhat freaky staring ten years of jail down in my future.

The personality of prison was that it had a face—one low enough, but not so low not to be able to reach cranks and buttons—and high enough for its will to be felt in other parts of far-away society. To wrap it up it could sink a boat instead of christen one. Picture men who left the system more angry than when they went in. It would be framed in the Louvre in Paris, France.

Catching up with Loro was an option, but anybody had more socks. As long as I felt comfortable, I shouldn't bother her. I just didn't learn the terrain between here and the Carib-bean when the subject came up in school. What was I saying? It wasn't important anyway.

Chapter 28

Nine forty five plus fifteen minutes was when I made it to the stakeout right on time. It was safe being with policemen. I had been to my place to take along donuts and coffee and found out nobody was there. She told me so, and why didn't I believe her? Great. But I did have a place to crash or live or something—the place to myself. I wasn't homeless. But it'd be much too easy for me to become that. My wife would have to refuse to go to the Caribbean—what kind of miracle took her back? I would create one that God would be proud of. And the botched trip would have to be my fault. Now why miss out on the multi-millionaires? Did anybody know of one? She didn't. What were they like? And they were making such a hard trip to get there—both sides, the men and the women.

"You wouldn't believe what I was up to an hour ago," I said to Mon and Con.

"Where? Jail? You smell like prison," Mon said.

"You're right," I said.

"You know, going to jail and going out again so many times makes a body schizophrenic," Con said.

"Tell it to the judge," I said. "He makes his own schizophrenics like they come out of a kit. My number is 03961102. Got any glue?"

"We have," said Mon. "Sally, the meter maid, gave Bill a piece of her mind when he came out of court waving and flapping his arms toward her, scared he'd get a ticket. He was parked in a handicapped space. Maybe living with only one arm in the past was good enough in his picture stuck on the windshield; but he had that arm reattached. And if he was still disabled, he should have the proper sticker."

"You want me to ticket his car and really get him riled up?" I asked.

"No, that would be like having a dry run on arresting him. We can't do that, either," said Mon. "Get out there and turn that trance on. Maybe they'll come to us. They downright hate your peskiness so far. Honest men should make up the difference. And we're honest, aren't we, Ben?" Mon and Con fist bumped. The Big Move was beginning to hover. That's what to watch out for, but both sides didn't really know what it was exactly, since the last catastrophe.

"It'd take ten to fifteen schizophrenic criminals to take us down, but they're behind schedule. They switch clothes with us and fool you as you come driving by. Bill is a big talker on the phone. But he prepared. This sounds like a diversion tactic. It's too stupid to be real. Look out for something to smash us." And then they got real nervous, cranked the car on and revved it with all the gas! Mon and Con looked around for an attack. They twisted, they peered, they went crazy with defending themselves. And then they turned the car off again, until the problem went away. It might not have been there to begin with, but they wanted to be sure.

So I popped a donut in my mouth and stepped outside the car. I didn't know my trances turned themselves on and off at the drop of a hat, and none happened to me. What I heard made up for it. Tod's parrot had been loose for a while and was lodged up a tree next to the car.

"Let's go to the river," the bird said, "and dump the body in the boat for now. Then after the judge and Smith make it over here, we'll shove off to the sea. They say Ben will be dead after they tie up Mon and Con. They won't see them coming." That last part was the diversion. They were pretty sneaky. And it said more! "Who cares who to blame after Ben's death? We'll be out to sea on the way to the Caribbean. Bill's boat is seaworthy, and he knows how to sail that puff-the-magic thing. If we can make it to the islands, we can make it anywhere." The wheels of the Big Move were in motion—right where our courage was.

Man, that bird was smart! And it sounded just like Tod. But what I couldn't figure out was if Tod was doing the talking, who was he talking to?

It wouldn't be James. He wouldn't go so far down South with any of them. He was probably back in the mental hospital. So why care who the extra hand was? I'd go and see. And then I put on the brakes. The bird was still talking!

"As sure as I'm gabbing with you, Loro, we're going to make it—a new life for the both of us. How much are you sitting on—one hundred and fifty thousand? Ben didn't know what he'd miss, seeing how he never took you out. And now you crave coffee and donuts? I'll get Smith and the judge to give you some after they raid his stash," said the bird, some more.

That was enough for one parrot. I'd have to walk it off to see if any of it was applicable. For this to be recorded by the bird, Loro had talked to Tod a very long time ago, like the day I lost my job. But who could blame her? She's stuck in an offensive crowd and would have to dig herself out of it—no pun intended. It seemed the unbelievable events proved I was out of my head, so I imagined sniffing out Tod's dead wife, a new adventure having nothing to do with Loro-and right on the money for our investigation. I strolled up the hill between the two sides. Why not hope for a psychiatric neurosis to make me feel better? My

The Court Blamed Me

senses were hungering for a reason to like this trash. But that bird was real! Now there was another side to Green Street. The window shade lights were turning on again, the stars were shining, and it was a picture-post-card night—nothing was wrong if you looked on the surface. I knew the lights on the right side of the street were sensing me, but were the criminals on the left side able to do it? With each step my gun got heavier and heavier. Then the cave-in trapped me for the coming tornado and hurricane, blowing one right after the other—my heart in motion. I was a novice at this. The words, Big Move, sounded like a Hollywood title, and who was the star?

"Hold it right there, Ben!" The judge and Smith had me at gunpoint. "That, uh, is the Big Move! I got him. He slipped out of my jail," said the judge.

"He ran amuck in my mental hospital," said Smith.

"His wife agreed to go to the Caribbean. He's, uh, not worth it," said the judge.

"But after him is Mon and Con," said Smith, shaking in his boots.

It was evident the judge had found what looked like Smith's chance of getting out, while the judge was looking for him. Completely moving to the next state over would have done it, but the judge thought of it first, and came down on him with a business proposal. The judge would get a hold of a million fine-tooth combs and Smith would give them all out to the police department. And Smith's head was dry enough to suck up rainwater. It put the cops all off track. But as soon as the judge was giving out combs for only bald people, the cops knew there was something off kilter. Then the lights went on and off in the row of houses to the right, and they were so staccato-like, it looked like the houses were blinking. It was some kind of weird signal. What happened was twenty or thirty convicts from the last few court cases had holed up in Smith's house, not saying Smith also condoned murder, but one house that had plenty of space. He had run to and fro gathering up the cons. It was certainly uncomfortable with the judge there, and his case against me, Ben, was not very well known.

The cons using the house that Smith built were runaway prisoners inside the underground railroad where Smith concentrated his rag of a mind. And believe it or not, Smith had them all stacked in his house like in a bubble gum machine, without the judge knowing. Smith was never going to bow in the presence of murder. In fact he was against the heavy hand of the law. It was only a one-night stay, so give up a few jokes they could share if the judge wasn't around. One got out.

Paying attention to the jury's sense of timing, the cons learned that it was only their own fistful of adventure and not the truth that the same jurors presided in all the court cases. The blinding glory of law and order against them happened all the time. They were wrong, but the joking of it would last well into the night. Joking was so much better free. This was yesterday. Tonight there was the blinking. One way or the other, this was the cue for them to go, and it was already rehearsed. So the ten to twenty hard-core convicts burst through the doorway filled by Smith and the judge, trampling them, but mostly the judge—he wasn't practiced except for the surprise of it all. It was like a ten dollar gold piece had fit into the slot, and all the bubble gum rolled out. The judge was one of those colorful round treats, so he had no idea. Of course, this cleared both of them from using their gun on me.

With no reason the convicts piled on. They had a hard time moving the judge out of the way: he kept getting back up. Stirring was next. Shots rang out as they fell, but the bullets cracked way above my head. The judge got back up but fell again from the last of the burdened convicts making it through. The Big Move was ultimately a nighttime bowel movement pushing out into the street! Do you get that from bubble gum? Initially, there were only a few wayward men, but Smith's hard work reached

The Court Blamed Me

far and wide coming up with a more sizeable number. Each time the gavel bit into the bench of the judge's fine decision, Smith imagined more coming his way. They could scrape by doing something only big muscular guys could do. Each ex-prisoner weighed as much as a pro-tackle football lineman, something quite different from the answer to the question, "Let me get up!" His gun had scared them enough.

This is when I saw Loro sandwiched between the fallen two. She had sunglasses over her round spherical colorful body, like I wasn't to know. It was so striking to want to pop her in and chew. The sunglasses didn't work. It was Loro. During their Big Move and "shoot-out," I did wave and smile at her. She didn't respond, thinking of course, of new renting possibilities. She needed to guard that thought.

The jailbirds had to go and fill up the cars to the next stop. They were victims of the judge's harsh sentencing. They both were not enlightened, but Smith and the judge were arch enemies! The lights to my right went off, and two cops came out of the darkness to handcuff the both of them. By then they had to break up a fist fight! Mon and Con came to the rescue, but the policemen all agreed for them to continue the stakeout. Mon and Con went back to their car, and I continued. It was over that quickly.

"How am I doing?" I asked them, kind of chuckling about the two old men waging war until they got handcuffed. All the prisoners escaped—a wrong for the judge, and a right for Smith.

"You're doing great!" they said, and gave me the thumbs-up signal. A couple more doors slammed, and Mon and Con were devouring donuts and coffee. Watching them made me want some.

But I trudged onward. That was the Big Move, an opportunity for accreditation for our police department. Defense was a bigger move. I was almost up the hill, when Bill drove by and opened the passenger door for a body to roll out! This was at my feet! I danced to get out of the way. It was James! He had been beaten pretty badly and bruised, so he was unconscious by the time I knelt at his side. I attended to him while the sirens took over. There were two sets—one on our car and another on a new car parked in a corner past Green Street on my right, where the lights had blinked. The two cars joined in conversation, and it was decided the new car, saving face from not being with us before, took to itself a thin presence to chase down Bill. The razor blade hit a few bumps and missed a close shave of some precious moments; Bill was already toweling off ready to captain the boat all the way down at the river.

Would the cops find him there? Bill didn't know he was lonely at the top of his "gang" even after contributing.

The square-looking ambulance came for James. What had he done now—threaten one or two of them? Maybe he was part of the "vote" to have honesty in the lead. Yeah, we all knew there were a few spots vacant in the local church choir. They say they had the "light." All the lights came back on and shooed the darkness away. We didn't need street lamps to know we were machines of knowledge. Just plug your boss up to an outlet. He'll rattle and roll! And you'll be done with that job in no time. To be impressionable is the better view of ourselves, if we have it. Plug everybody up, and watch the seismic graph send someone directly to your house.

It looked like there were not many passengers to board the boat. Maybe the only one was Tod. Wouldn't it be great if his bird remembered a clue and flew over to where I was—and sang again? I needed all the help I could get. I think it flew down to the boat, right when I was at Done's house. All the lights went out down the street. Oh, no. I knew that was a foreboding "remark" of some kind, if communication had not been screwed.

One window couldn't yell at the other to say when to come in or to go out. They were in separate houses. They probably were having so much fun, they didn't want to go outside and talk

The Court Blamed Me

to me. I thought about going inside.

Now, I had pretended to smell that corpse on my way up my beat all the way to the river, but were my olfactory glands imagining it, or was this real? I was actually too quick, but I was sure I smelled something dead. Maybe it was road-kill or something, but no, it was like a rock in a pond with ripples. The stench was getting stronger, the water nearing sludge; releasing the smell, I got further from Done's house to the fresh air. Maybe the breeze was from off the hand or the shoulder of Loro. I sure was missing her. One time, she said that in a hundred years all caskets inside would smell like the day they were buried. She sure knew how to relate. She could make anything smell good. Back to stinking—it wasn't from Tod's new house. I could tell. And it wasn't at the boat down by the river. The buzzards on the night shift weren't circling down there. They were flying like little feathered wind-ups ready to dive to earth and spring back up with their gourmet meal at Done's castle.

Before I slipped completely out of reality, I got a phone call from Con about how I didn't clue them in about the motives these five suspects on Green Street had—why they were so mischievous. It took me by surprise. I hadn't told them about the Caribbean?

"There are women down there, and the suspected neighborhood wants a piece of the action," said Con. "They're more than prostitutes. If you were talking, you'd say these were cultured women, who tried love and lost. Now, it's a money game, isn't it? Why didn't you say anything? This is a whole side of life. It should have its own anniversary and birthday cake."

"I don't know why I overlooked the possibility you were interested in their women."

"I know why. It's because you're sick. These guys live for women. They attracted all the men, and Bill has a boat to get them there. It's a motive they all lived with as neighbors—the questionable business they each wanted immunity for. And the worse part is they jailed all the husbands to pry the wives out to get it all started. We found out by tapping their phones," said Con, again.

"Sounds like the law is being broken," I said.

"You're broken!" said Con. "This isn't something insignificant. We could have interrogated Done to a pile of urine, if we knew his ties to the Caribbean. We get along with the police just fine down there. Half the force needs a little more sunshine, and we have bottles that would cork a note in them by an assault of men who know how to stuff their own message in an international industrial line. Just think of those warm breezes—OK?"

"It's easy to figure them out, and you know I had to worry about it, since my wife is on her way down there. She left me in jail," I said.

"No, I didn't know that. You must hate us—"

"I just keep myself from trusting you too much," I said.

"But why twenty or so schizophrenics are in jail for years for being inappropriate or a little crazy is inexcusable!"

"Con, I'm sorry," I said.

"You have one plea that makes sense. You're not guilty for the reason of insanity, a law in Congress. You aren't—see, the reason Tod killed his wife was because he had another one waiting for him down there on that hot island. We all would have had no trouble seeing the weakness of why James didn't help more. It's pure business to clue us in, get it? We may have lost a life, but we don't know, yet." I struggled with my emotions.

"Why don't you put that gun down? You're not getting another stakeout with us anymore," said Con. "We're against you. You won't become a policeman with us. So that's why you were such a hot shot. You thought you knew everything. You don't know anything. You're a schizophrenic! We hope you lose your court case! Your mistake, if you didn't do it on purpose, is not acceptable. So get back over here to the car." Then he hung up.

The Court Blamed Me

But then it hit me. A trance was inevitable, because I didn't believe what my eyes told me. Out of a corner of my eye-I didn't want to look straight ahead—was a Ferris wheel full of clowns dispensing themselves one at a time to the ground below. It was like a tape with the round holder of the roll and the straight part sticking out, where the clowns clumped and then thinned out to fall in line. They were running right for the boat and then congregated or stuck to it. Bill wasn't there to tell me they were real, so I didn't know.

The clowns saw me and waved and yelled, turning in circles and old clown stuff. But I was at a precipice. It was either accost Done or broaden my range in seizing the boat single-handedly. I wasn't sure I had the strength of mind and body to do either, since Con and Mon were against me. So what I did was to ask the cumulative crowd of clowns at a distance to go this way, or to ask the clowns to go Done's way. I used hand signals like on a game show with the audience responding. I wasn't going to lose my method of happiness from what Con said. Believe me, it was a trust issue at least in my defense. At first I held up my arms toward the boat. Most of the clowns were waving me off. Then I held up my arms pointing at Done's house, and they led me to the affirmative. First at the boat-no way; then at Done's—yes, way. So that was my decision. If Done wanted to know why I picked him, I'd have to fight back with "Why are you not dead?" And the scuffle would be whose explanation was first, the most important? It had to be his, of course. There was a hidden but substantial meaning that begged the simple question: why help out a murderer? And I'd give it to him, because that was what he was doing. Whatever—I'd dispense of him soon enough to return to Mon and Con.

I went up to the house in question, but when I turned the way to my left, I gave one more look to the river on my right, and the boat where my wife boarded. Yes, believe it or not, there she was about to make a mess of her life, too. She'd tell me all about it when she came back, though. I wasn't going down there. The clowns probably knew she was part of the formula that kept me from getting in serious trouble. You don't want to be too sensitive—or too insensitive. I was going back. No, I would be against the majority. No, she gave me the socks. No, she was always into money.

No, no, no!

"What do you want?" Done said, as he opened his door. I was standing on his doorstep like I had been there for ages. It was me now I didn't have Mon or Con backing me up. We had the same thing in mind, but he didn't want to admit it. It smelled worse when he opened his door.

"Do you smell that?" I asked, innocently at first.

"What smell?"

"The one coming out of your house," I said.

"I don't smell anything, you donut-and-coffee syringe," he said.

"Well, I just thought—"

"You thought?" he asked. "Wait until I thought, and I thought long and hard about this!" He slammed the door shut, and I cussed myself out I wasn't a policeman, yet; maybe never be. I couldn't arrest him. But I could hear him through the door cussing to himself about how the Big Move should've got rid of me. I didn't dare crack a smile.

Well, that was the end of that trip. I should ask for permission if I wanted to go to the dock all-alone, but I knew what they'd say. I looked one more time down there and saw what the bird was saying. Tod was gazing at his future in my wife's eyes. She was helping with the ropes, but she was only pre-tending. If they rushed off, she'd stay on the dock. Leave it to me. I would bring her a donut. Bill, the captain, was talking to the cop and wouldn't be included in their dirty accusations. Once they were floating down the river, the cops had no re-course but to give up—from this end. I didn't know if police-men had their own boat or not. And would they have enough firepower to include the clowns? There were about twenty or thirty now on board. So that was the end of the Big Move.

We had burned the neighborhood down with our suspicions and the slippery actions of the criminals, but we hadn't brought Tod in. I faced the truth. Would he get another court case to prosecute? Maybe not, and I would win. But he would be free, too. Something had to improve, and I was working my tail off. Then I smelled that dead body again. Was it true? I looked over my shoulder. Sure enough, there was Done behind me heaving that heavy body on his back going the same way I was. I kind of speeded up. Then he did. He was chasing me! I hit the gas. I didn't want that dead body all over me. Safety was two houses down. And I wouldn't eat anymore donuts. I wasn't hungry for anything, for I don't know how long. I turned toward him and fired my gun! I was a crack shot, but I hit the dead body, and wow.

The head came off. I was at full speed when I finally ran to the stakeout car. I jumped inside and locked my door.

"He's probably going to place the body in its former hole," Mon said. They had been watching. I was panting.

"More coffee?" they asked.

"Sorry," I said. "Don't make me eat."

"They radioed us and said they took Bill in for aggravated assault and had later options of calling it attempted murder. That shouldn't have happened. You're lucky you got away with only a hospitalization during our stakeout."

"Yeah, James was a great help," I panted. "Bill deserves it. Ask me to testify if you need a schizophrenic." I waited a moment for them to reply, but no word was said. I was trying to lighten up the mood. It looks like they were sure about the diagnosis, whether I was or not.

"Aren't you going to bust Done?"

"We've got time. Don't you want to disagree and watch the boat on the river?" Mon asked. "Listen, you're sick. You need help. It's not that we don't like you. We do."

"I guess." They fist-bumped and made a high-five like they were back being all jokes, and they were. But there went the big argument I'd prepared. The only way to kick a schizophrenic when he's down is not to believe a word he said—that's just your imagination, or you need more medication.

We saw Loro and Tod, barely, but there they were. The boat was charted for the Caribbean. It was floating down the river to the sea. Tod and Loro. Most normal people would give up on her, but I loved Loro. Worse case scenario—she had to come back by the old-age time of life, or it wasn't part of her good nature to look so good and be so bad. I told her she could be a model. This is what we worked for. Nothing else mattered, and I was used to it, but in smaller doses. The further she left me, the funnier it would get, to look back on. Old age would be terrific. Our love was that strong. She was just getting me for calling her ugly.

And whatever Done did with the body, it buried the Big Move, as if there was anything left of it.

"Clowns! That's your new word, Con," said Mon. Did they see clowns? I wasn't going to ask.

"Great! So I lost count," said Con. "Ben, we're going to miss you."

Chapter 29

I'd make it to court on time, thank you, though I didn't have any idea what was to come. I had enough time in my apartment to wash the grit off myself and get to bed for a few hours, but I was rudely awakened by every shadow and silhouette. Maybe it was the paperboy this time. I had to admit my subscription was overdue, because I didn't have the money. Court stars like me didn't receive a discount, even if I were in front of the public; and as rumor had it for the next assemblage a news camera would be on. The grogginess in me had to be gone if I were to keep my edge.

My trances were bad enough. Thinking back on it, I probably imagined those clowns right inside my own brain. Then again, they had led me in the right direction. However, this one was a lighter trance than the ones proceeding. Heightened senses were becoming a normal part of me. The fear from working like a cop had spun my attentiveness into a top that began spinning. I had it naturally the whole time and just needed an adrenaline kick. Whatever, if I did have a form of schizophrenia, I was working it out.

I opened the door. "What?"

"Your mama!" It was Jon again and his helper with a future. "Don't worry. We're not taking you to the mental hospital. Tod's orders are to take you straight to court, so you won't escape. You'll be wearing this." He held up a straight jacket. The real reason for wearing one was probably because Tod didn't want to be pointed at in the heat of the battle. But why was he prosecuting anybody? Didn't he go down the river? Oh, well, maybe the Coast Guard picked him up. They caught small-time rogues on the river before. I lost word on Loro. She could be the accomplice, but I didn't believe she did anything wrong. Laughter was hard to come by when I first told jokes. Now, their punch line made them even worse. So I caught on. Tod being with Loro was the end to a joke? What was funny about that? She was on the back pew watching every last one of us. I did the cool thing and didn't wave. Then the humor opened up. She would laugh at Tod's jokes and make him less strange. That would be really funny, since he sounded like his parrot these days.

So I took my seat on the witness stand—why was I always the only one? Then the judge came in, the regular one. And everyone stood up and sat down. Tod, out on bail, took his rich presence and stuffed it in his chair, where all the prosecutors reclined. And my defense attorney was in the same row across the aisle. We were there early again, but I don't think this mattered. After all, the judge had a couple days on vacation, but he was finally there with a sea horse on his lapel.

"Did you respect the court, uh, by standing, uh, on the royal way we deserve?" the judge asked me. He was also out on bail. Tod and he were a couple diehards, let me tell you, both out for bloody murder now that Big Move blew up in their faces. But to tell you the truth, I had forgotten whether I stood or not, that jacket being the price of concentrating on some-thing.

"No, it's kind of slippery here in the box seat," I said, as a few of my marbles accidentally fell out of my pocket onto the floor. They were for my brother if he got too close to my face. "But for

The Court Blamed Me

you, I'll do anything." Here comes the contempt of court I always got. I cringed, waiting...

"Stand up and sit down!" he yelled. It was like great comedians of the past when they said, "Wake up and go to sleep!" But I did it. I stood up and sat down. There, was he satisfied? "Prosecutor, call, uh, your first witness," the judge said.

"I object!" said my defense.

"Overruled!" said the judge. "But, uh, you better watch yourself."

"I'd like to call Ben Packin," Tod said. "I mean I want to. You know, I'm calling Ben Packin to the stand." And then our eyes met. But his blew up balloons, and mine knifed them until the blood vessels popped and the bleeding never quit.

"I'm already on the stand. Can you take this straight jacket off of me?" He didn't.

"OK, then," said Tod. "I only have a few questions. Is it true you had a breakdown with your job at Hamerston and Owen? He had left his seat, staying a good distance from me, but he did cover his area like an experienced lion on the hunt. He was just getting started.

"I prefer to call it because and only because of my position at Hamerston and Owen. It was too much for me," I said. The people in the gallery of the courtroom were riveted, the bailiff was in and out of smiles the entire time, and the jurors were very interested by the looks on their faces. If we had sky lights on the ceiling, there'd be a number of kids forming a crowd and frothing from the mouth to claim the best view face down.

"Do you know what schizophrenia is, Mister Packin? I'll tell you what it is. It's being so mindless and inappropriate that one germ, now I mean it, one germ from one schizophrenic to a healthy person by way of a train of molecules in the air would make them go berserk! I say to you and to the rest of the court, you, Mister Packin, are one. You're a schizophreniack!" And he about fell over, he pointed so hard. I was humored he stepped on one of my marbles by his body language, but he didn't. I thought, not based on reality, that he must have grazed one.

The crowd was in an uproar. Some were blaming, and some were complaining. The gavel went up and down, like the judge wanted quiet, but he really didn't. My defense man got up and said, "I object. I object to the crowd, don't you, judge? Call it quiet."

"Ben's a schizophrenic? Has that been determined?" the judge asked. "No."

The defense said, "No."

"I said no," the judge said.

"But he has a straight jacket on," said Tod.

"Ben," the judge bent down and said. "You'll save us a lot of time and, uh, trouble if you, uh, agree with your brother and ride that one little train. He's, uh, not the best, but if you were at your best, uh, it'd never reach the bottom of his shoe. You're no diehard or martyr. Come clean, uh, I'll give you a television set for Green Row. Everybody wants one." He was talking to me like a child, but it's like Con talking down to me. He still liked me. Just make room for the sickness.

"I heard that, and I agree, judge, your honor, sir," said Tod. "No more questions at this time."

Then the defense stood up and tugged at the seam of his vest with both hands, spun on his heels to get an eyeful of the courtroom layout, and pointed his finger in the air. My man was as cool as they come. He did everything but put James Brown on the stereo. They were all kids at heart. They were never broken.

"There were no more questions coming from the prosecutor," my defense man said. Then he sat down knowing what would happen next. At first everybody was quiet and pliable to the rules and demeanor of the case, watching with polite fervor, but this didn't last.

"He didn't ask me anymore questions either," said one fry, in the gallery package to go, "And I saw everything!" The court

The Court Blamed Me

didn't know what to do. Whoever said those words wasn't on the witness stand. Concerning myself, the spirit was there.

"He asked me one question, and then he kicked me in the pants. I'm sorry for poverty. Blame it on me," said another, moved by the heart of where this was going. They all shared the same heart.

"I asked him one question," said a guy, who thought enough of the proceedings to stand up. "I asked him why he killed that one man."

"You saw him do it?" asked the judge. We snagged him! That's all he had to say.

"Yes." After he got that answer the judge folded like a dying spider, sorry he asked anything. You see, the press had their claws in this travesty and appealed by television for all witnesses of my dad's murder to come forward. They were sitting here and there in the courtroom. They had come in droves. Their fight to get a seat was too much of a contrast from the omnipotence of a hardened criminal. The lawbreaker couldn't be inspected under the light that reached the whole room, or he'd be found out. So after a little shouting, all the witnesses took a seat and got comfortable.

"I went to the prosecutor's court case, and there weren't any witnesses, and I repeat, no witnesses. None. Zilch," said another warm fry. They were all warmed-up food to me as I piled it on my plate. I was getting to the point of taking a bite out of these wonderful people. At least they were food for thought. Many people aren't broken. When I "went," schizophrenia must have filled the space left by the break. So I was not dying of this disease, even if it was trying to take over.

"I have another question for the defendant," said Tod.

"Yes?" asked the judge. The defense had already sat down, meaning he hadn't stood back up again. But they had on the stand someone who needed a support group, when all of his acquaintances had moved on. If only I had kids—three little ones who knew everything. Between an empty home and no comfort money to spend getting away from it all, the layers of defense were slowly peeling off one by one. And if there were a child within me, I was breaking its bones with my own hand, not knowing when to quit.

"Do you deny," and Tod moved a little closer to me, stepped on one marble and slid awkwardly to the floor! But he quickly got up and kicked the marble as hard as he could. "I'm all right."

"It's got brains, doesn't it?" I asked, raising my eyebrows a few times.

"It was just a marble, sir," Tod said. "It hurt me more than it hurt itself. But let me continue. Do you deny? (The longer the questions were asked, the more the judge felt his nerves take over, like Bill's had.)

"Did the cleaning crew remove that robe stuck to the floor?" I asked to weigh down the little nerve Tod was bran-dishing.

"Do you deny your wife left you, because you were a schizophreniack? And there's no one else in the stand, and we're good enough brothers to tell the honest undeniable truth to God himself and us down here, doing the best we can." And he spun around and pointed at me. I tried but failed to loosen myself. The jacket could've been sewn by Loro, the way things were going. I rocked back and forth, trying to get loose, but my magic skills were down to "Thumbs up" if I remembered the thumb.

"She left because I wasn't good enough for her," I said. Nobody was getting the real story. "It was a marriage that didn't work from the beginning. We decided to skip all tender moments until we got old and gray." Then I hung my head and couldn't say anything else.

"C'mon guy."

"Buck up, man. He killed people."

"We both didn't want to share any love. We had found each other, not to want anything, but to grow old with some-one. This is what we hoped for, and it wasn't good enough for any one of

The Court Blamed Me

us."

Wow! Was I going to divorce her? That's what it sounded like. It was so sad. What I said about us was so close to the truth, I actually enjoyed confessing. But the harsh reality of spitting it all out and taking it in was as bad as canned toilet water. Just like what happened at Green Row, what I didn't say about our relationship made what I did say sound like a big lie. I didn't want the court to know about our personal lives together. I was fighting in my soul the littlest step—believing she was still mine. And if we did get back together, there'd be no great outpouring of love, anyway. Life is predictable, as long as you trust the right people.

"You were in and out of schizophrenia, she said," said Tod.

"Hearsay!" said the defense.

"I'll allow it," said the judge. "Clear it up soon, Tod. You're skating on thin ice." Then he halfway smiled at me. Yeah, judge. That's how you do it. I smiled back.

"She could say anything she wanted to," I said. "That was a proponent of our marriage. The love was an old-man's love or a woman's. Nothing would count until we got sixty or seventy. What we talked about was how old was old."

"Do you remember putting objects around the room, each at a specific distance or place or order?" Tod asked.

"Do you remember blinding our sweet-old dad's eyes with that fake optometrist? So he'd have to have help crossing the street?" I countered.

"That wasn't in his murder case! And it should have been. Now we're turning with honesty," said a beautiful golden fry in the courtroom pan. They were all Southern browned fries, and I had gotten bored of my own cooking. So stack them up, gentlemen. Keep them coming so they're hot. We were winning as long as this kept up. I looked to see if Loro was checking us out, but she wasn't.

"There were a lot of things missing in Tod's case," said

another. People were getting really uneasy of how Tod had been defended a few months ago in the murder case. Was he a murderer, and the court a sham? The judge was turning a feint shade of red, but he always did that.

The press got a hold of the floor. "Ladies and gentlemen, we're historically seeing the pants of the judge of this travesty of justice turn inside out. A past case of the prosecutor had exonerated him, when it appears he was guilty as sin. Stay tuned. This is WXBO. Use the best deodorant."

"I push for a new court case against the prosecutor," said one, as he stood.

"You can't try me twice, even if I killed the old man," said Tod, with his teeth in the law, like a shark's jaw. "I rest my case, your honor."

The gaping mouths of the jury if there was anything to be done, was filled up with what the judge had-his big foot. They became divisive on which court case this was.

And then the defense ordered the lights down low. He unpacked his projector and inserted one slide. It was a picture of Tod's house with the pink polka dots and the imposing fence erected by the neighborhood, the giant target painted over his front door and beyond, and the toilet paper strung everywhere with some chopped-down trees.

"This is what the neighborhood thinks of the luxurious Tod and his life. Ask them. This is what you do if someone murders an unsuspecting innocent, young thing, because the cops can't do anything but go on a stakeout after it's over and done with."

"Wait a minute," I said. "He's going down. Mark my words."

The crowd "oohed" and "ahhed." The picture agreed with the jury and the crowd in court with what they thought of Tod. And we had at least five of the jurors on our side. The murder case had gone awry to a sour point.

Schizophrenia could be what I had so that I saw everything backwards. But was I schizophrenic? No. Tod was inches from the evil pit. Don't give up yet. It's just too good to be true.

The bailiff whispered to the judge, "Call Tod on contempt of court, and we'll have the time to whisk him away to some remote island down in the Caribbean." They had caught him, too—the reach from Green Street! What were they using for bait? And what were they going to do with him? They had courts down there. But the judge turned to the audience.

"What the court, uh, is concerned about at this point of the proceedings, uh, is the outbursts from people who, uh, haven't been sworn in. Any more, uh, admissions from personal recollections that can be held separate, uh, from this court will be taken with a grain of salt." Down went the gavel. Sore thumbs are created there. That's why no one is invited up to the bench, other than the lawyers, and they took classes.

"I have all the salt I need," said my man, Buck, the defense man, and he heard the following: he had no witnesses, he had no prominent opinions by experts, he had no prosecution by anybody we know of, and he didn't even get arrested, we think. "You call this a court? Maybe this one is a sham!"

The judge was having another case of embarrassment, and he turned more red.

"I did, too," said Tod, meekly. "What do you want me to do with this trash—prosecute myself? I had a great big court case. My wife enjoyed the whole thing."

"From the grave?" a person asked.

"Did you have bail?" someone asked.

"I posted bail," said Tod.

"And she handed the money to them?" Everybody laughed!

"There is no bail for murder! And no exceptions for the dead wife," said someone. The crowd was definitely murmuring. "And now we've just about proved there are too many dead people around this guy. It gets worse instead of better."

"We'll, uh, retry him," said the judge. He knew he couldn't, but it might settle everybody down.

"You can't retry him by law," I said, "but you can damage his reputation. Tod, beloved brother of mine—you stink. Now take this jacket off."

"You're not a schizophreniack?" he asked. "The mental hospital put that on you."

"I remember what happened," I said. "I crossed the street after the bus rolled by. I saw you waving our dad across in the way of the city bus."

"I'm the bus driver," a middle-aged man said, out of nowhere. He had stayed out of the limelight for the longest time. It was very traumatic. "I saw everything. The blind man was coaxed into the way of my bus by Tod, the prosecutor—simple as that."

"You don't want an innocent man to go down in flames?" asked the defense.

"I don't want an honest man to die in jail like my cousin is on Green Row." He continued. "Now we can't find him. May-be we could prove this man in charge is sending other innocent men to prison. The whole thing is rotten to the core." And the orchestra one by one threw apple cores at Tod like snow-balls. They weren't playing after this court session was over.

"Maybe we could have a wrongful death suit against this bundle of dishonesty," said another fry. I bit into that one. The crowd started chanting here, and if they rose up, violence had nothing else but to extract Tod and send him to be hanged—though they weren't that enraged. They did agree as a multitude that something had to be done.

"I can't handle a wrongful-death suit," said Tod. My eyes crossed his again, maybe for the last time, but he blinked them away. He couldn't look at me anymore.

"You'll have to," said someone in the crowd. And every-body agreed. They cheered and clapped.

"You're rotten to the core," I said. "Please take this straight jacket off."

"Say he's in contempt, judge," said Tod.

"I can't do that anymore," the judge said. "I'll go down some, but not taking orders from you from this day forward will keep me from falling forever. I call this court over and done with," said the judge. And he banged down the gavel!

The whole courtroom stood up and cheered!

"It's over?" asked Tod. He stood right up, but the crowd made his head swim. Everything was a blur, and when I talked, it was like I was blowing bubbles with both of us being underwater.

"Your life is over," I said, as I climbed out of the well-worn witness stand. He thought I was physically going after him. I still had the jacket on.

"My life?" he asked, and then he clutched his chest.

"I'm going to give you a heart attack!" I said.

"We," said two cops, coming from obscurity, "have picked up the pieces of the body that fell when you moved it to its new residence. A finger, a nail, some skin, and clumps of hair that had rubbed off yours and Done's jacket as both of you walked and lead us to the stinking flesh. It was inside where you had it displayed as a conversation piece. But nobody came by, did they, Tod?

"You're under arrest—for murder!" they said, holding up the dead woman's head in Tod's face.

Tod jumped out of his skin and hit the ceiling!

"It's over," I said, wanting to go over to him and smack him on the cheek.

Then he bent over. "I think I'm going to die," and fell on the floor.

"Good for you!" I said, and lost every little bit of my energy. "Was it over? Is he dying? Does he have an abundance of dead molecules?"

He clutched for life, flailing away with his arms and coughing quite a bit. He was going to be dead in another moment. On the floor he went into convulsions twitching all over.

The judge leapt from his bench and hurried as fast as his round jelly-making plump body could go and bent over Tod.

"He's choking! Get that robe out of his mouth!"

"Sorry," said the judge.

"Turn him over," somebody said.

"Ahhh, that's a knife in his back!" People crowded around. "Take it out."

The judge pulled it out, while he saw a shadowy figure leave the courtroom.

"Put a tourniquet around his back. He's bleeding profusely." There were three or four more kneeling beside him.

"You mean around his neck? Look!" And there revealed a noose tightened to him and the ceiling. "How did we miss that?"

"Take it off! Has anybody called an ambulance?"

"No."

"Then I'll call," said the judge. "Excuse me," and he sought some privacy in the hall. The newest criminal pointed his gun on the judge.

"My name is Gomez, but you probably knew that."

"Look at that. He has a bomb stuck to his shoe!" as the attention went back to Tod. Somebody tore it off and let it fly, which landed in the arms of the dumb criminal, who threw it to the judge. The judge threw it at Gomez. Gomez threw it to the judge. The judge threw it away, and it bounced down the stairs. Gomez shot once and ran away. Nobody knew if it blew up or not, but the judge was safe. He wasn't hit by the one bullet or the bomb.

The ambulance came and shoveled Tod to the present dirt pile in the hospital, which didn't exist, but some wished it did. When he thought he had a chance of living, and many doctors were working on him, he spit out his cyanide pill, but half of it was gone. At the very bottom was his heart attack, but no one

The Court Blamed Me

could get to it. It was that far down. They left him for dead and closed up shop.

Tod was guilty and actually defended at court—but not this one. There he met life itself, raw and uncensored, and it was against him, a good lesson for the people in the court-room. I waited for the obituaries in the newspaper and also for the money to pay for them. But I did feel better knowing I had been freed from my charges. With a good run at it from when Bill was the judge, we finished in style with the real McCoy trying to fight it off.

"Wow," I said, while I was shaking the hand of my defense attorney. "They finally took the straight jacket off. My feelings are hardly contained. Is he dead?"

"Let's grab a cup of coffee together," Buck said. "I'm buying. I want to let you into a secret. You've been approved by the police department to be a full-fledged cop."

"Does it include donuts?" I asked, and we both laughed.

"There was so much weight on your shoulders from the court case, Mon and Con saw enough to forgive you from one blaring error. This is in effect as long as you won."

I was exhilarated. I wanted to shake the hands of everyone in the jury, but they didn't even have to vote. What I really wondered, knowing some of his true life on Green Street and the prison, how did the judge stay honest toward the end? And why was I so pooped? I was in the right, but Tod had evil powers. He had…and I lost it. I cried like a baby. The defense attorney had a good shoulder to cry on. And then we went for coffee to talk it all out. The bottom line was right there in between the living and the dead.

Chapter 30

Tod was dead. He had his own article in the paper, where he had the distinction of it being made official. He couldn't lead anybody anywhere—no more Tod.

"You're in contempt of court! Do you hear me?" asked my wife as I came through the door, not expecting anybody—especially her.

"You're back?" It was such a simple question. She could win the marathon of Antarctica in a bikini, and things would be the same. I saved it all for old age—and a few lies to tide us over. It looked like I had cut up hope, but I didn't, keeping my insides free.

"Do you want me back?" Loro asked.

"You haven't left," I said. "Want some coffee?" I laughed. It was funny, but that's as much as it was worth. Her absence in jest is what I grabbed a hold of.

"Sure," she said. I poured her a cup, and we both enjoyed the silence. I knew it'd be hilarious to ask her at seventy what her intentions were, and I wondered about when she boarded Bill's boat with the promise of a murderer, Tod, talking too much to her. He'd incriminate himself if he were still around. To her this

The Court Blamed Me

was obvious, but not to me. She was thinking why, and would ask me, why I didn't consider Tod a threat, when he stopped everything to go for her jugular. To him it was impossible to dig his grave any deeper.

It was like I did it on purpose, sending her out with him.

She thought I would break, the longer her rope was.

This was our silence, full of anything and everything. She was going for blame, and I knew I'd eventually be convinced. But to be back, things had to be livable. That was one of my demands. Hence, mercy. I hadn't told anyone, but she had put my soul on the rack, and I couldn't take that again.

There was a knock on the door. It was about eleven o'clock, and I needed sleep from partying with my own defense attorney, Buck, and Mon and Con. Two weeks had gone by, and enough crime was punished to receive that coveted badge. That made me a genuine policeman. So I yelled through the door, easier to ward off the eager-beaver sales-man.

"What?"

"Your mama!"

I wished I had the keys to hell. Here we go again, and Loro was laughing. By this time I had the badge, and I knew I could arrest them for harassment.

"I will love you so much," I said, on my way out.

"I'll love you, too," Loro said.